WELCOME TO THE LAND OF LOONS

Cal Blevins is starting his life over at 62 years young. Newly divorced after 40 years of marriage and laid off from his job of 22 years, he heads to his fishing lodge on scenic Lake McDowell in the North Georgia mountains to contemplate his future. There he finds a quirky, mysterious woman renting the cabin next door; Lauren Talbot, a history teacher from Tennessee, vacationing with her stroke-addled father, Edgar. Cal, against his better judgment, becomes infatuated with Lauren's odd charms, and ends up falling head-over-heels for her. Cal is then shocked when Lauren reveals she has deep feelings for him as well, telling Cal that she fell for him the first time she heard him playing his guitar.

Cal and Lauren become inseparable. Early on in their newly-spun relationship, Cal begins experiencing what can only be described as supernatural events. Lauren also experiences happenings she cannot explain. To complicate matters, Edgar's behavior becomes increasingly erratic.

Cal learns of Edgar's strange obsession with the loons that populate the lake. Could it be that Lauren's handicapped father has a special connection with these nocturnal birds? Cal is aware that the Cherokee of the *Tsi-s-Qua* clan living in South Birdtown have worshiped loons for centuries, but doesn't know the details of their reverence.

Cal takes Lauren and Edgar on a fact-finding trip across the lake to South Birdtown, where the villagers still practice the old ways. While there, they witness a *Tsi-s-Qua* loon ceremony, a Cherokee ritual so bizarre that it stuns both Cal and Lauren to silence. But none of it seems to faze the old man. To Edgar Talbot, the inexplicable experience in the Cherokee village is as natural as daylight.

Events continue to spiral out of control as Edgar pulls Cal and Lauren into the ways of the loon. Near the end of Cal's and Lauren's torrid two-week affair, Edgar Talbot commits one final act of desperation that changes all of their lives. The shocking ending is sure to stay with you long after you read the final word.

THE WISDOM OF LOONS is a tale of offbeat romance between two unlikely lovers. But the novel is much more than that. It's also about love and loss, life and death, comedy and tragedy. It is a story that peeks into the furthest corners of the human heart—both the light, whimsical corners where music and laughter reside, and the dark, shadowy places where our assorted demons run amok. Mostly it is a tale of eternal hope and the power of the mind. After reading *THE WISDOM OF LOONS*, you will never again question the possibility of anything.

THE WISDOM OF LOONS

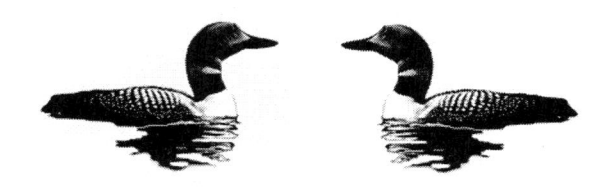

a novel

by

Jeff Dennis

This is a work of fiction. The events described are imaginary. The characters and settings are fictitious. Any references to real persons or places are included only to lend authenticity to the story.

THE WISDOM OF LOONS

FIRST EDITION

All rights reserved.
Copyright © 2009 by Jeff Dennis

Cover Photos/Design © 2009 by Linda Davidson

ISBN-13: 978-0-9819572-1-0
ISBN-10: 0-9819572-1-8

Nightbird Publishing
P.O. Box 159
Norcross, Georgia 30091

Web site: www.nightbirdpubs.com

e-mail : info@nightbirdpubs.com

PRINTED IN THE UNITED STATES OF AMERICA

10 9 8 7 6 5 4 3 2 1

Prologue

THE LOON CRIES AT DUSK

Magic surrounded his canoe.

FishHawk felt it as a physical presence, vibrating through the cedar hull, rising the length of his torso, zipping through his arms to his hands. His fingers tingled. His mind buzzed with strange clairvoyance. Many times today he questioned whether he'd been struck by lightning.

But he knew it wasn't lightning. This was magic. Kiko-Ru's special magic.

The village shaman had worked another miracle. Kiko-Ru performed his ceremonial christening on this splendid dugout before its maiden launch this morning. FishHawk had barely paddled clear of the village inlet when he'd noticed large schools of fish following in his wake. Big fish came from the far corners of the lake, attracted to the boat like buzzards to a fresh kill. More experienced fishermen had told him what to expect, but he had been a doubter.

He no longer doubted.

FishHawk paddled. The enchanted canoe rode low in the water, burdened by the day's catch. He looked over his haul with pride, the bow stacked three high with large bass and lake trout, glimmering in the late afternoon sun like silver medallions. His fellow villagers would eat well this week. FishHawk thanked the Great Spirit for Kiko-Ru's masterful conjuring. Fishing had never been so easy.

He breathed in the pungent fishy scent, the bright tangy smell of freshly carved cedar. FishHawk felt great honor to be selected to pilot this grand canoe. It was a fine craft, steady in the rapids, solid and durable. He admired the craftsmanship of the prow, intricately chiseled into the head of an eagle, the painted eyes so very lifelike. He believed those eyes could actually see. FishHawk was convinced that the canoe was a living creature with a mind of its own. All he had to do was paddle. The canoe seemed to know where to go.

Some mysterious inner communication told him to stop paddling. The magic at work.

He pulled the paddle in, let it clunk on the floor. The lake was but a whisper of breeze, the tinkle of softly rippling currents. He leaned over the side, saw his painted face in the wavy reflection of the water—the whiteface, the bold red and blue slashes streaked across his cheeks and forehead, the porcupine hair headdress that looked like a bird's nest atop his head. He felt drops of sweat trickling down his chest beneath the rawhide vest. All master fishermen of the village—the *a-su-hi-is*—wore this garb. The paint made his face feel tight. The headdress made his scalp itch. The vest chapped the skin on his shoulders. He was uncomfortable, but FishHawk wore the fisher's outfit with pride. Today was his first day as one of the respected *a-su-hi-is*, and he sat tall in the canoe.

Beneath his reflection, FishHawk saw a gathering of largemouth bass, gliding back-and-forth the length of the canoe. He knew they were waiting for his command. He dipped his fingers into the water and moved his hands in slow circles. The bass began to sway in unison, moving languidly as blades of swamp grass rustling in a slow current. His power over these lake creatures fascinated him.

He stood and snapped his fingers, left hand first, then the right.

With each sharp snap, a bass leaped from the water into his hand. FishHawk snapped and caught, snapped and caught . . . hands a blur, catching and tossing the flying fish onto the pile in the bow. Within minutes the hold over-flowed with flopping, writhing fish. FishHawk wished he could take more, but even a boat possessed by magic had its limits.

FishHawk sat, retrieved the paddle.

The rowing required much more effort now. He felt a tired ache in his arms as he paddled across the wide lake. But it was a good ache. A *productive* ache.

As he paddled, FishHawk took in the incredible sunset. He marveled at the low-lying sun peeking through the trees, setting the far shore ablaze in a crimson fire. The surface glowed a brilliant orange, the color of ripe pumpkins at the fall harvest. He squinted against the glare, thinking how beautiful this land was, the land of his people. So peaceful and undisturbed were the surrounding hills and tiny pine-scrub islands that dotted the lake.

In the distance he heard the mournful cry of a loon, a lonely call that signaled the turn of day into night. He heard the call a second time, echoing over the water, eerie yet reassuring.

The loons watched over the Cherokee like proud parents.

FishHawk heard the lonesome cry a third time. A thin smile creased his painted face. He knew he would arrive at the village safely.

1

CALL OF THE WILD

Starting over at age sixty-two is like jumping off a cliff tethered to a frayed bungee cord.

Cal Blevins envisioned himself dangling at the end of that cord: the rubber unraveling with each shriek-inducing swing over a deep gorge, the pulse-pounding excitement followed by moments of sheer terror.

This free-flying scenario played in Cal's mind, over and over. It consumed him in a dark way as he drove north from Atlanta. Like a film loop of some tragic news event. For ninety miles he had watched himself hanging on for dear life. Like he was some fool contestant performing an idiotic stunt on reality TV.

Things really aren't that bad, are they? Cal figured this new start should be a positive development. So why the bleak outlook?

He turned his attention back to the road, thinking about his destination, trying to chase the image of himself as a bungee jumper. This area of the Blue Ridge Mountains, carpeted by the Chattahoochee National Forest, had been his sanctuary since he was a boy. Cal looked forward to living at his Loon Mountain fishing lodge, a place that had always smoothed out his rough edges. Situated on cozy Lake McDowell, his summer home had long been a refuge from his hectic corporate executive life in the traffic-clogged skyscraper madness of Atlanta. He and his ex-wife

Sandra bought the lakefront property and built the three-bedroom cabin twenty-five years ago. Back when the marriage was a happy union and the kids still believed in Santa Claus. Lumpkin County Chamber of Commerce brochures referred to Loon Mountain as "The Emerald Throne of Georgia." Cal couldn't have put it better himself.

He turned onto Mountain Road, the meandering ribbon of asphalt leading up to the lake. Moby yipped appreciatively from the back seat. Cal glanced in the rearview. The black Lab sat next to Cal's guitar case, slapping his tail against the door, sticking his nose through the crack in the window to get a sniff of the sweet Georgia pine. Moby knew where they were headed. The dog loved Loon Mountain. Especially Lake McDowell. Lots of squirrels and chipmunks for him to chase. Cal smiled. He knew Moby had his little canine mind set on the lake and a brisk swim. Somewhere in the hound's ancestry lurked a creature with gills and fins. Had to, the way that dog took to the water.

Cal steered his Explorer under the thick canopy of trees. Twilight shadows stretched across the road. He turned on his headlights and the asphalt uncoiled in front of him like a large black serpent. An earthy aroma drifted through his open window. Cal smelled the lake in the distance, an inviting mossy scent. He inhaled deeply. Up ahead, a deer darted across the road, the dusky blur of a small buck.

He thought about recent events that led him here. His layoff from Southwick Packaging after 22 years of dedicated employment. Marketing Director had been his title on the day they gave him his walking papers. No gold watch or retirement dinner. Thanks for everything and best of luck, they'd told him. Just three years shy of a full pension. Then there was his divorce from Sandra, a marriage that had slowly unraveled over 35 years. Sandra had the 'growing apart' explanation down to Jungian precision. Cal was still working on his assessment. And as usual, the only winners were the lawyers.

Time for a fresh start. He should be ecstatic. And yet his future never looked so uncertain. The bungee-jump scenario seemed appropriate.

He passed the signpost that announced Loon Mountain's population of 837, passed familiar billboards for Lonnie's General Store and Carleton's Boat and Bait. The Cherokee Lane turnoff branched into the woods to the right, a narrow tar-and-gravel road that led to the first group of residential properties on the lower ridge. Mountain Road switched back to the left, following Brighton Creek. Cal could see the tops of smooth boulders dotting the middle of the stream and the browned river reeds lining the banks. Not much rain since his last trip up here.

He passed several outlying cabins—hunting lodges, dark and unoccupied. The small game season didn't begin for another three weeks. Once the season opened, this hillside would be crawling with orange-vested hunters and the ridge would echo with the sharp cracks of gunfire.

The Explorer climbed the mountainside, Moby getting more excited the higher they went. Cal circled the east side and broke into a clearing—Ellery's Pass—that offered a breathtaking view of the valley below. The dying sunlight threw spangled shadows across the ridge, the rolling forest resembling a bejeweled patchwork quilt.

Just as quickly, Mountain Road forged into a dark tunnel of trees. The grade steepened and Cal felt the four-wheel drive downshift. Up ahead, the road brightened with the lights of a construction crew. Cal slowed as he came into an area with enough halogen rigging to rival a Hollywood set. Several half-cleared lots, lit up bright as high noon. A backhoe and a grader spewed plumes of oily black smoke as the machines labored to topple trees and level the earth. Further up the road, Cal saw new construction, three houses in various stages of completion. He heard the pounding of hammers and the whine of a saw, could smell the sap of fresh-cut lumber.

Moby growled at one of the carpenters walking along the side of the road. These workers were an affront to Moby. The Lab didn't appreciate their loud intrusion; they were trespassing in his kingdom.

"Easy, big fella," Cal said. "They're just doing their job. We don't own this mountain, after all."

Moby looked at Cal, a sad cast to his eyes. Whined a little, then backed away from the window.

Cal shared Moby's outlook. For years there had been no new development up here. Cal's cabin had been one of the first built on the lake, and remained for many years one of just a handful of developed properties scattered along Lake McDowell. Loon Mountain—the Emerald Throne nestled between the Appalachian Trail to the north and the ghosts of the Dahlonega gold mines to the south—had been a rustic paradise, a place of solitude and introspection. Then, five years ago, *Atlanta Magazine* published an article about this area, complete with stunning color photographs, and suddenly there was a yuppie stampede. Cal started passing more BMWs and Mercedes and Saabs on Mountain Road, began seeing larger homes being built. The corporate yuppies from the big city a hundred miles due south had a new place in which to compete.

He turned onto Dogwood Lane, the gravel road leading to his property. Tiny pebbles pinged the undercarriage of the Explorer, sounding like popcorn exploding in the microwave. As Cal approached his house, he saw a mini-van parked in the driveway of the cabin next door. Tennessee plates. The *For Sale* sign that had been planted in the yard for close to a year was gone. Cal didn't think the place would ever sell, and he felt a keen sense of disappointment that it had. He pulled into his driveway and shut off the ignition, got out and stretched his road-weary limbs. Moby darted out behind him and headed for the lake. Cal heard the distant splash and Moby's yips of joy, the dog thrashing around in the water.

He looked back toward the minivan—a dark green Dodge Caravan—trying to gain some perspective on his new neighbors. Bright orange University of Tennessee Volunteers decal plastered to a side window. Next to it was a peeling bumper sticker of Hank Williams, Jr. with the legend *HELL YEAH!* inscribed in bold lettering under the outlaw rocker's bearded face. As Cal walked past the vehicle, he saw the torn-up front end, the jagged shards of metal beginning to freckle with rust. The headlight on the driver's side was smashed out and the bent edge of the radiator peeked out from under the crumpled hood. The chassis was pushed in against the engine block and contorted into a pretzel shape. The bumper had been reattached with baling wire. Cal wondered how the thing had made it up the mountain.

He glanced toward the house. Lights on downstairs, second floor dark. He caught a whiff of barbecue, could hear muffled voices. Canned laughter from a television coming through the open living room windows.

Cal grabbed his things from the back of the Explorer—two canvas duffels full of clothes and his guitar. The front steps groaned under his weight. He set the bags down on the porch and fumbled the key into the lock. Pushed the door open. Flicked on the lights in the living room. The house embraced him with its musty warmth. The familiar smells of hamburger grease and cigarette smoke and stale beer assailed him. Memories of his last stay. Six weeks ago, a long weekend with his musician friends—Chuck, Glenn, and Albee—one of their semi-regular pick-n-grin get-togethers. Three days and nights of singing and strumming, living on bottled beer and burgers cooked on the grill. Live music and cold brew, with a little fishing thrown in. Life didn't get any better.

Cal opened windows to air the place out. Took his bags

up to his bedroom. He grabbed a Heineken from the fridge and took his guitar out on the rear deck. Darkness had descended over the lake. A beautiful orange crescent moon hung over the treetops, reflecting a finger of fire across the surface of the calm water. He could see the outline of his dock and the silvery shine of his bass boat below. The trail of flagstone steps leading from the house down to the dock glowed like marshmallows in the bright moonlight.

He opened his guitar case and pulled out his Taylor, basking in the rich scent of the oiled wood. Cal owned several guitars, but this acoustic was his pride and joy. A Leo Kottke Signature Model with the spruce top and mahogany back and sides, the jumbo body that gave Cal the booming sound he loved. He only wished that owning this ultra-expensive Kottke-edition Taylor guitar would enable him to play even half as well as Leo.

He warmed up with "Angel From Montgomery," then broke into a standard blues riff, but was interrupted by a very wet Moby. Cal laid the guitar back in the case and went to attend to the dog, who gleamed with a sheen of lake mud.

Cal smiled at the Lab as he toweled him off. "You been going after those turtles again, Mobes? Some day one of those snappers is gonna bite your nose off, partner. I don't care how well you can swim."

Moby just wagged his tail, basking in the attention.

Cal threw the muddy towels in the utility room next to the washing machine and returned to the rear deck, Moby following close on his heels. He sat and retrieved his guitar, began picking some random notes, just doodling. Moby sat at his feet, tail sweeping across the baked cedar boards like a whisk broom, chocolate-brown eyes wide with expectation.

"Okay, I'm taking requests," Cal said, launching into their time-honored routine. "What would you like to hear, Mr. Moby?"

Moby yipped twice, a redundant whimper, flopped his ears. Sat at attention.

Cal took a swig of beer and wiped his mouth. "I believe I remember how to play that one." He snuggled the guitar up against his belly and strummed the opening chords to "American Pie." Moby barked appreciatively, then stretched out on the deck floor to listen in earnest. Moby was a musician's dream audience. It never mattered to the Lab what Cal played. Cal could run boring scales for an hour or sing horribly off key and Moby would still listen attentively. Something about Cal's voice and the melodies he produced from the large acoustic guitar had a hypnotic effect on the dog.

Two hours and three beers later, Cal packed the guitar away and was headed inside when he heard something strange in the distance. A moaning-mewling sound, barely audible at first, then gaining in volume. Moby's ears pricked up, listening, his body rigid and on full alert.

Cal set the guitar case down and went to the deck railing, listened. There it was again, louder, a desperate sound echoing across the lake. A wounded animal? A possum or raccoon? A loon? No, Cal decided, the sound was too throaty for a loon. A coyote perhaps? Caught in a trap? A wolf, maybe?

And then a chill ran through Cal as the moan escalated to a scream, closer now.

Moby barked and lunged against the side railing.

Another feral scream, the cry of a disembodied spirit.

Cold fear squeezed Cal's heart as he realized the screams came from his neighbor's cabin.

2

SCREAM THERAPY

High-pitched wails pierced the humid night, like a banshee crying through agonizing death throes. Cal's heart raced with each caterwaul. The hair-raising screams incited Moby to furious barking.

And then, as quickly as it started, the cacophony stopped.

Cal went to the railing, craned his neck, trying to get a look at the cabin next door, but all he could see through the treetops was a section of roof. Moby whimpered through labored breaths, his snout stuck through the slats of the deck enclosure. Cal waited, listened. Heard a burst of angry voices—a male and a female—followed by the thump of a sliding glass door.

Great, he thought, recalling the beat-up minivan with the Tennessee plates. Some dysfunctional trailer trash bought the property next door. Just my luck.

Cal leaned his hip against the railing. The night returned to its usual quiet night sounds: cicadas, bullfrogs, crickets.

"Come on, boy," he said to Moby, "let's go inside."

Cal retreated to the air-conditioned cool of the living room, plopped down on the couch and punched the remote to turn on the television. Moby hopped up on the sofa and occupied his usual position at Cal's feet. On TV the eleven o'clock news anchor reported the litany of daily Atlanta tragedies—three teens killed in an auto accident; a family of five burned to death in a house fire; two car-jackings near Lenox Mall. Cal shook his head. No wonder anti-depressant sales were through the roof. If you were to believe the news media, the world was swirling down the toilet on its last flush. Never any good news. Cal had long been fascinated by this conundrum of capitalism—the way the media dished out a continual stream of death and mayhem to sell cars and jewelry and pharmaceuticals. Keep the consumers scared and drugged and lusting for material things.

He switched the channel. A standup comic doing a routine about Viagra. This is more like it, he thought, stretching out on the sofa, settling in. Moby stirred at his feet, trying to get comfortable. Cal's eyelids fluttered. The long day and the beer were putting the finishing touches on his exhaustion. He struggled to keep his eyes open. Drifted in and out of wakefulness through the next couple of comedians.

Sooooo tired.

He was straddling the murky edge of sleep when a sharp rapping at the front door brought him awake. Moby bounded off the sofa, barking with convincing intimidation. Cal bolted upright, sending a cushion to the floor. More incessant knocking. He stood, disoriented, each knock piercing, like a dagger stabbing his ear.

He heard a female voice, though he couldn't make out any words the way Moby carried on. Cal got the dog under control and flipped on the front porch light.

"Yeah, who is it?" he said through the door.

"I'm sorry for bothering you at this late hour," the woman said, her voice whiskey-soaked with a Deep-South drawl. "I'm your new neighbor. Lauren Talbot. Down from Chattanooga. I saw you pull in earlier and wanted to come over and introduce myself, but—"

"It's close to midnight," Cal said. "Not the best time for introductions."

A slight hesitation, then she said, "I know you must have heard the commotion coming from my cabin a while ago. I, um … I just wanted to explain things before you got the wrong idea and called the police."

Cal thought a minute, then said, "You call the cops up here on this mountain and they might get here day after tomorrow. Besides, I figured it was just a party that got out of hand. No harm done. Go home and sleep it off."

"No, it wasn't a party," Lauren Talbot persisted. "That's what I wanted to explain to you."

"I'm sure it will keep until tomorrow. Good night."

"No wait! Please, open the door and I promise I won't take more than two minutes of your time."

Cal let out a heavy sigh. "Look, I've had a long day and I'm really tired. This would go much better in the morning."

A long moment of silence, but Cal didn't hear any footsteps.

Finally she said, "I've heard tell there are bears in these parts. Nocturnal predators, they are. You wouldn't want to be responsible for me being mauled by one would you?"

Cal smiled. He had to give her points for creativity. "No, I guess not," he said. "And I'm in no mood to clean up the mess it would leave on my porch."

She laughed, a soft giggle. "Please," she said. "I'll be quick and to the point."

Cal had to admit he was intrigued. He glanced at Moby, who lay sprawled at the foot of the door, sniffing through the oak and wagging his tail.

Cal threw back the dead bolt and opened the door. Before him stood an impossibly tall woman. Cal was six feet tall, but he had to raise his head slightly to look Lauren Talbot in the eyes. She had to be six-two. Gangly, with a long slender neck. Short-cropped hair that clung to her head like ginger shag carpet. Narrow face that was all sharp angles, intelligent liquid eyes peering out from behind dainty gold-framed lenses much too large for that face. Wide mouth and fleshy lips. Long, stiletto-thin legs that seemed out of proportion with the rest of her body. All neck and legs. Cal flashed on a giraffe munching the greenery from the top of an acacia tree on the African plains. Lauren Talbot wasn't exactly homely, but then again. Her height was the sole reason she would turn heads in a crowd.

"Howdy, neighbor," she said brightly, extending a thin hand. "And you are?"

"Cal," he said, taking her hand in his, alarmed at how bony it felt. "Cal Blevins. Come on in before the bears get you."

"Thank you," she said with a touch of a smile. She walked past him, into the foyer. "I'm sorry that we have to meet under these conditions, but—"

Moby was all over her, tail and tongue wagging, snout firmly implanted in the crotch of her jeans.

"And who is this little rascal?" Lauren said, trying to fend off Moby's amorous advances.

Cal watched Moby sniff the woman in strategic places, then mount her right leg and begin humping.

"MOBY! Get down! NOW!" he yelled. "I'm sorry," he said to the Talbot woman, realizing that his faithful companion was lost in his sexual frenzy.

"It's okay," Lauren said, wrestling with the excitable dog, straining through a smile. "Boys will be boys."

Cal went to help her get Moby under control. She smelled freshly dusted with baby powder. He noticed under the bright living room light that Lauren Talbot was ten years older than he first thought. The tiny lines etched around her eyes and at the edges of her mouth, splotches of gray at the roots of her hair, age spots on the backs of her hands. The woman was pushing fifty, though the agile, energetic way she moved made her seem younger.

"Moby," she said with affection, scratching the now restrained Lab behind a floppy ear. "Such a cute name ... such a *handsome* fella . . ."

Cal watched as Moby bonded with the woman, Lauren bending down, petting him, wooing him with baby talk, Moby beaming like the prince of canines with all the attention. Cal's ex wife never liked dogs. Sandra never reached a level of comfort with Moby. She was a cat lover. Moby knew this and did his best to avoid her. One thing you'd never see in the Blevins household would be Moby humping Sandra's leg. Just wouldn't happen. Moby saved his gigolo affection for females he knew would return the attention. Unlike Cal, the Lab had a sixth sense about women.

"So what is it you wanted to explain to me?" he said.

Lauren stood, kept one hand on top of Moby's head, scratching him with her long index finger. "Well, it has to do with those screams you heard."

"What about them?"

"It wasn't a wild party like you thought."

"So who was the lunatic screaming for his life?"

"My father."

"Your father? Was he drunk?"

"Hardly. Daddy doesn't drink." Her Tennessee Valley twang made Daddy come out as *Dead-y*.

"Sounded pretty convincing to me."

She smiled demurely, leaned back against the sofa. "I know. And I'm sorry about the disturbance."

"So, what was it all about, then?"

"Well . . ." she looked down at Moby, who was sniffing her feet around the leather straps of her sandals. "Daddy isn't quite right in the head."

"How so?"

"He, um . . . some of the wires are frayed in his brain."

Cal remained silent. This was going from strange to bizarre. Had an elderly schizoid moved in next door?

Someone who hears voices instructing him to scream like a madman across the lake?

"It's not what you're thinking," she said.

"How do you know what I'm thinking?"

"It's written all over your face. You look like Sherlock Holmes pondering the case of Jack the Ripper."

"Well, what do you expect?" Cal replied. "When you tell me somebody's not right in the head?. That some of the wires are frayed? After that screaming from your porch. I'd say it's open to that kind of interpretation."

"Daddy had a stroke. A few years ago. He's doing great, but there are still a few things . . .'"

Cal waited for her to finish the sentence, but she left it hanging. "What? He likes to get naked and howl at the moon? Maybe your father thinks he's a werewolf now?"

"I'm glad you find this so amusing, Mr. Blevins—"

"Please . . . it's *Cal*."

"—Okay Cal," she said, her shoulders slumping, "let me inform you that there is nothing the slightest bit funny about Daddy's condition."

"Sorry," he said, "I was just trying to keep things light."

"I appreciate that. But you must understand what a burden this has been on me."

Cal studied her, her long frame slumped against the back of the sofa, the bluish-white light of the television reflecting off the lenses of her glasses. Lauren Talbot looked tired, defeated. Extremely worn down by life.

"Please, have a seat," he said, pointing at the couch. "I can make some coffee if you'd like."

"Oh, no," she said, waving him off, "I can't stay. I can't leave Daddy alone too long. If I do, he tends to get, um . . . *ideas*."

"Ideas?" Cal said, curious about the perverse way she said it.

"Yeah. Without supervision he gets into mischief."

Cal listened as she went into great detail about her

father's condition, about the stroke that affected the part of his brain that controlled learned behavior. The way he experienced periods of extreme lucidity, moments when he could recall events in his adult life, when he could relate to adults on their level, but how, most of the time, he thought and acted like a child. She told Cal about the medical diagnosis, that it was a rare form of stroke, one that induced a kind of juvenile autism. A stroke that messed with his speech and memory, but not his neurological functions.

"Daddy has the energy and curiosity of a young boy," she said. "I have to watch him constantly so he doesn't hurt himself."

"So why was he screaming?"

Lauren Talbot let out a deep sigh, leaned back against the sofa and crossed her arms. "When we got here last week, Daddy heard the loons making their strange calls out on the lake. He's been trying to imitate them ever since. He's obsessed with them."

Cal almost laughed, but held it in check as he saw the strain on the woman's face. "Surely you're aware that your father will never win any bird-calling contests."

She eyed him warily for several long seconds. "Is everything a joke with you?"

"No," he said, "I just don't see any reason to take things too seriously. Keeps my blood pressure in line."

"I have to go," she said suddenly, turning and walking to the door, Moby trailing her like a four-legged servant. Her hand went to the doorknob. "This was a mistake, coming here. I'm sorry we disturbed your evening."

Cal was about to respond with "No bother at all," but the door slammed behind Lauren Talbot, leaving the words trapped somewhere between his brain and his vocal cords. He heard her clomp off his front porch and scrunch across the gravel driveway.

Moby sat staring at the closed door, his look forlorn.

"That is one seriously uptight lady, Moby."

Moby raked a paw against the bottom of the door, let out a high-pitched whine.

"You're an incurable horn dog," Cal said, scratching the Lab's head. "One sniff of woman scent and you're over the edge."

And then he heard the screams again.

The Loon Mimic was back practicing his craft.

So much for a peaceful retirement.

3

ANGEL BIRDS

He was playing his guitar again. Such lovely music he made on that acoustic, such sweet melodies he produced with those hands. Hard to believe these beautiful sounds came from the same man she met last night. The guy who thought nothing should be taken too seriously.

Obviously, he took his guitar playing seriously.

Lauren sat on her back patio, sipping lemonade under the shade of the billowing deck umbrella. An early-afternoon breeze moved through the trees, ruffling the flaps of the umbrella and bringing the boggy smell of the lake with the sound of live music from next door. She listened to Cal Blevins playing "Angel From Montgomery," captivated by the way he drew the lyrics up from some deep wound in his psyche and sang from his heart with whisky-drenched abandon. His voice wasn't the greatest, but he sang from his soul, giving passion to the kind of raw-edged bluesy-folk selections he favored. She wondered if he knew any other John Prine songs. Maybe "Paradise" or "Speed of the Sound of Loneliness."

She listened as Cal started into another song, one about Santa Fe she didn't know. Lauren wished she could watch him perform, but the neighboring cabins were built with privacy in mind. From this angle she could see only a corner of Cal's deck railing. So she listened, sipped her lemonade. A Hank Williams standard followed by a jazzy instrumental, and then a Gene Vincent tune, of all things. It was difficult for her to associate this kind of versatility and musical talent with the balding, beer-gutted man she met last night.

Last night. God, but she had been a fool. Rushing over there like some kind of damsel in distress after one of Daddy's episodes. What was she thinking? Laying her problems on a complete stranger like that. At that hour of the night? Lauren tried to justify it as exactly what she had explained to the man—that she didn't want him calling the police. But it was more than that. Lauren knew she wanted to meet the man the moment she saw him lugging his guitar case up the front steps and into his cabin. Something about him. Something familiar, a vague attraction she couldn't pinpoint. Of course, she'd always had a thing for musician types. Especially guitarists. But this was different some-how. She should have gone over and introduced herself earlier, *before* Daddy went into his Loon Prince act. She wouldn't be feeling this embarrassment now had she thought it through a little better.

Near the end of an Everly Brothers song, she realized time was getting away from her. She had put Daddy down for his afternoon nap after doctoring his apple sauce with a crushed-up sleeping pill at lunch. That gave her an extended window of time to pick up some much-needed groceries. She would love to sit here all afternoon, enjoying Cal Blevins's music, but responsibility beckoned.

Lauren went back into the house, closing and locking the sliding glass door behind her, cutting short Cal's spot-on cover of Harry Chapin's "Taxi." She grabbed her purse and grocery list off the kitchen counter, then checked on Daddy, who was sleeping soundly in the second bedroom. She leaned over, planted a soft kiss on his cheek. He seemed to be doing better since they'd been here at Loon Mountain, last night's episode notwithstanding. This lakeside hideaway was good for him. For Lauren, too. She watched him stir in his sleep, felt her love for him swelling in her chest, a tingly lightness there, as though her heart had been inflated by helium. She wondered what his dreams were like, whether he dreamed at all. Did he dream of Mother? Did he dream of himself and Mother when she was alive, when they were young and in love? Lauren could watch him sleep for hours. He looked at peace when he was asleep.

She went out to the Caravan and climbed behind the wheel, struggling for breath in the sauna-like heat. She fired up the old minivan in a cloud of noxious smoke and gravel dust. The air-conditioner blew revitalizing cool air in her face. Her sweat-soaked blouse clung to her heated skin like a thin layer of ice. She checked her watch, noting she had about an hour before Daddy would be up and around.

She headed to Lonnie's General Store, three miles around the western side of the lake. Lauren pulled in under a big wooden sign with sun-faded red-and-blue lettering that proclaimed: *Last Stop Before Heaven!* A pair of ragged bullet holes splintered the wood just above *Heaven*. She didn't know whether to laugh or worry.

She parked and got out, smelling the woodsy-sulfur scent of the lake and the tar of baking asphalt. Her glasses steamed up, and she paused a moment until her lenses cleared. The heat of the day radiated through the soles of her sandals and traveled up her bare legs. No other cars in the lot at this mid-afternoon hour.

She checked out Lonnie's General Store, a long, narrow, two-story aluminum structure shaded by towering oak and poplar. The building backed out onto the lake, and she could see a section of a wooden dock stretching into the pristine water of Lake McDowell behind the store. A rusted hydraulic lift dominated one side of the dock, cradling two small boats in harnesses just above the waterline.

Lauren entered the cool sanctuary of the store, a bell

jingling overhead as she closed the door behind her. Sharp, tangy smells engulfed her—coffee, spices, scented candles, produce. Soft music played—a mandolin, a fiddle, and a flute—something close to bluegrass, but with a distinctive Native American feel.

The place was cluttered with stock. Boxes and bags spilled over into the aisles. Canned goods overran shelves. Half of one wall was a glass-fronted bank of frozen foods, frost-rimmed items jammed into every available space. Overwhelming. Complete sensory overload. Only the high ceiling kept Lauren from suffering a claustrophobic breakdown.

Her eyes were drawn to the checkout area. A gold antique cash register sat at one end of an immense mahogany counter, gleaming like King Tut's throne. A sign behind the front counter made her smile: *IF LONNIE DOESN'T HAVE IT ... IT DOESN'T EXIST!* Looking around, Lauren couldn't argue with the claim. Below it, in smaller letters, another sign: *Your Cherokee Nation Credit is Always Good at Lonnie's.*

She scanned the array of Native American arts and crafts clustered around the burled wood counter. To the right sat a rack of colorful beaded medallions and hand-painted dream catchers, leather medicine bags trimmed with shells and feathers. Dozens of hand-woven tapestries in rich earth tones, each bearing the Cherokee Nation seal, were draped over display racks. On the floor sat lacquered clay pots, designed in a turtle motif. Lauren knew from her reading that the turtle represented long life and prosperity for the Cherokee. In front of the counter, perched on prongs made to look like tree limbs, were a dozen or more hand-sewn birds, each crafted with meticulous care. They were striking, with their riveting red eyes, glossy black heads, black-and-white checkered backs, white bellies and wing linings, the white rings encircling their throats. She plucked one from its perch. The cloth was a fine texture, a silky feel, and she delighted in rubbing her hand along the stuffed bird's back. She turned it over, noticing the writing stitched in black thread on the white underbelly:

I'm a loon-atic!
Lake McDowell
Loon Mountain, Georgia

"One of our biggest sellers," a man's voice boomed behind her, startling her. "Quite a beautiful bird, *a-se-hi*?"

She turned to see a short, squat man with a dark leathery face. Two platinum-white braids of hair hung over his shoulders, dangling across his blocky chest. He wore a black fedora with a snakeskin band, a denim shirt, chino shorts, and black high-top sneakers without socks. Difficult to guess his age; the man had a timeless essence about him that would put him anywhere between forty and eighty.

"Lonnie Whitefeather at your service, ma'am," he said, smiling, revealing gaps in his teeth that lent his speech a lispy-whistling quality. "Fourth generation Cherokee, descendant of the Terrapin clan—the *Uh-La-Na-Wa*—and proprietor of this fine establishment. And how has Lonnie pleased the gods to be blessed with the presence of such a beautiful *a-gi-ya*?" He offered his hand in greeting, gold and silver rings on each finger shining in the overhead light.

This one's a charmer, Lauren thought, noticing his eyes travel the length of her body. Normally such obvious behavior would bother her, but the man's diminutive stature and whistling speech rendered him non-threatening. Lonnie Whitefeather was just a charismatic retailer trying to make a buck.

She cradled the stuffed loon against her belly and took his outstretched hand in hers, his rings pinching the skin of her palm. "I'm Lauren Talbot," she said, quickly taking her hand back.

"My pleasure, Ms. Talbot. New to the mountain?"

"Yes. First time here. It's a gorgeous area."

"Sure is. Best land south of the rez. My ancestors used to own it all . . . that is, until Sam decided to become landlord. I tell ya, Ms. Talbot, that Sam is one self-serving uncle . . ."

Lauren looked down at the stuffed loon in her hands, avoiding eye contact with Lonnie as he went on about the injustices the government had brought on his people. The last thing she wanted was to discuss politics with a bitter Native American. Lauren knew all about the Trail of Tears, the way the government had stolen Cherokee land and murdered thousands of its people. She had taught a gener-ation of Tennessee schoolchildren about this tarnished period of American history. But it wasn't her doing. She came here to buy groceries, not discuss the greed and avarice and inhumanity of long-dead generations.

"Oh, I'm terribly sorry, my dear," Lonnie said, noticing her discomfort. "I didn't mean to go on about—"

"It's okay, really," Lauren said, placing the bird back on its perch. She pointed at the display of hand-sewn loons. "Why is this bird so special in these parts?"

Lonnie's weathered face softened. "Ah, the bewitching and mystical loon," he said, his gap-toothed smile returning. "These birds are the original landowners, here long before my people showed up. Direct descendants of the dinosaur, they are." Lonnie picked up one of the stuffed birds and looked at it with great affection. "These little fellows possess magical powers. They are sacred to the Cherokee, believed to have supernatural links with the soul of this land and the waters of Lake McDowell. They fly with the angel spirits, swim with the fish, and nest in the fertile soil along the shore. They move comfortably between three planes of existence—wind, water, and earth. Makes them special among the animal kingdom. Have you seen one yet?"

Lauren nodded. "A quick glimpse or two. We hear them almost every night. My father is quite taken with their call. He even tries to imitate them."

"Ah!" Lonnie exclaimed. "Your *do-da* is enchanted with the song of the loon? They have him under their spell?"

Lauren couldn't help but snicker. "Something like that, yeah."

"That is not so unusual, Ms. Talbot. The call of the loon is very hypnotic. My people have been under their spell for more than two hundred years. We call them the angel bird—the *a-da-we-hi Tsi-s-Qua*—the bird of peace and tranquility. We Cherokee hear the loon's call as the whistle of beauty and generosity."

"Interesting," Lauren said. "I thought loons were a northern bird ... you know, indigenous to Canada and Michigan, the northern New England states."

"Ah! You sound like an experienced birder."

"Not really. I just always assumed that loons were like Canada geese."

"They are, to a point. Most loons are migratory, just like the majestic geese of Canada. They spend the summer months up north, mating and nesting, then come south for the winter. But our angel birds are different."

"How so?"

"They don't migrate. Our loons stay here year-round."

"How can that be?"

Lonnie Whitefeather scratched at the gray stubble on his chin, thinking. "What would be the point?" he said finally. "Where else can angel birds go once they've found heaven?"

Lauren thought about the sign out front, the one that claimed Lonnie's was the last stop before heaven. She said, "So, you think this area is heaven? The lake? This mountain?"

"Absolutely," Lonnie said. "Spend some time here and you'll see. Ancient Cherokee tales tell of the angel birds finding heaven here at the top of the mountain, on Lake

McDowell."

She grabbed a stuffed bird off its perch. "And you learned of heaven from these loons?"

"Yes. They have been our guiding light since we arrived. My people have lived in perfect harmony with these special birds for centuries. They even did their best to protect us from the invasion of Uncle Sam's army. The United States government drove my people out of heaven for a while—sent them to a terrible hell as a matter of fact—but even the might of the U.S. military couldn't eradicate the loons. They tried, oh yes indeed they did. The cavalry soldiers called them 'Big Hell Divers' and 'Devil Birds' and tried to kill them every chance they got. But the loons were far too crafty and intelligent. According to Cherokee legend, the angel birds fought back against the white man. They used the land that they knew so well as their main weapon. They lured soldiers into treacherous areas here on the mountain and then entrapped them. Those soldiers were never heard from again. It is also documented that many soldiers drowned mysteriously in Lake McDowell. Cherokee legend says that the loons hypnotized the U.S. Army with their calls and made them take dangerous risks. Risks that always proved to be fatal. Yes, indeed, these angel birds are quite sacred to us. They kept the Cherokee spirit and consciousness alive during the years that my people were gone from this area. We owe them and will protect them with our lives."

"Interesting," Lauren said, rubbing the crimson marbled eyes of the bird she held in her hands. "These are really nice. Excellent craftsmanship. Do your people make them here on the reservation?"

"The Cherokee rez is up in western North Carolina, in the Qualla Boundary. Here on the mountain we have a small settlement, directly across the lake. It's called South Birdtown—*Tsi-Gaduhv*. Three hundred or so. My people hand-stitch these birds there. They make all kinds of arts and crafts there, some of which I sell here. Have you been over there yet?"

"No. I didn't know about it."

"Ah! You're in for a treat," Lonnie said enthusiastically. "The people of South Birdtown believe in the old ways of the Cherokee. They left the rez up in Qualla and all of its evil casino money to return to this area. They live simply, off the land and the water, just like we once did. You owe it to yourself to get over there. It's really quite an experience."

"I'd like that, yes," she said, looking at the angel bird in her hands, thinking how much Daddy would love one of these stuffed loons. "I don't see a price on these. How much?"

"I never tag them," Lonnie said. "That would be disrespectful. How can you put a price on something so divine?"

"So they're free, then?"

"Ah! You are very quick, Ms. Talbot. I would love to give you an angel bird for free, but Lonnie has to put food on the table."

"I understand. How much?"

A female voice answered from the next aisle. "They're fifteen dollars each, sweetie."

Lauren heard footsteps, then saw the source of the voice—a short, stubby woman wearing a bright Indian serape and a scowling expression directed at Lonnie. Lauren noticed Lonnie recoil a little at her appearance.

"I'm Amitola," she said to Lauren. "*Mrs.* Whitefeather."

"Pleased to meet you," Lauren said, thinking that Amitola Whitefeather could be Lonnie's female twin they looked so much alike, except Amitola was more shapely and had more teeth.

"I always have to rescue customers from my husband. Lonnie will talk your ears off if you let him get started."

Amitola looked at Lonnie. "We might actually make a little profit if he worked more and talked less."

Lonnie said, "My wife has never understood the finer points of salesmanship."

"I understand salesmanship completely," Amitola quipped. "I understand that if you spend fifteen minutes talking up a customer to make a fifteen-dollar sale, you'll never be profitable. And Lonnie, how often must I remind you that not everyone is interested in the plight of the Cherokee?"

"I was just being friendly, dear," Lonnie said defensively.

"Well, go get friendly with the new shipment that just arrived out back!"

Lonnie doffed his hat at Lauren. "Duty calls, Ms. Talbot," he said, then shuffled off to the rear of the store.

Amitola watched him leave, then said, "I love that man dearly, but sometimes he can be so *nu-da*."

Lauren didn't know what *nu-da* meant, but she had a good idea. "I'll take two of the stuffed angel birds, please."

Amitola looked at her as though she was crazy.

"I guess there must be something to your husband's salesmanship, after all."

Amitola Whitefeather's hint of a smile said she agreed with Lauren's assessment.

4

THE HANDS OF THE FISHERMAN

Cal loved being out on the water this time of day. Just before dusk. The magic hour, when the lake shimmered with the day's dying heat and the surface laid flat and smooth, mirroring the overhead sky. The sweet scent of fireweed and wintergreen mingled with the cool, moist balm of the water, energizing him.

So quiet out here in his boat. So peaceful. Just he and Moby and a cooler full of beer. Fishing rod propped up between the twin outboards, the thin filament of line trailing lazily, glimmering in the fading sunlight like a strand of spider silk.

They drifted. Cal sipped his beer while Moby slept under the overhang of the bow. A quick swish of water drew Cal's attention off to his right. A water moccasin cut an 'S' pattern on the placid surface before going under. Cal loved snakes. Their languid movements mesmerized him.

He crushed his empty beer can and tossed it near Moby, who came awake with a start.

"Welcome to reality, lazy butt," he said quietly. "You just missed a spectacular snake."

Moby got to his feet and yawned, scratched himself.

"You have absolutely no appreciation of nature, my friend."

Moby took that as his cue. Tail wagging, he padded

over to Cal and Cal stroked him behind an ear, rubbed his back.

Cal looked inside his catch bucket. Two puny crappie and a small bream flopped in the bottom, the sum total of today's catch. Moby stuck his nose into the bucket, then backed out quickly, let loose with a sneeze.

"Hey, it's nothing to sneeze at, buster! It's three more fish than you've caught! Even if they are pipsqueaks."

Moby just sat there, giving Cal that look of resigned innocence that Cal had never been able to resist.

He stood, snatched the rod from between the motors. "If I'm reading this correctly, we're floating on top of a school of anorexic fish. Let's head in. Got to be better action along the shore."

He reeled in the line with a clicking whine. His tackle was light, streamlined, easy to control. He liked the fluid feel of his fishing rig, the no-jam snap of the well-oiled reel, the whip action of the rod, the no-drag float of his bismuth walking sinkers. The latter was an answer to the longstanding Lake McDowell ban on lead sinkers, a fish and game ordinance put into effect to protect against lead poisoning of aquatic wildlife.

Cal fired up the motors. A flock of brown thrashers scattered from the treetops on Loon Island, about a half mile to starboard. He sat behind the Plexiglas windshield and grabbed the wheel with both hands, turned the boat a smooth one-eighty and headed for shore at full throttle. Moby hopped up on the shell of the bow. The dog loved the cool breeze against his face. Cal laughed every time he watched the Lab trying to catch the wind with his long, droopy tongue.

He throttled down and maneuvered the boat into a small cove. The dim inlet was studded with pond reeds. Branches of live oak reached out overhead, creating a ceiling of greenery. Silvery mosses hung from the limbs like tinsel from a Christmas tree. Small creeping buttercups threw splashes of color along the shoreline. Cal breathed in the thick loamy air.

He cut the engine and anchored. Cal couldn't risk letting the boat drift. Too easy to get caught up in a web of reeds or run aground on the rocks. He'd had some good fishing luck in this cove in the recent past. Largemouth bass had a habit of escaping to the cooler shadows of these inlets when the heat of day became too much out on the open lake.

Bullfrogs croaked from their hiding places. A pair of bats whizzed past Cal's head, which started Moby on a barking jag.

Cal slid his tackle box out from under the bench seat and affixed a chartreuse walking sinker to his line, then tied a silvery fly to the rig. Normally this kind of close detail task made his hands hurt. Today there was no pain. Two days up here in the mountains and the rheumatoid arthritis that often made his life miserable was all but gone. He'd noticed it earlier this afternoon, when he was playing his guitar. His hands felt stronger. He could play bar chords that normally made the joint between his thumb and forefinger ache.

He cast his line near a clump of lake grass and sat back, watching Moby contend with a dragonfly that pestered him. "Just bear with me a while longer, Mobes," he said, reaching into the cooler and cracking open another beer. "Give me a chance to catch a decent dinner and then I'll let you go swimming."

Moby understood that word—*swimming*. The Lab's ears perked up. The dog lusted for the water.

Cal sat and drank, occasionally gave the rod a tug to make the silver fly skip across the surface like a juicy water bug.

Time passed.

The sunlight receded to the furthest corners of the inlet, shadows stretching across the water. The encroaching darkness threw a sepia-toned veil over everything.

Cal focused on the silver fly. He worked it across the shallow water. He drank. Worked the rod some more. Waited for a strike. Waited for a big bass or striper to come out of the reeds and hit that thing, take it down.

Nothing. Not even a ripple broke the placid glass surface.

An owl hooted from the near woods. Sounded to Cal like the bird was mocking him.

He reeled in his line and recast, hoping to get the fly in a better position. As soon as his walking sinker hit the water, Cal heard a large splash.

Moby jumped to attention on the bow, tail rigid, head tilted to the side. His inquisitive stance.

Cal looked toward the splash, beyond a clump of reeds in a dark corner of the cove that was backlit by the low-lying sun. He strained his eyes, trying to make out movement there.

Moby stood erect, concentrating on whatever was going on behind those reeds.

As Cal's eyes adjusted to the shadowy light, he saw something he couldn't explain. A dark-skinned man—an Indian, probably one of the young Cherokees from South Birdtown—pushed through the reeds in a crude dugout canoe. The man's face was painted white with red and blue slashes running down his cheeks. A rawhide band held his long black hair back off his face. A short leather vest showed off a muscled abdomen.

The Indian stopped, laid his paddle down in the canoe and kneeled, leaned over the side. Placed the palms of both hands flat against the surface of the water, slowly moving them, back and forth . . . back and forth . . . the motion hypnotic, freezing both Cal and Moby in a kind of trance.

Back and forth . . .

Back and forth . . .

The Indian's hands never stopped. The rhythm never

varied.

Then, suddenly, the man stood in the canoe and snapped his fingers. Once ... twice. Incredibly, on the first snap a giant spotted bass leapt from the murky water into his right hand; on the second snap, a plump largemouth jumped into his other hand. Quickly, he dropped the two prize fish in his canoe and snapped his fingers again. Same result, but two very big stripers this time.

What is going on? Cal's mind did somersaults over the logic. Fishing through hypnotism? Mind control? Nah! Impossible.

But then the Indian repeated his act a third time. Two more prize-winning bass.

Surely Cal hadn't polished off *that* many beers.

Moby could hold back no longer. The Lab took off running, nails clicking across the fiberglass of the boat's bow cover. A leaping dive off the front of the boat and a yelp as he belly flopped into the marsh.

When the wake cleared, the Indian and his crude canoe were gone.

5

THE TRIALS AND TRIBULATIONS
OF EDGAR TALBOT

She heard him playing his guitar again. Lauren could set her watch by it. Every day, same time, same place. His rear deck. Those big hands of his coaxing beautiful melodies from the instrument. She heard him singing, his voice carrying out over the lake and echoing back to her with a full resonance.

Lauren was trying to muster up the courage to go over there, to visit Cal Blevins. Watch him play in person instead of eavesdropping from her back porch like some Peeping Tom groupie. Every musician needed an appreciative audience. That's what she told herself . No time like the present, she decided. She had just tucked Daddy in for his afternoon nap.

Lauren couldn't remember the last time she had been blindly infatuated like this. Certainly not since The Big Humiliation, when Paul Monroe had torn her heart out and held it aloft for the world to see her beating, pulsing pain. The jerk had left Lauren standing alone at the altar on her wedding day. She remembered the look of pity on the preacher's face as he called it off, the mumbled regrets from her bridesmaids and guests as she rushed from the church in tears. Practically cured her itch for the male of the species once and for all.

So why did Cal Blevins intrigue her so? Why did this man she had just met stir her to action? Was she taken with Cal's musicianship or the man himself?

Time to find answers to those questions.

She went to her bedroom and grabbed the stuffed loon she planned to give Cal, hoping he wouldn't think the gift to be too goofy. She would tell him it was an apology for Daddy's bird mimic disturbances.

Why couldn't Daddy be content just observing the birds who flitted around the feeders in their back yard? Why couldn't he be happy just listening to their lively songs? Why did he feel the need to participate? The two-note whistle of a bob white or the cry of a jay always got Daddy started. He would lean out over the veranda railing and attempt to answer them, tentatively at first, then building in confidence as he perceived his sour warbles to have the desired communicative effect. Then, near dusk, when the loons launched into their wild falsetto calls, sounding like maniacal laughter, Daddy joined them in full-throated glee. After dark, when the whippoorwills began their shrill chants, he ramped up the screech. No way could Daddy let the birds have all the fun.

She went to check on him, cracking the door to his bedroom and peering in. Daddy was sprawled out on the bed in a dead sleep. In his arms he clutched the other cloth angel bird she purchased at Lonnie's. Lauren smiled at the memory of his reaction when she had given him the bird yesterday. Eyes big as saucers, a look of joy spreading across his droopy face. His shouts of *woon! woon!* that both delighted and saddened Lauren. Edgar's stroke-affected speech rendered him incapable of pronouncing words beginning with the letter "L" so loon came out as *woon* and Lauren came out as *Warren*. To see her 76-year-old father happy gave her pleasure, and yet, watching her father cuddle a stuffed animal reminded Lauren of everything Edgar had lost.

She closed his door and walked through the living room, taking in the riot of chaotic colors. Hundreds—maybe thousands—of Daddy's jigsaw puzzle pieces were strewn across the floor. She smiled as she spied the paper bags lined up under his work table, bags Lauren knew contained puzzle pieces that Daddy had grouped according to color or pattern. Since the stroke, puzzles were the only thing Daddy could focus on more than ten minutes at a stretch. Lauren's father preferred puzzles over television or reading or even bird watching. He spent hours in absolute concentration, biting his lower lip as he went about the trial-and-error task of matching jagged pieces to slots on the boards. Lauren thought things would be okay if he could work just one puzzle at a time. But Edgar Talbot always possessed a grand vision, and that wide scope extended to his post-stroke puzzle obsession. Currently, he had half a dozen puzzles in various stages of completion.

She went to the kitchen, grabbed two turkey sandwiches and a Tupperware container of fruit salad from the refrigerator. Hopefully Cal Blevins would put his guitar down long enough to eat some lunch. As she put the food and bottled water into a picnic basket, she wondered again whether this wasn't a foolish pursuit.

But that intangible something kept pushing her forward. As if in a trance, Lauren found herself on his front porch, knocking on his door. She heard the music stop. Footsteps clomping through the house. The dog barking. Moby? Wasn't that the dog's name?

The door opened and Cal Blevins stood before her, taking in the picnic basket and the stuffed loon sitting on top. His irritable look told her she was wrong to interrupt his practice session.

"Is this a bad time?" she said, eyeing his baggy Bermuda shorts and blue muscle shirt.

"Bad time for what?"

Moby sniffed around her ankles and lower legs, his wet

black nose quickly discovering the picnic basket.

"I thought you might be interested in some lunch," Lauren mumbled.

"I already ate, but thanks." Cal kneeled to grab Moby by the collar. "And you've eaten, too, Mobes, so leave the woman alone."

An uncomfortable stretch of silence. Lauren looked down on Cal's broad shoulders, the tufts of coarse silvery hair that covered them, the top of his sun-freckled head, the thin fringe of gray hair circling his shiny dome. She felt like running and hiding. What had gotten into her, coming over here like this again?

"Would you like to come in?" Cal said, looking up at her while holding back Moby.

Lauren felt her iron-clad grip relax on the handle of the picnic basket.

"I wasn't doing anything special," Cal said over his shoulder as he led her through the house. "Just doodling around on my guitar."

"I would say it's a bit more than doodling," Lauren said, following. "I've been listening. You're a very accomplished player. I love that John Prine stuff you do."

He stopped suddenly, turned. Lauren bumped into him awkwardly and she mumbled an apology. He looked at her, an odd expression crossing his face. Had she said the wrong thing? Maybe she shouldn't have admitted she had been eavesdropping on his practice sessions.

"Here," Cal said, brushing her hand on the picnic basket, "let me take that."

In their exchange, the stuffed loon fell to the floor.

Lauren bent to pick it up. "This is for you," she said, standing, thrusting the stuffed bird at him. "A genuine, world-famous Cherokee loon. Made right here in South Birdtown. They're so cute and cuddly, I had to buy two of them . . . one for Daddy and one for you."

Lauren watched Cal take the loon from her with his free

hand and study it. She felt like the world's biggest fool. Did she really just refer to this stuffed animal as *cute and cuddly*? You're losing it, old girl, she thought. All this time with Daddy is making you revert back to your own childhood.

Cal Blevins smiled. "Well . . . thank you. I see you've met Lonnie Whitefeather."

"Yes. That's quite a store he has."

"Yeah, it is. And Lonnie's the consummate salesman. He could sell ice to the Eskimos. Probably has, for all I know. Did you meet his wife, Amitola?"

"Yes, I did. Seems like she runs the show."

"She does. Ami is the brains and discipline, Lonnie is the personality. It's been a winning combination for more than fifty years. They've been working that store since the days I started coming up here as a kid."

"Oh, so you're a native then?"

"I wouldn't call myself a native, no," Cal said. "When I was a student I worked summers at a couple of the camps on Lake McDowell. Bought this place as a summer home to keep the tradition alive." He held the picnic basket aloft. "Excuse me while I put this stuff away. Make yourself comfortable. Can I get you anything? Beer? Coffee? Soft drink?"

"I'll take one of those bottled waters."

He rummaged through the basket. "You want one of your sandwiches, too?"

"No thanks. I already ate lunch with Daddy."

He smiled at her as he handed her the bottle. A knowing smile, as if saying *I knew lunch wasn't the real reason you came over here.* But there was nothing accusatory in his look. In fact, Lauren thought she detected a warm twinkle in his eyes, an inviting openness that suggested he might be glad for the company.

He turned and disappeared into the kitchen. Moby trailed close behind, following the scent of food. Lauren heard the refrigerator door swish open, containers moved around, plates clanking. Cal telling Moby he had his own food.

She entered the living room, sunk down into the clutch of the battered sofa. The small room surrounded her in a depressing mix of drab browns. The wood paneled walls coupled with the décor gave the room a dark and gloomy essence. A thin layer of dust covered everything. It smelled like a biker bar she had been in during her younger, wilder days—cigarette smoke, stale beer, male sweat and testosterone. A place literally screaming for a woman's touch.

She spotted a framed photograph on top of the television. A slightly younger version of Cal and an attractive woman of about the same age with grayish-blonde hair. His wife? They wore color-coordinated outfits—dark blue oxford shirt for him, powder blue blouse for her—against a light yellow background. Lauren's eyes scanned the walls—a couple of fly-fishing prints in cheap gold frames, a lighted Budweiser clock, an unframed poster showing a selection of guitars. What little furniture existed—two beat-up end tables, coffee table, a dilapidated easy chair—were of the thrift store variety. Of the two lamps, one was missing a shade. Certainly the wife could not be part of Cal's life here, she thought. Definitely a bachelor pad. No woman who spent any time here would allow this complete disregard for interior decorating.

Lauren's eyes strayed to the only other source of color in the room, a cherry red electric guitar in the corner, propped up against a small amplifier. A compact disc stereo system against the wall, stack of CD jewel cases on top, more cases fanned out on the floor. Everybody has their obsessions, Lauren thought, reminded of Daddy's jigsaw puzzles cluttering her own living room.

"So, when did you buy the place next door?" she heard Cal say from behind her. "*Lauren*, right?"

She turned, saw the bottle of Heineken in his hand, watched him down a healthy slug before moving to the far end of the sofa.

"Good memory," she said, feeling the cushions shift under her as he plopped down. "I didn't buy the property. We're just renting for a few weeks. Daddy and I could never afford such a place."

Cal broke into a wry smile. "Your father . . . the bird caller?"

"Look, if you're going to make fun—"

"I'm *not* making fun. I listened to his performance last night and he's almost got the whippoorwill nailed. Still needs work on his loon call, though. It's getting better, but it still sounds more like a cat in heat. Actually, an *orgy* of cats."

Lauren couldn't help but laugh.

"Where is Birdman now?"

"His name is Edgar, *not* Birdman. You *are* making fun."

"Sorry. Where is Edgar?"

"Sleeping. He takes a nap every afternoon. It's the only time I get much peace and quiet."

"So how come he's your responsibility?"

"There's no one else. Mama died years ago. Daddy's an only child. I have a younger sister, Claire, who had all four of her children late in life. She has her hands full. That leaves me. I was always closer to Daddy anyway."

Cal took another slug of beer. "And you are . . . alone?"

"Oh, no. I'm never alone for very long," she responded, her stock answer to this frequently-asked question. "My students keep me engaged."

"A teacher, huh? What do you teach?"

"High school. American History and Western Civilization. Been teaching in the Hamilton County district in Chattanooga for half my life." She went on to tell him she got her undergraduate degree at Vanderbilt, her masters in

Secondary Education from George Peabody College in Nashville. She realized she was talking too much. Nerves did that to her. Shut up, girl, you're boring him, she chided herself as she drank from her water bottle.

Cal filled in the silence. "You should be proud to be a teacher. It might be the only honorable profession left."

She looked at him. "You think so?"

"I *know* so."

Lauren sighed. "Sometimes I think the importance of history is lost on the younger generation. Most days I feel like I'm not getting through to them. Not connecting in any meaningful way."

"You've been teaching in the same school district for half your life, as you say. You must be doing something right, Lauren. I'm sure you're a wonderful teacher. You have a very generous nature about you."

She looked away, flushed with embarrassment. "You're sweet to say that, Cal, but you don't really know me."

"I know enough to know you brought me a picnic basket of food and a stuffed animal. I would say that illustrates generosity . . . thoughtfulness. Every great teacher in my checkered academic past had those qualities."

They both sipped their drinks in silence. She heard the dog whine, and both she and Cal turned to see Moby scratching at the front door.

"Excuse me," Cal said standing. "It's time for Moby's swim."

She heard the front door open and the dog's nails clicking across the porch, the door close.

"You let Moby swim in the lake unsupervised?" she asked Cal, as he returned to his seat on the sofa.

"He's not a child. Moby knows these woods and the lake better than I do. He's been coming up here with me his whole life. Besides, he gets cranky if he isn't allowed his afternoon hike and swim."

Another long stretch of silence. Lauren was suddenly conscious of her long legs. She pulled them back, up against the couch. She searched for something intelligent to say, but came up empty. Something about this man caused her brain to freeze.

Suddenly, Cal said, "Tell me something. Do you believe in the supernatural?"

Her surprise made her dribble water from the corner of her mouth down the front of her blouse. She turned to him as she dabbed at the spill. "Whatever prompted that question?"

Cal looked down into his beer bottle. "I don't know. It's just something I find intriguing. Supernatural forces. Do you believe in them?"

Lauren detected that Cal was more troubled than intrigued. She wanted to answer him honestly, but how to do so without coming across like a New Age kook?

"Yes," she said finally. "I believe in certain kinds of supernatural forces. There are things that defy logical explanation. Why do you ask?"

"No reason," he said, lifting his head, meeting her gaze. Preoccupied, seeming to look through her rather than at her. After a long moment, his eyes focused on her. "Why did you really come over here, Lauren?"

"I—I wanted to watch you play your guitar. You play so beautifully. I would give anything to be able to play the way you do."

Cal's wide face spread into a smile. There was a rugged grace about Cal Blevins when he smiled.

"Well, in that case," he said, standing, setting his empty beer bottle on the coffee table, "let the concert begin."

Suddenly, they heard footsteps slapping the boards on the front porch. The door burst open, letting in a flash of afternoon sunlight and heat.

"What the—?" Cal said, standing, his mouth open in surprise.

Lauren twisted around, looked over the back of the sofa, then shrieked, "*DADDY?*"

Edgar Talbot stood in the doorway in all his glory. Completely naked. He held the stuffed loon in front of his privates.

"I'm hot, Warren," Edgar said through his uncooperative mouth.

"Who's Warren?" Cal inquired.

"Uh—that would be me," Lauren said, feeling an overwhelming sense of embarrassment.

Edgar held the loon out in front of him, exposing himself. "Woon!" he said proudly. "He's my friend!"

Lauren heard Cal mutter something in surprise as she jumped to action, bolting from the sofa and running to Edgar, throwing her arms around him and shielding him from Cal.

What a nightmare! Lauren thought, feeling her father shiver in her embrace. She steered him toward the door, covering him with her body as she hurried him back to their cabin.

6

MELANCHOLY COVE

Dusk.

Cal and Moby sat in the boat, searching the cove for the Indian who fished with his hands.

Nothing. No breeze stirring the reeds. Not a ripple on the water.

Same story the previous two evenings. Cal had even gone in with his hip-waders last night, searching the area around the cattails where the vision of the Cherokee-Who-Hypnotizes-Fish appeared three nights before. Cal flushed out some big bass, but no signs that a canoe had been there. No broken reeds or flattened swamp grass. No disturbance of overhanging tree limbs.

He sat back, frustrated, perplexed. Had it been an apparition or reality? Cal was fairly certain the Indian fisherman had been real. Moby had seen him, too, or at least something that spooked him.

Cal slid back his Atlanta Braves cap and scratched his head, stared at Moby who lay with his chin resting on his front paws on the bench seat next to him.

"Whaddaya think, partner?" Cal said, his voice cutting through the thick silence. "You think it's possible we're both going crazy together?"

Moby sat up, whined, licked Cal's hand.

Cal scratched the top of his head. "Well, Mobes, you're

okay. But the fact that I'm out in a boat talking to a dog about a ghost Indian and expecting an answer makes me the one who's bonkers."

Another whine from Moby, louder this time.

"You don't have to be so quick to agree with me, old boy."

They sat, waiting quietly as the sunlight faded. The anchor line groaned as a stiff breeze whistled through the inlet. A woodpecker worked a tree deep in the woods, the machine-gun *rat-a-tat-a-tat* sharp and distinct.

Cal's thoughts drifted to his ex-wife, Sandra. He'd tried calling her several times the past two days, needing to talk to a friend. He wanted a sanity check on this ghost Indian. Sandra would be straight with him. Since the divorce became official, their talks were more frequent, certainly more civil. Now that the legal baggage of marriage was behind them and the splitting of assets complete, they had become best of friends again. Just like the early days of their relationship. They talked two or three times a week, and Cal looked forward to their discussions. But since coming up here to the mountains, he hadn't been able to reach her by phone. Sandra's phone just rang and rang. The answering machine she relied on to screen her calls never picked up. No chance getting her on a cell phone, either. Cal cursed Sandra's aversion to cellular technology. She had seen several reports on television about how cell phone use caused brain tumors, and she had taken it as gospel.

A pair of loons interrupted Cal's reverie, their calls eerie and mournful, yet somehow gleeful, sounding like wild demented laughter. The loons reminded him of Edgar Talbot. Cal hadn't seen Birdman or his daughter since the afternoon day before last, when Edgar burst into Cal's house like some kind of crazed nudist. Hadn't seen either of them, but he had heard Edgar doing his birdcall act the last two nights.

Cal figured he hadn't seen Lauren Talbot because of

her embarrassment over her father's naked faux pas. Granted, it was an awkward moment, but it was over quick. Lauren seemed like the type who dwelled on misfortune. She seemed rather fragile that way. Like a six-foot-plus Olive Oyl. She wore her hurt like a designer outfit. Her anguished demeanor made a statement; Lauren Talbot had that wounded animal defensiveness about her, like the abused and abandoned puppies Cal had seen in the kennel when he was looking for Moby.

He wished there was some easy way to let her know that he understood her father's mishap the other day. But he couldn't. Not without revealing more about himself than he wanted to. Cal saw Edgar Talbot as courageous. The man Lauren called Daddy was strong—a survivor in every sense of the word—not weak, as outward appearances might make him seem.

Meeting Edgar brought back Cal's near pathological fear of stroke. Cal's own father, Max, died from a series of strokes at the tender young age of fifty-six. Cal would never forget seeing his once strapping, gregarious father reduced to a drooling, vacant-eyed, bed-ridden lump after the first stroke put him down. Max hung on for almost a month, a month in which he suffered the worst kind of human indignity—complete loss of bowel and bladder control, no way to communicate except by scratching out arcane messages on a notepad, no escaping the prison cell of his bed without assistance from two big orderlies. Cal remembered watching the hospital staffers walking his father down the hallway, Max shuffling along like some kind of zombie creature in a late-night cable horror movie, visitors and other patients staring at him with a mixture of pity and fear. And then Max Blevins suffered the second massive stroke that blessedly rescued him from his suffering. His indignity was over.

Lauren's father had suffered plenty and lived through it. In Cal's view, Edgar Talbot should be commended for winning his fight, for surviving his terrible ordeal, no matter how strange and bizarre he might come across now. So what if he had a thing for mimicking birds in obnoxiously loud ways. So what if the man liked to get naked and sleep with stuffed animals. Edgar Talbot was alive and embracing life. That was more than could be said for a lot of people.

And if Edgar was strong, what did that make Lauren? A saint? Cal had called her generous, but the word generous didn't begin to define her giving nature. He doubted he could have done for his father what she was doing for Edgar. Maybe it was a stretch to call Lauren Talbot a saint, but not much of one. He certainly admired her selflessness.

Cal's only regret from the other afternoon was that he didn't get a chance to perform for her. Maybe he would pay her a visit tomorrow. Bring his guitar and give her the concert he'd promised.

Moby's wet nose nuzzled his arm.

"What is it, Mobes?" he said, looking down, realizing how dark it had become. All he could see were the whites of the black Lab's eyes. "Time to go home, huh?"

Cal scanned the section of the inlet where they had seen the Indian fisherman three nights ago. Fireflies blinked orange dots all around the tall reeds. He heard the high-pitched drone of a mosquito buzzing his left ear, and he slapped at it, squashed it against his neck.

"Okay, partner, let's head in," he said, firing up the outboards. "So dark now even ghosts can't see to fish."

7

THE HAND THAT FEEDS

Lauren flipped burgers on the grill. The *sizzle-pop* of the dripping grease brought a wave of smoke to her face and smeared the lenses of her glasses.

She and Daddy had spent the morning shopping at Lonnie's General Store, where Edgar became fixated on a new-fangled bird feeder. Lauren finally relented to his constant begging and bought it, assembled it, put it on the railing at the far end of the deck. Daddy had been out here watching it ever since.

Edgar sat in one of the plastic deck chairs, mesmerized by the finches and sparrows zooming in on the three-tiered feeder. He applauded and laughed appreciatively when a bird performed an impressive aerial stunt. A large cardinal perched on the rail and spread its wings, dramatically showing off its striking plumage. Edgar oohed and ahhed at the display.

Maybe the feeder is worth its weight in gold, Lauren thought, smiling, returning to her cooking.

As she slid the last burger onto the plate she heard the doorbell chime through the house. Her stomach fluttered. Could it possibly be Cal Blevins? Lauren was thinking about him earlier, wondering why she hadn't heard him playing his guitar this afternoon. Nah, couldn't be Cal, she surmised. Not after Daddy's emperor-with-no-clothes routine three days ago. No man in his right mind would want to visit them after that. Had to be the mailman or a delivery. Maybe Lonnie Whitefeather bringing her something she left behind at the store.

She left Daddy with his birds and took the burgers to the kitchen, heard insistent knocking at the front door. "Just a minute," she called out. Lauren paused to clean her glasses with a towel, then check her reflection in the oven window. She sighed and shook her head. After all these years with the same long, narrow face and fuzzy head of hair, did she really expect to see a beauty queen in her reflection? Maybe growing her hair out again would help. Nope. Still the same old ugly duckling, she thought gloomily.

She opened the front door and tried not to show her surprise as she saw Cal Blevins standing there with his guitar case in his left hand, a small cooler on the floor at his feet.

"Cal? What a pleasant surprise!"

"Yeah, I'm here to give you the concert we never got around to the other day. I'm a man of my word."

She looked at him, debating whether she should apologize for her father's naked intrusion. Lauren noticed he was freshly shaved, could smell a soapy scent wafting off of him on the warm breeze. He wore an Atlanta Braves baseball cap, freshly pressed polo shirt with a fox emblem on the breast, khaki Docker shorts with black rubber Speedo sandals. He had cleaned up for his visit, which pleased her for reasons she couldn't explain.

"Have I sprouted a second head or something?" Cal asked.

"Oh, I'm sorry. I—uh . . . didn't mean to stare. It's just that—"

"I would have called first, but I don't have your number."

"We don't have a phone here. Trying to get completely

away from civilization for a while, you know."

"That's always a good idea," he said, stooping to pick up the cooler. "Where should the band set up?"

She caught a whiff of lime aftershave as he stepped into the foyer. He stopped, turned, waited for her response.

"Um . . . Daddy and I are about to eat lunch."

"Oh, I don't mind playing for the lunch crowd. In fact, you should know that very expensive government studies have concluded that music aids digestion."

"Is that so?" Lauren replied with a smile. She turned and looked out at the front porch. "Where's Moby?"

"Moby's not a band member on this tour. He does his best work in the studio."

Lauren closed the door. "You're impossible, Cal Blevins."

Cal shrugged with a *What can I say?* attitude.

"Follow me. We're having hamburgers out on the deck. Can I fix you one?"

"No thanks. Tough to sing with my mouth full."

She led Cal out onto the deck and reintroduced him to Daddy, whose eyes lit up when he saw Cal. Lauren held her breath, hoping for the best.

"Call me Birdman," Edgar said to Cal in his labored tongue. "Birdman better than Edgar."

Cal looked at Lauren, questioning with his eyes. Lauren had let it slip to Daddy that Cal Blevins called him 'Birdman.' She'd explained to her father that she thought it was derogatory, but surprisingly Edgar loved it.

She raised her eyebrows at Cal, the look conveying *Whatever Daddy wants.*

"Good to see you again, *Birdman*," Cal said as he opened his case and pulled out his guitar.

"I'm wearing clothes today," Edgar stated proudly.

"Yes, I see that." Cal sat on the edge of a chaise lounger, began checking the tuning on his guitar.

Edgar pointed at Lauren. "Warren told me I was bad

when I was naked. Why is that? Birds are naked and birds aren't bad."

This was headed in a direction Lauren didn't care to go. She said, "I'm quite sure Mr. Blevins doesn't want to hear your philosophy of nudism, Daddy. Now I'm going to the kitchen to fix our burgers and I want you to behave yourself. Understand?"

"We're okay," Cal said, gingerly placing the guitar back in the open case. He opened the cooler, grabbed a bottle of Heineken, popped the cap and took a swig. Went over to where Edgar sat. Looked at the triple-decker feeder that held Edgar in rapt fascination. "That's quite a contraption you've got there, Edgar—"

"*Birdman*!" Edgar insisted.

"Right . . . Birdman . . . Sorry."

Lauren said, "I'll be right back." She went into the kitchen and cracked the window looking out onto the deck so she could eavesdrop on their exchange. She wasn't comfortable leaving Daddy alone with her neighbor for very long. No telling what might come out of his mouth.

"Birds are fascinating creatures, aren't they?" she heard Cal say.

"Yes, yes, yes," Edgar replied enthusiastically. "It's fun watching them fly. I wish I had wings so I could fly."

"Me, too, Edgar—uh, I mean Birdman."

"If I had wings I'd fly to heaven, Mr. Cal."

"Heaven, huh? You'd need a huge pair of wings to fly that far."

Edgar watched a large blue jay move in on the feeder, scattering the smaller birds. "Woons fly to heaven," he said, "and they don't have big wings."

"How do you know loons fly to heaven?"

"I've seen them, Mr. Cal . . . Yes, yes, yes . . . I have indeed."

"Do you think heaven is a real place, Birdman?"

"Yes, yes, yes . . . absolutely. Don't you, Mr. Cal?"

Lauren saw her father looking at Cal Blevins as though Cal's answer was of paramount importance.

"Well, I suppose heaven is whatever you think it is," Cal said. "If you think it's a real place, then it is."

Cal's nebulous answer seemed to satisfy Edgar.

"I see you're quite good at working puzzles, Birdman."

"Yes, yes, yes . . . Jigsaws . . . they're my friends." Jigsaws came out as *yigsaws*.

"I saw some of your work on my way in. I'm impressed."

Lauren saw Daddy beam with pride. She hadn't seen him this happy in months.

Cal said, "You have to be pretty smart to work big puzzles like that."

"Nah . . . Nothin' to it, Mr. Cal."

Lauren chuckled softly as she broke out a head of lettuce and sliced up a tomato.

Daddy's attention went to the feeder. A pair of aggressive sparrows attacked the seed pole. Their ferocity startled him. He pushed back from the feeder in a panic. Dismay pinched his mouth.

"Relax," Cal said, touching his arm. "They won't bite the hand that feeds."

Edgar looked at Cal sharply, fear clouding his eyes. "*Bite* me?"

"No, Edgar, no. They *WON'T* bite you. They only like seeds. You're not birdseed are you?"

"B-bird s-s-seed?" he stammered. "Me?"

Lauren knew Daddy was getting tired and she willed Cal to keep his communications with him simple. She looked at Cal and could tell from his expression that he realized he wouldn't be able to communicate with Lauren's father on any kind of sophisticated level.

"Don't worry, Edgar," Cal reassured him, "you're safe. Hey, how about I play some music for you?"

Lauren brought out the burgers and chips and fresh

drinks as Cal settled in behind his guitar. Cal took several long slugs of beer as he watched Lauren help Edgar to the picnic table and pin a bib around his neck. Edgar dug in while Lauren fixed her own place setting.

"This first song," Cal said, striking a chord on the guitar, "I would like to dedicate to my new friend, Edgar Birdman Talbot, the most dedicated birder this side of the Audubon Society." Cal began picking out the introduction to "Blackbird" by the Beatles, going into a voiceover rap, improvising, poking fun at Edgar's bird mania as he played the extended intro over and over. Lauren couldn't stop laughing long enough to take a bite of her burger. Daddy never stopped chomping, the ketchup and mustard splatters turning his bib into a colorful, swirling-fire art deco piece.

Cal began singing the verses, and Daddy tuned in completely. By the time Cal hit the second chorus, Edgar was singing along and clapping his hands, doing a pretty good job of staying with Cal's rhythm.

Lauren listened, appreciating Cal's talent. She loved the delicate way his big hands massaged the strings, the way his meaty fingers nimbly traversed the neck of the guitar. The sounds he produced were sweet and true. Never a false note. No strain. He made it look easy, which Lauren knew it was not. She remembered her futile attempts to learn the guitar. She even paid for formal lessons but quit after four sessions, her fingertips bloody, her head cluttered with scales and fret board positioning charts. Singing in the shower was more her speed. Much easier than trying to coax palatable music out of a stringed instrument.

Cal finished playing "Blackbird" and Lauren applauded wildly. Daddy followed along, slapping his hands together with loud smacks and yelling, "Blackbird—yes, yes, yes!"

When the applause subsided, Daddy said, "That's awful, Mr. Cal . . . simply *awful*."

Lauren saw Cal's smile vanish, his chest deflate. Heard him say, "You looked like you were enjoying it, Edgar."

"Yes, yes, yes . . . I enjoy!" Daddy said, his eyes bright, his head bobbing excitedly with each *yes*. "Simply awful, Mr. Cal."

"He's confused, Cal," Lauren said. "What my father means to say is that you are *awesome*, not awful. Isn't that what you meant to say, Daddy? Cal is awesome?"

"Yes, yes, yes . . . awful!"

Lauren and Cal exchanged smiles as Cal launched into his next song, a difficult flat-picking bluegrass instrumental Lauren had heard him play before. Amazing, his well-honed dynamics, the way he brought the tune down to a whisper before accelerating back into the rapid arpeggio runs that were the song's signature. Very muscular yet precise.

She and Daddy finished their lunches as they listened to Cal play three more songs, one an obscure John Prine tune that pleased Lauren, returning her momentarily to another place and time. As she listened to Cal play and sing, she thought he was good enough to be on tour. She could see the name Calvin Blevins lighting up marquees in Nashville.

"Looks like your father really does think my stuff stinks," Cal said, nodding past Lauren to the lounger nearest the bird feeder.

She had been so wrapped up in Cal's music that she hadn't seen Daddy slip away from the table. He was fast asleep, every third breath or so ending in a snort.

"Poor man," Lauren said, going to him and draping a light blanket over him. "He's had a busy day and it's way past his nap time."

"It's hotter than Hades out here," Cal said. "Why the blanket?"

"Blood thinners. Dr. Spangler has him on strong drugs. Daddy gets the chills pretty easily."

"What about the other day? When he showed up at my place in his birthday suit?"

"Well," she said, wishing he hadn't brought this up.

"Daddy runs hot and cold. Dr. Spangler says his stroke knocked his internal thermostat out of whack. Daddy doesn't care much for doctors—we've been through a few of them—but he gets along real well with Doctor Spangler. Daddy's also sweet on his nurse, Julia, who stays with him when I'm working. It took a while, but we finally got him the kind of care he needs. Daddy can be a handful."

Cal laid his guitar back in the case, uncapped another Heineken. "Yeah," he said, sucking down a swig of beer, "I can tell Edgar was probably a force to be reckoned with back before his illness. What was he like?"

Lauren looked at her father, a touch of sadness darkening her mood. "He was one of the most articulate, outgoing people you'd ever want to know. Daddy had a way with words like you do with your guitar, Cal. Could have been a great evangelist if he leaned that way. Instead, he became a motivational speaker ... very much in demand, I might add."

"Motivational speaker?" Cal said with a half-laugh. "No, I never would have guessed that."

Lauren noticed the thick line of drool at the corner of Daddy's mouth. She plucked a napkin from the table, went to him, gently cleaned him up. "Daddy started out as a salesman," she said, dabbing at his cheek. "He sold insurance for years and brought home a very good paycheck. We never lacked for anything, really—Mom, and my sister Claire and I. Daddy made sure of that. He was always wise with money, very prudent. Then, when most people are beginning to contemplate retirement, he parlayed his savings into his own business, and his life took off. Daddy became big on the corporate circuit, teaching sales and marketing types the power of persuasion. He made tapes of his lectures and sold them at his appearances. Several publishers approached him about a series of books. He got about halfway through the first manuscript when he was cut down by the stroke."

Lauren went on to tell Cal that when Edgar started getting better, she tried to recharge his interest in the partially completed manuscript, thinking maybe it might be a good project for him, something to keep him occupied. But he pitched a fit and tore the thing to shreds. That's when he got interested in jigsaw puzzles, which he never seemed to tire of.

"Sounds like he led quite an interesting life."

"Yes. He was a great man. He accomplished so much. Claire and I always idolized him. You would have liked him a lot, Cal."

"I like him now."

"You do?"

"Yeah. Why does that surprise you?"

"I don't know," she said, coming back to the table. "Just the way he . . . *is*. Daddy tends to make people uncomfortable. Even most of his old friends have abandoned him."

"That says more about his old friends than it does him. When I look at your father, I see a great strength and ironclad will. I see a unique man who observes the world through the curious eyes of a child. I like those qualities. I like the old guy. Edgar's got more inside him than most."

"You're a sweet man, Cal Blevins."

"Not really," he said, sipping at his beer. "I'm an *understanding* guy, not sweet. I understand what your father has been through. I know how tough things are for him now."

"How could you possibly know that?"

"Because I watched my father go through much the same thing."

"Your father is a stroke victim?"

"*Was*. He only made it a month or so after the initial stroke. Just fifty-six years old when he died. It tore me up."

"Oh, Cal, I'm so sorry," Lauren said. She scooted next to him on the picnic table bench and unconsciously rubbed his back.

"It's okay," he said, the hint of tears at the corners of his eyes. "It happened more than thirty years ago. I should be over it by now, right?"

"Some things we never truly get over."

He pushed back from the table, grabbed his beer. "Hey, how about I play another set for you? I hear the management gets a little testy when the band takes long breaks."

"More of your music would be wonderful. But Cal? Tell me one thing. Does your father's stroke have anything to do with that question you asked me a few days ago? You know, if I believe in the supernatural?"

"No. They're not related."

"So what's the supernatural thing about?"

"I'll tell you when I figure it out. I'm not sure how to put it into words right now."

"Come on," Lauren prodded. "You're killing me with this. All week long I've been trying to guess what it is. You can't just lay a question like that on a woman without explanation. Can't you give me some kind of clue?"

"Okay," he said slowly, thinking. "All I can tell you right now is that I saw something very strange out on the lake. Something I can't explain."

"And you think it's supernatural in origin?"

"I—I really don't know, Lauren."

"It could be a mirage of some sort, don't you think? I've read that certain conditions on large bodies of water can cause optical illusions. You know, light and shadows reflecting off the surface?"

"It wasn't any mirage. Moby saw it, too. Or at least he saw *something*."

"Oh," Lauren said, now more intrigued than ever.

She thought about it through the next hour as Cal played and sang for her.

When the music stopped, she came to a conclusion: Cal Blevins is an enormously gifted musician and a deep, complicated man.

A loner, just like her.

And lonely.

Lauren wondered whether Cal handled his loneliness better than she managed her own.

8

IN SEARCH OF THE FISH HYPNOTIST

Cal and Moby were on the water just after dawn. A layer of mist rolled over Lake McDowell, and Cal maneuvered the boat through the fluffy fog carpet. Misty tendrils grabbed at the hull like desperate ghostly fingers. Moby occupied his usual spot at the front of the bow, his eyes scanning the water, getting into the adventure.

Cal wanted to beat the early risers to Lonnie's General Store. If anyone knew about what Cal and Moby saw out here the other day, it would be Lonnie Whitefeather.

As they made their way through the soupy conditions, Cal thought about yesterday afternoon and all the fun he'd had making music for Lauren and Edgar Talbot. It had been quite a while since he'd played for a live audience, and it rejuvenated him. He could have stayed there all night playing and singing, but he didn't want to impose on them. Lauren had her hands full with the old man. But Cal did detect a trace of sadness in her when he announced he needed to get home to feed Moby.

Interesting woman, Lauren Talbot. Not at all Cal's thing in the looks department, but intelligent and an excellent conversationalist. They had talked for a while after he finished playing, and the give-and-take had been free and easy. Mostly about Cal's guitar playing. She seemed genuinely interested in his musical ability, asking him questions about how long he'd been playing (since he was 14), what made him take an interest in guitar (Elvis Presley and Buddy Holly), his musical pedigree (played in too many bad bands to count and several solo stints at weddings). Yet she wisely avoided any forays into his personal life. Not one question about his marital status. No inquiries about his family or previous life in Atlanta. Cal liked that about her. She put him at ease.

But then Cal had opened his big mouth and gone on about his father's fatal stroke. Even broke down a bit, which embarrassed him. Why had he let that slip out? It wasn't like him to volunteer information about his personal life. Something about Lauren Talbot allowed her to get behind the wall Cal had so carefully erected around his emotions. Something about her made him open up. And she did it with ease.

His thoughts returned to his ex, Sandra. When Cal got home last night he'd tried calling her several times. Still no answer. Still no recorded message. Four days running now he'd been unable to reach her. He wracked his brain, trying to remember if she had said anything about taking a trip this week. Even if she went somewhere, her answering machine should have picked up. Strange, too, that Sandra hadn't called him, to see how he was adjusting to retired life. That was her style. Not complete silence like this. What to do? If his computer wasn't on the fritz, he would have tried to contact her via e-mail. Maybe he should plan a day trip back to Atlanta to check on her, make sure she was okay.

He wanted—*needed*—to hear Sandra's voice. Cal needed that familiarity in the face of all the weirdness he'd experienced since arriving here at the lake. Oh sure, she would needle him about the way he was losing it. Probably throw in something about how you have to be crazy to spend so much time fishing. That was Sandra's style— sarcasm tinged with respect. Cal would give anything to hear one of her quips right now.

He steered the boat around Maple Point where the lake opened up wide. The mist scattered and the better visibility allowed him to gun the throttle. Moby yipped with delight as his ears blew back. The dog loved speed and wide open spaces.

Ahead, a couple of miles on the left, Cal saw Lonnie's General Store, looking like a scale model from this distance. The sun peeked through the tree line, throwing a mosaic of shadows across the roof. He could see activity out on the dock behind the store, a boat moored there. Fishermen refueling and stocking up on bait and supplies.

As they got closer, Cal spotted Lonnie near the fuel pumps, the Indian's braids sprouting like platinum vines from under his trademark black fedora. Cal called out to him and Lonnie doffed his hat, signaled for him to pull his boat to the far side of the dock. Moby stood at the prow and barked. Moby loved Lonnie Whitefeather, mainly because Lonnie always had tasty doggie treats for him.

Cal maneuvered the boat into the designated slip and tied to the piling. Moby bolted onto the dock with purpose, going straight for Lonnie.

"Hey, buddy," Lonnie said, bending to pet Moby. "I suppose you're expecting something from Uncle Lonnie, aren't you?"

Cal stepped up out of the boat and onto the pier, pointed at Moby and said, "He's quite the mercenary when it comes to food."

"Well, how can anyone possibly resist a handsome stud like this?" Lonnie said, pulling a dog biscuit from his pocket. "Here you go, fella." Lonnie Whitefeather was the unofficial canine Pied Piper for all the dogs on the mountain.

Moby snapped up the biscuit and devoured it on the spot. Wagged his tail in anticipation of another.

"Let's not get greedy there, Mobes," Cal said.

"Ah, he's all right," Lonnie said, producing another biscuit and bending to feed it to him. "It's been too long since I've seen my favorite *gi-li*." He stood and looked at Cal. "You, too, stranger."

"Yeah, I know. I've been away too long," Cal said, clasping Lonnie's arm with a Cherokee handshake. "How are you, Lonnie?"

"Good. I hear you're back up here permanently."

"Where'd you hear that?"

"Your new neighbors—the Talbots. They were here yesterday. The tall woman told me."

"Yeah, I finally took the retirement plunge."

"Good for you, *gi-ne-li*," which Cal knew meant friend. "And your wife? Is she with you?"

"No. Sandra and I finally called it quits."

"Oh, I'm so sorry, Calvin."

The use of his formal name sounded strange to Cal. Lonnie Whitefeather had known him since he was a boy and still preferred the name used by summer camp counselors all those years ago.

"Don't be," Cal said. "It's for the best, as they say. And what about you, Lonnie? I'd say you're long overdue for retirement."

"Hah! Tell that to my wife. Ami never lets down for a second. Always work, work, work. Always on my back about how time is money. I swear that woman will be pushing me even after I'm dead. There is no justice in the Cherokee Nation, *gi-ne-li*."

Cal laughed, and Lonnie laughed along with him.

"So what can I get for you today?" Lonnie said. "Dog food? Beer?"

"Yeah, both. Plus some human food and gas for the boat. But mostly I'm here to ask you a few questions."

"Oh? About what?"

"Something I saw out on the lake earlier this week . . . something I *thought* I saw."

"Whereabouts?"

"Over in one of the inlets east of Loon Island."

"I see," Lonnie said, craggy face turning serious. He glanced up the dock at the store. "Tell you what," he said, "set your gas tanks up here on the dock next to the pumps and I'll fill them while we chat. Last thing I need is Ami coming out here and getting on me about goofing off."

As Cal retrieved the tanks, a boater on the other side of the dock fired up an outboard motor. The sound was deafening. A cloud of gasoline-scented smoke engulfed the dock area.

Cal brought the gas tanks to where Lonnie stood at the pumps. Lonnie watched the boat move out into the deeper water, leaving a trail of black smoke in its wake.

Cal noticed the sad tone in Lonnie's voice as the Indian said, "I swear I'll never understand people with money; Jake Vinson's got enough *a-de-la* to buy a new yacht, but he won't replace that motor. Thing's older than me. Makes me mad, Calvin. Vinson doesn't care that he's polluting the lake. His kind isn't concerned about the wildlife here."

"Why don't you report him?"

"Are you kidding? Jake Vinson is one of our best customers!"

Lonnie began filling the first fuel tank. "Okay, now what was it you think you saw near Loon Island?"

"Well," Cal began, not sure how to approach it. "It sounds so . . . bizarre that I—"

"Just tell me, Calvin. I've seen a lot of strange things out here over the years."

Cal watched Lonnie pull the nozzle from the first can and insert it into the second. Heard the gasoline tinkling against the aluminum, smelled the noxious fumes. Maybe the best way to handle this was through questioning. "Lonnie, this is weird, I know, but do you know of any of your Cherokee brothers who fish out of an ancient dugout canoe?"

"Sure. Quite a few of the fishermen over in South Bird-town use the old dugouts. In fact, most of my people over there observe the old ways. You know that."

"Yeah, I know. But there's more."

"I'm listening, *gi-ne-li*."

"Okay. This fisherman I saw? He was in a dugout and wearing full face paint."

"What did the markings look like? What colors?"

"Whiteface with red and blue slashes running down his cheeks."

"Ah. The markings of a Cherokee *a-su-hi-is* . . . a master fisherman. They paint their faces that way to attract the fish."

"Really? Does the face paint make the fish jump out of the water and into his hands?"

"What? That's what you saw?"

"Yeah," Cal said sheepishly. "But the fisherman knelt down and put his hands in the water first. Moved them around slowly on the surface . . . kind of like . . . I don't know . . . like he was hypnotizing the fish or something."

Cal looked out over the lake, saw Jake Vinson's smoking boat disappear around the bend. He could feel Lonnie Whitefeather's eyes on him.

"That's a new one on me, Calvin."

"You think I'm nuts, don't you?"

"No, I don't. Like I said, I've witnessed a lot of strange things on and around Lake McDowell. All I'm saying is that's a new one. I have to ask you this, though," Lonnie said, replacing the nozzle at the pump and screwing the caps back on the two fuel tanks. "Have you been under a lot of stress lately?"

Cal met Lonnie's wizened stare, saw the concern in his eyes. Stress? Just two of the top three—divorce and job loss. The only one he hadn't suffered through lately was a death. Cal had thought plenty about these stress inducers. Could divorce and job loss make him see things?

Hallucinations? An apparition? But Moby had seen it, too. Or at least Moby had seen *something*.

"Yes, I have, Lonnie, but—"

"Look, *gi-ne-li*, I'm not implying anything. I think the best thing for you to do is to go over to South Birdtown and talk to someone who might know more about it than I do."

"I haven't been over there in years. Who would I talk to?"

"Um . . . I'd suggest you see Walter Yanegwa, also known as Big Bear. He oversees much of the fishing in the village. He could tell you if what you saw was real."

"Yanegwa . . . Big Bear . . . Got it," Cal said. "But will he talk to me? I mean, I know some of the old line Cherokee are very standoffish with us white folks."

"Not Walter. Big Bear is very friendly. In fact, most of them over in Birdtown are. Still, it's probably best that I contact Walter first, let him know you're coming. Tell you what, Calvin. I'll go see him tonight after we close. Give me a call at the store tomorrow, and I'll let you know the best time."

"I appreciate it."

"Oh, and Calvin?"

"Yeah?"

"You might want to take your new neighbor with you, that Talbot fella? He wore me out with all his questions about loons. He's obsessed with birds. Even insisted that I call him Birdman. I kinda feel sorry for the old coot."

Cal chuckled, knowing how Edgar could be. "Can Walter Big Bear fill us in about native birds?"

"No. Izzie Kalanu is the village expert on birds. Kalanu is known as Izzie the Raven."

"The Raven? Will he talk to us?"

"Don't let the name fool you. Izzie is very approachable. Loves to talk. In fact, he's the official South Birdtown storyteller. Izzie will tell you more than you ever cared to know about our winged friends, especially the loons."

Loons and bears and ravens. Cherokee warriors who hypnotize fish?

This wasn't at all the way Cal had envisioned his retirement.

9

BIZARRE GUITAR

Cal tied off the boat, slipped the canvas covers over the motors and gathered up his groceries, began walking up the flagstone path to the house. He was thinking about his visit with Lonnie Whitefeather when he heard loud screeching sounds coming from inside his house. Moby came to an abrupt halt in front of him, ears pricked up like two furry radars, head tilted to the side.

The sound was discordant, a painful shriek.

Someone was in his house, playing his electric guitar. Or at least trying to play it. Cal grimaced as he listened to the howling feedback and buzzing distortion.

Moby took off running, realizing there was an intruder invading his territory.

And then the roaring din stopped, replaced by a warbling voice singing the chorus of "Blackbird."

Cal shook his head and trudged up the path.

The front door stood wide open. He went to the living room, saw Edgar Talbot sitting on the stool, Cal's Fender Stratocaster across his lap. Moby sat to one side licking Edgar's hand. Some watchdog!

"Mr. Cal!" Edgar shouted. "I played guitar! Did you hear?"

Cal flushed with anger, but the emotion quickly passed. How could he go off the deep end at this unfortunate old man who didn't know any better. At least Edgar was playing Cal's beat-up old electric and hadn't found his priceless Taylor acoustic.

"Yeah, I heard you, Edgar," he said. "What are you doing here?"

"Playing music, yes, yes, yes."

"How did you get in?"

"Front door. It wasn't locked. I-I-I—"

"Slow down, Edgar. It's all right."

"—I knocked once . . . yes I did, Mr. Cal . . . Honest."

"I believe you. But still, you really shouldn't just walk into other people's houses when they aren't home. Folks get arrested for that."

"I know," he said, dropping his head dramatically. "I was bad. I'm sorry, Mr. Cal."

"It's okay," Cal said, feeling foolish for reprimanding a man who was fourteen years his senior, talking to him as he would a child.

The amplifier sputtered and popped behind Edgar. Cal figured he had the volume turned all the way up. "Where's Lauren?"

"Warren's asleep. She's tired a lot."

Cal could certainly understand that, having to care for a father who was all revved up with no place to go. Suddenly an idea occurred to him. "You like the guitar, Edgar?"

"Yes, yes, yes . . . very much. I wish I could p-p-plaaaay it like you do."

"Tell you what," he said, "Let me put up these groceries and then I'll show you a few things. How's that sound?"

"That'd be great, Mr. Cal! Teach me how to play 'Blackbird'."

"I don't know, Edgar. That's a difficult song for a beginner. Why don't we start with some basic chords?"

"Okay," he said, the disappointment obvious in his voice.

Cal went to the kitchen, set the grocery bags on the

counter and opened the refrigerator, began stacking the frozen dinners in the freezer compartment. He could hear Edgar experimenting with his guitar, producing some of the most godawful noise Cal had ever heard. Cal wondered if he was capable of teaching the old man anything, whether he had the patience.

He went to his bedroom and grabbed his Taylor from the closet, then rejoined Edgar in the living room.

"The first thing one must learn when playing an electrical instrument," he yelled over the noise, "is the proper volume at which to play." Cal set his guitar case on the floor and went to the amplifier, twisted the volume knob all the way down. The screeching ceased.

"Hey!" Edgar protested, "I can't hear it now."

"I'm going to be playing my acoustic," Cal said, unsnapping the latches on his guitar case and pulling out his Taylor. "You'll drown me out. You'll never learn anything if you can't hear me, Edgar."

"My name's Birdman," he said petulantly. "Much better than Edgar."

"Of course . . . *Birdman*," Cal said, pulling up a chair and sitting across from him. "Now I'm going to show you where to put your fingers on the fretboard to make some beautiful sounding chords. Are you with me?"

"Yes, yes, yes, Mr. Cal."

Cal showed him the fingering positions for the open E, A, and D chords, the three easiest to learn in terms of simplicity and hand positioning. Three chords that required no stretching. But quickly he realized that Edgar had very little strength in his hands. The old man could grasp the pick and strum with his right hand okay, but after five minutes, his left hand shook noticeably. The chords sounded worse with each attempt. The E sounded like the A, which sounded like the D, all due to Edgar's palsied left hand and his inability to keep his fingers on the right strings. Try as Edgar might, he couldn't produce a clean sound. All that came out of the amplifier was a muffled buzz.

Cal was exasperated. How did teachers do it? How did Lauren Talbot cope with her slower students? Where did she get the patience to continue guiding them when she knew they would never get it? Cal remembered her comment to him, when she told him she was a teacher: *"Sometimes I think the importance of history is lost on the younger generation. Most days I feel like I'm not getting through to them. Not connecting in any meaningful way."* Cal had long thought that teachers deserved much bigger paychecks for their efforts.

He watched Edgar, who sat across from him, trying to get his reluctant fingers to cooperate. The old man bit at his lower lip, the determination on his craggy face wrenched with pain and defeat.

Cal tried to keep the frustration out of his voice when he said, "What say we take a break. Looks like you could use a rest."

"B-b-but we just started, Mr. Cal."

"I know. But you have to understand that it takes time to build up the strength in your hands. It takes time to learn theory and technique. An Olympic athlete needs years of training to compete. A baseball pitcher doesn't start out throwing ninety-mile-an-hour fastballs. It's the same for musicians. Guitarists need hours and hours of practice to get good. *Years* even."

"But I don't have years."

"Sure you do, Edgar," Cal said, laughing, clapping him on the shoulder. "I believe you'll outlive us all."

Cal began picking out the intro to "Blackbird" on his Taylor, and Edgar became transfixed. The old man set Cal's electric back in its stand and listened, joining in singing with Cal on the chorus. When he finished the song, Cal knew he had Edgar where he wanted him. This was a chance to ask him some things he'd been wondering about.

"Lauren tells me you were a motivational speaker."

"I don't want to talk about that."

"Why not?"

"Because I don't talk so good anymore."

"You do just fine, Edgar. Lauren tells me you were a crackerjack insurance salesman and that you were writing a book about positive thinking and motivational sales techniques. I'd like to read what you wrote sometime."

"Ah—fuggleshine!" Edgar said, waving Cal off as though this was insignificant.

"What? I'm interested, is all. Why don't you finish the book? I understand you had a publishing deal."

"Those pirates! Th-they'd s-st-steal from their own mothers, that bunch."

"But still, why don't you finish it?"

"Can't."

"Why not?"

Edgar hung his head, brought his liver-spotted hands up to his ears. He didn't want to hear any more. "Can't. Don't wanna talk about it . . . no, no, no."

"Edgar, I know people who would kill for a book deal. It's quite an accomplishment."

Cal watched Edgar's face transform into a mask of rage. "I can't r-re-read anymore, okay?" he screamed, veins popping in his neck. "Are you h-h-happy?" And then, just as quickly, his rage passed, replaced by a look of utter defeat, his eyes heavy with tears. "The words get all scrambled in my head," he said softly, on the verge of sobbing. "Reading's too hard. Writing's even harder."

"I'm sorry," Cal said, "I didn't mean to—"

"That's why I do p-puzzles. Pictures are easy. The bird sounds, too. W-w-words are hard."

"I understand now. Thanks for sharing that with me. Things can't be easy for you."

Edgar nodded. "It's all hard now . . . everything."

"I imagine so. Listen, at the risk of making you mad

again, I'm curious about something. As long as you're pouring your heart out to me, I was wondering if you could tell me something."

Edgar looked at him skeptically, wiped at his eyes. "Maybe . . . depends."

Here goes, Cal thought. "When you suffered your stroke, did you feel anything? I mean, did you see a bright light at the end of a tunnel? Did your life flash past like a speeded-up movie?"

Edgar stared at him for a long time, then finally reached for the electric guitar. "Sh-show me the E chord again. P-pl-please?"

"I'm serious, Edgar—"

"It's *Birdman*, remember?"

"Okay . . . Birdman. I really want to know what it was like . . . your stroke."

"Why?"

"Because I care."

"Oh, fuggleshine!"

"Really. I've read accounts of people who have had near death experiences. I want to know what yours was like."

"You are morbid, Mr. Cal."

Cal laughed. "Well, I reckon that's one way of looking at it."

"The answer is nothing."

"Nothing? You felt nothing?"

"Yes, yes, yes . . . only numbness . . . f-float-floating."

"Floating, but no pain?"

"No pain."

The exact same answer Cal's father had given him before he died.

Edgar looked at him with a quizzical expression. "Why are you asking me this?"

"Because my dad also had a stroke."

"Really? Where is he now?"

"He's no longer with us, Edgar. He wasn't as tough as you."

"Oh."

"It happened many years ago, but still, I think about him a lot."

"You really think I'm tough?"

"The toughest of the tough."

A smile lit Edgar's face. "You're a good man, Mr. Cal. I like you much more than Paul Monroe."

"Paul Monroe? Who's that?"

"The jerk who was supposed to marry my daw-daughter."

"Lauren?"

"Yes, yes, yes . . . Warren."

"When?"

"Long time ago. Before I got sick."

"What happened?"

Edgar shrugged his shoulders, threw out his hands, palms up. "He disappeared . . . on their wedding day."

Wow, Cal thought. The runaway groom. The ultimate humiliation for a bride-to-be. "Did he ever contact her?"

"No. Good thing. Warren might have killed him."

"So Lauren's not married now?"

"Nooooh—she hasn't even had a date in years."

Cal noticed the twinkle in Edgar's eyes, and said, "Now don't you go getting any ideas about matchmaking, Bird-man."

"B-but she likes you, Mr. Cal. I can tell. She—she talks about you."

Cal was about to respond when he heard footsteps clomping up onto his front porch. Moby awoke from his snooze on the floor and started barking.

The front door creaked open. Footsteps in the foyer.

"There you are!" Lauren said, bursting into the living room, gasping for breath. "You had me worried sick, Daddy! You know you're not supposed to leave the house without me."

Cal looked at her and said, "Doesn't anyone in the Talbot family knock or ring the doorbell?"

"I played music, Warren!" Edgar exclaimed. He grabbed for the electric guitar. "Wanna hear me?"

Cal and Lauren shouted, "NO!" in unison.

10

HARMONIC CONVERGENCE

"Does he always fall asleep that fast?" Cal pointed at Edgar, curled up on Cal's sofa.

"Not often enough," Lauren said. Daddy had yapped continuously for an hour after she arrived, then promptly dropped off into a deep slumber. While Edgar slept, Cal played and sang for her, even doing a few obscure John Prine tunes at her request.

She looked at Edgar. "Daddy's been rather keyed up the past couple of days. It's all catching up with him. Did you really give him a guitar lesson?"

Cal harrumphed, repositioned the guitar in his lap. "Let's just say he'll never be Andres Segovia. But he tried. A little."

"You're nice to do that. Most men would have been tempted to take a swing at him, the way he broke into your house and all."

"Oh, I was plenty steamed. But it's impossible to stay mad at Edgar. Your father's charming in his own way. We had a nice chat."

Lauren stared at Daddy, laying with his head back, mouth drooped open. She could see the underpinnings of his dental work and the sprouts of nose hair that looked like gossamer strands of fiberglass in his nostrils, the loose turkey flap of skin under his chin that fluttered as he breathed. She wished Cal could have known him before his illness. "So what did you two talk about?"

"Well, this and that. I asked him about his work and about the book he was writing before he, uh—"

"Oops . . . Not one of Daddy's favorite topics."

"Yeah, I discovered that real quick."

"Did he get upset?"

"Oh, yeah. I changed the subject fast."

"To what?"

"I asked him about his stroke. If he remembered anything about it. If he felt any pain."

"Wow, Cal . . . Out of the frying pan and into the microwave. What'd he say?"

"Said he couldn't remember much."

"And you asked him about this because of your own father? Maybe to settle your own fears?"

Cal nodded slowly, a reluctant admission. "Don't you ever worry about it, Lauren?"

"No. If I worried about getting sick, I wouldn't be able to focus on living, would I? I wouldn't be able to enjoy the moment. Worry only leads to self-fulfilling prophecy."

She could tell by Cal's reaction she had struck a chord in him. She wanted to tell him that maintaining a carefree attitude got her through tough times, but thought it would sound too self-righteous. Also, it would be a lie. Her father caused her great anxiety and plenty of worry, truth be told.

Cal said, "Did your don't-worry-be-happy attitude help you get over Paul Monroe?"

Hearing her ex-fiancé's name trip off Cal's tongue made her dizzy. She searched his face for signs of malice. Saw only curiosity. She glanced at Daddy, sprawled out on the sofa, sleeping comfortably, his eyelids quivering with dreams. "He got to running his mouth, didn't he?"

Cal shrugged. "Yep."

Lauren groaned.

Cal leaned over, touched her arm. "Hey, it's nothing to

be ashamed of. Anybody who'd go AWOL on you clearly doesn't have all their wires connected. The guy was a fool. Consider yourself fortunate he took off *before* the marriage became legal."

"I reckon," she said, thinking how pathetic it was that this man knew something so intimate about her. Lauren felt violated. She hated her father at that moment. Daddy was her babbling loose-cannon ball-and-chain, and she despised him. "What else did he tell you?" she said, her eyes burning holes in Edgar.

"Are you sure you want me to go there?"

"Please. Every word. The truth."

"Okay. Edgar told me you hadn't been on a date in years. But I paraphrase. He might have said *months*, I don't know."

She felt her anger consuming her, eating her from the inside out. She let out a snort, a sound of disgust.

"Look, Lauren. If it helps, I think you're a terrific lady—"

"You don't know me," she snapped.

"I know enough." He smiled at her. His words and thoughtful way he looked at her had a calming effect.

"This isn't fair," she said.

"*What* isn't fair?"

"Well, you know a lot about Daddy and me, but I don't know much about you, other than you're a very accomplished guitar player and you like to fish."

"That's about it for me."

Lauren spied the framed photograph on top of the television, the one with a younger Cal and an attractive woman. She pointed at it. "What about that? Is she your wife?"

"Was. That's my ex . . . Sandra. We went the separation route for a couple of years before the divorce was finalized last month."

"Why do you keep her picture in your living room?"

He looked at her askance.

"Fair is fair, Cal. You know about my most humiliating failure—"

"Your runaway groom wasn't any failure on your part. And I don't consider my marriage a failure, either. We had a lot of great years together, Sandra and me. She's a very special woman and I still love her. Just not in a husbandly way."

"Yeah," Lauren said absently, looking back at the couch and her sleeping father. "Love's a tricky thing, isn't it?"

Cal thought for a long moment, picked out a few random notes on his guitar.

"You and Sandra have any children?"

He looked away, as though contemplating whether to answer. Then, "Two . . . a son and a daughter. Both stay in touch with their mother, but not me. I keep up with them through Sandra."

"Why don't they talk to you?" Lauren sensed by his sour expression that she had pushed him too far. Something going on there with his children. Her mind reeled with possibilities.

"Look," he said, "both Charles and Andrea are grown and lead their own lives now."

Cal's reaction only stimulated her female curiosity. How best to get him to open up? "Any grandchildren?"

Cal squirmed in his chair and repositioned the guitar in his lap. He eyed her warily and sighed.

"I'm sorry, Cal. I didn't mean to pry—"

"Yes you did."

Lauren emitted a nervous laugh. "Fair enough," she said, feeling like one of those nosy old crones she despised. "Look, I'm sorry for being rude. I wouldn't ask if I wasn't interested."

She looked away, embarrassed, saw Moby stretched out on the floor in the corner near the door to the kitchen, then glanced back at Cal. "Can I ask you one more thing?"

"That depends. If you're going to ask me whether I prefer boxers or briefs—"

"Why Mr. Blevins," Lauren said with an affected Southern debutante accent, "I believe you have me confused with a woman of ill repute. A lady of my exalted social status would never stoop so low as to discuss a man's underthings." She fanned herself with her hand. "The very thought of it gives me the vapors!"

Their laughter was light and airy, chasing the tension. Even Moby seemed to be smiling.

"So you're fully retired now?"

"As of last week, yeah."

"What are you going to do with all your free time?"

"Same thing I've been doing . . . enjoying the life of leisure. I've earned it."

"Oh, I'm sure you have. It's just—"

"Just what?"

"Just that . . . you're so young. You've got a lot of years left. You just going to wile it away playing your guitar and drinking beer and fishing up here?"

"Sure. I can't think of anything else I'd rather be doing. Isn't that what retirement's supposed to be?"

"Well, yes, but—"

"And I'm not young, either, Lauren. I'm sixty-two."

"Like I said, you have plenty of years left."

"Maybe . . . maybe not. No way to know for sure."

"That's true. But it's no reason to give up on life."

"Who's giving up?" he said, voice rising. "Way I see it, I'm just *beginning* to live." He squinted at her, sizing her up. "I know what you're thinking," he said. "You're wondering where my ambition's disappeared to. Isn't that right?"

"Well, yes . . . kind of."

"I left it in Jack Ardsdale's office at Southwick Packaging. He's the nice man from Human Resources who handled the details of my early retirement."

"You sound bitter."

"No. Not really. They did me a favor, the way I see it."

"What did you do at Southwick?"

"Director of Marketing. Yep, twenty-two years with that company. Same old song and dance—employee sells his soul to the corporation, who in turn promises employee the sun, moon, and stars . . . employee learns too late that the universe promised by his employer is just a stage set. Lots of false facades and a cast of bad actors."

"Director of Marketing! I'm impressed."

"Don't be. There're only so many ways you can sell corrugated packaging. Talk about your dead-end career path."

"Twenty-two years doesn't sound too dead-end to me. Most people don't last five years with companies nowadays, what with all the reorgs and acquisitions and mergers and all the other euphemisms corporations use to trim their payrolls and improve their bottom line."

Cal looked impressed. "You have a keen insight into corporate America."

"I learned a lot watching Daddy go through it. That kind of thing makes me glad I opted for a career in academia."

Cal nodded. "I don't mean it was all bad. Southwick paid me well. Allowed me to buy this place and the home where Sandra now lives."

Lauren smiled at him. "A creative soul trapped in a corporate prison, right?"

"Something like that, yeah. I masqueraded as an exec for more than thirty years. I feel like I sold out. Now I can play and sing any time the mood strikes. No more time-wasting meetings to attend. No more windowless office to keep me imprisoned. I feel much better in this skin. My days as The Great Pretender are behind me. Hallelujah!"

He began picking out notes on his guitar. Lauren

recognized the melody of "The Great Pretender" by the Platters.

"Enough talk," he said. "Time for more music. Anything in particular you want to hear?"

"You know any Beatles?"

Cal knitted his brows in mock surprise. "Do I know any Beatles? the lady asks. No, I don't know any of them personally, but I can do a fair representation of most of their songs. Which one did you have in mind?"

"'Norwegian Wood'?"

"Ah, quite a beautiful tune," Cal said, strumming the intro.

Lauren listened to the plinking, slow-shuffle beat, Cal playing it note for note, sounding just like the record she had worn out years ago. She listened to him sing the first verse. When the first chorus came around, Lauren was ready. She launched into the high harmony part, overlaying his tenor with her sweet alto. The living room filled with the most gorgeous two-part harmony Lauren had ever heard. It was magical, like they'd been singing together for years. Cal hesitated, slowing the chorus a bit due to his surprise. But then he smiled at her and nodded encouragement, got the song back on tempo. They sang three more verses and the bridge before Cal brought the song to a close.

They sat facing each other for a long astonished moment, stunned at the music they had just made together.

Suddenly the silence was replaced by applause. Edgar was awake and sitting up on the couch, clapping enthusiastically. "Bravo!" he shouted while continuing to applaud. "Very nice! Just like the Captain and Tenille!" The word 'like' came out as *wike*.

"Captain and Tenille?" Lauren gasped. "Daddy, please give us more credit than that."

Edgar quit clapping. Confusion darkened his face.

"It's okay, Edgar," Cal said to the old man. "I'm

honored that you think so highly of us." To Lauren he said, "It could have been worse. He could have called us Steve Lawrence and Edie Gourmet."

She laughed. "Or maybe George Jones and Tammy Wynette."

"God forbid."

"Or what about Sonny and Cher?"

"Shoot me now!" Cal said, laughing.

Edgar followed the exchange like a spectator at a tennis match, head swiveling back and forth. "Hey," he intervened, "how about another song from the Captain and Tenille?"

Lauren looked to Cal. "Whaddaya say, Captain?"

Cal smirked. "Sure. But just don't ask me to play 'Muskrat Love'."

The two of them shared a hearty laugh while Edgar puzzled over what they found so funny.

11

THE MAN IN THE ZOOT SUIT

Late afternoon heat shimmered off the lake in squiggly ribbons as the boat creaked in the gentle current. Cal and Edgar were anchored in the shade of the huge oaks near the eastern shore. A thin dusting of cattail pollen eddied around the boat like a living membrane. A pollen slick as large as this one usually meant great fishing, the large bass and lake trout congregating under such a slick to gorge on the bugs attracted to the fine, sweet powder. Not so today. He and Edgar had struck out. Not even a nibble between them. Cal attributed it to the ongoing drought.

Lauren had beamed when Cal suggested that he take Edgar out fishing with him. Cal thought it would be a kind gesture, allowing Lauren some much-needed time for herself. But was that all it was, really? An act of kindness?

He absently watched his line drift, listened to the buzz of insects along the shoreline. Thoughts of Lauren Talbot consumed him. Her quirky string-bean looks and innate intelligence were growing on him. Cal loved her gracious, weary smile and those arresting green eyes. This morning he'd felt something move in his chest when she looked at him. And that voice! Cal was becoming quite fond of her speaking voice—a whispery tenor inflected with her beguiling East Tennessee dialect. And when she opened her mouth to sing, a transformation took place. The lady had a voice like an angel! Yes indeed, they had made some beautiful music together. Cal couldn't wait to see the reaction from Chuck, Glenn, and Albee—his pick-n-grin guitar-playing buddies—the first time they heard Lauren sing.

Something definitely going on here, Cal had to admit. What it was, he didn't know. *Couldn't* know. Not yet.

"Hey, Captain Cal," he heard Edgar say behind him. "I don't think the fish are hungry here."

Cal turned, saw Edgar sitting with his back to him, concentrating on his line. The old man wore what he called his "lucky fishing hat"—a ragged golf hat with fish hooks dangling from strips of fishing line sewn around the brim. Ridiculous. Cal could only hope the old guy didn't put an eye out by moving his head too fast.

Edgar again: "Maybe we need different bait, Captain."

"The bait is fine," Cal said, trying to keep the impatience out of his voice. They had been on the lake a couple of hours now, and Edgar had kept up a near-constant chatter. The old man also snagged his line twice with his restless casting and knocked an expensive reel overboard. "Maybe you just need a luckier fishing hat, Birdman."

Edgar turned to face him, looking like he had been slapped. "I'll have you know I caught a record tarpon wearing this hat. Destin, Florida it was . . . 1976 . . . yes, yes, yes it was."

Cal sighed. "I know. You've told me twice already. You also landed a marlin off the coast of Fort Lauderdale in eighty-two. You gave the hat credit for that, too."

"Yes, yes, yes! *Big* marlin!"

"And every hook on your hat represents a big catch, right?"

Edgar's head bobbed up and down, the fishhooks jangling. "You got it, Captain."

"Well, seeing as how neither of us have caught anything tells me your hat might have run out of luck."

Edgar's rheumy eyes surveyed Cal from the far side of the boat. The white sun block slathered on his nose and cheeks gave him a clownish appearance, and Cal came close to laughing.

"Y-you think I'm cr-crazy, don't you, Captain?" Edgar asked with wounded sincerity.

Cal feigned surprise. "Now why would I think that? I wouldn't have brought you out here if I thought you were. But one thing's for sure—with all your jabbering and constant casting, you've probably scared all the fish to the other side of Lake McDowell. Maybe all the way to South Birdtown."

Edgar's shoulders slumped, his wiry body sagged in defeat. "I—I'm sorry, Mr. Cal."

"No need to apologize. What say we just concentrate on our fishing for a while, see if we can catch something. We've still got an hour of sunlight. Also, leave your line in the water, Edgar. Give the suckers a chance to take the bait. You keep jerking your line around, and even the hungriest fish don't want to make the effort."

"Okay. Good idea, Captain."

They fished in silence for the next twenty minutes, Edgar from the starboard side, Cal from the port side, their backs to each other. Cal became lulled by the gentle lapping of water against the hull, the reflection of the clouds on the surface of the lake. A soft breeze rippled the water and rustled the treetops along the shore. A clump of lily pads floated past the boat. In the distance, he heard the soft drone of a motorboat. Further off, the faint strains of a dog barking. Suddenly, Cal caught a whiff of cigarette smoke. Edgar doesn't smoke, he thought in the instant before he turned around. What could possibly—?

He swiveled on his bench seat, and what he saw made him gasp.

A man in his mid-fifties leaned against the captain's chair, sucking on a cigarette. He wore a vintage white zoot suit, circa 1942, complete with baggy pants, long-tailed jacket, black silk dress shirt, and broad white tie. Black-and-white two-toned patent leather shoes completed the ensemble. The white suit gleamed fluorescently in the late-afternoon sun.

"Hello, Calvin. Long time no see," the man said, exhaling a cloud of smoke.

Cal's heart pushed up into his throat. He nearly fumbled his tackle over the side of the boat. How could this be? He looked to where Edgar sat fishing. Edgar didn't seem to notice that a third person had joined them. Cal looked back at the man dressed in white. He recognized the man. And the suit. Cal had to be dreaming this.

There was no other explanation.

The man knocked the ash off the end of his cigarette and sat in the captain's chair. After a long moment he said, "I understand your shock at seeing me again after all these years, son."

Son? Cal knew he was going stark-raving bonkers now. He was out on Lake McDowell in his boat, face-to-face with his long-dead father, Stan Blevins. Thirty-two years ago, Cal had been a pallbearer at his funeral. More unsettling was the zoot suit. Cal's father used to wear it when he went ballroom dancing with his mother.

To Edgar's back, he said, "Hey, Birdman, do you smell smoke?"

"No. Should I?"

Stan Blevins held up his cigarette and said, "He can't smell this, Calvin. Only you and I can smell it."

Cal felt his gears slipping. "You hear any voices, Edgar?"

"Just yours, Captain Cal."

"I mean other than mine."

Edgar turned around to face him, worry etched into his face. "No, no, no . . . No voices and no smoke. Are you okay? You seem funny."

Stan Blevins grinned at Cal. "Your fishing buddy can't see me, smell me, or hear me. To him I don't exist. Just you and me here, son." He took another drag on his cigarette.

Cal shook his head, trying to chase what was surely a waking hallucination. But try as he might to clear his vision, his father still sat in the captain's chair, looking like the Man From Glad in his white dancing suit. Cal thought: *first the Indian who hypnotizes fish, now this.* "No!" he practically shouted. "You can't be real! This can't be happening!"

"Wh-what are you talking about?" Edgar said in a frightened voice. "Of *course* I'm real . . . yes, yes, yes I am!"

Cal's father laughed, clearly enjoying this little passion play. He flipped his cigarette over the Plexiglas windshield, the spent butt making a *sizzle-pop* sound as it hit the water. "I'd suggest not talking to me unless you want your angler friend to think you've flown the cuckoo's nest."

Edgar stood quickly, his jerky movement rocking the boat to his side. His rod and reel went over the side with a splashy *kerplunk.*

Cal winced. This was turning into an expensive fishing trip, it being the second reel Edgar had lost today. Edgar took one thumping step toward Cal and the boat tipped again.

"Edgar, stay right where you are!" Cal screamed. "I told you quick movements could capsize us."

Edgar stopped in his tracks. "I—I know. But I'm w-worried about you, Mr. Cal."

Cal looked back at his father; who smiled at him, exposing straight rows of nicotine-stained teeth. To Edgar, Cal said, "I'm okay, Birdman. *Really.* The heat is just getting to me. That's all." Cal only wished he could believe his own words.

Reluctantly, Edgar returned to his seat. "Ma-maybe we should head back in. If the heat's too much for you—"

"I'm fine."

Edgar looked out at the water where his rod and reel had gone under. "I wost my pole . . . can't fish anymore," he said forlornly. "I—I'm sorry, Mr. Cal. I promise I'll replace everything I wost today."

"Don't worry about it, Birdman," Cal said, thinking as he watched his father light up another smoke that he had bigger worries than lost tackle right now. "Edgar, remember I told you there was a good chance we might see some loons out here this time of day?"

"Yes, yes, yes! You think we will?"

"It's *very* possible," Cal said, looking out over the main body of the lake. The shadows of treetops stretched across the water like ebony fingers, the night closing in. "You have to be extremely still. This is their feeding time, but they won't come anywhere near us if they know we're here."

"Oh, goody, goody, goody! I wanna see a woon . . . yes, yes, yes!"

Edgar turned back to keep a vigilant watch from his side of the boat.

Cal's father winked at him. "You're very patient with him. Would you have been as patient with me?"

Cal thought the question to be ludicrous. But then, everything about this encounter fell into that category. "How'd you get out here? You're not wet so you didn't swim."

Edgar said, "I came out here with you, Mr. Cal. You know that."

Stan Blevins took a deep pull on his cigarette. "I told you to let me do all the talking, Calvin."

Cal's voice was strangely high-pitched as he asked, "What are you? A figment of my imagination? A ghost?"

"I'm neither and I'm both. I'm something you can't possibly understand right now, son."

"This is insane!" Cal said, shaking his head in dismay.

"You can't be real."

Edgar heaved an exaggerated sigh. "You're talking to yourself again. You told *me* to be quiet. You should practice what you preach, Captain, yes, yes, yes . . . we'll never see any woons this way."

"You're right, Edgar. I'm sorry. I'll keep my mouth shut." Cal looked back at his father, his wide-eyed expression saying, *"Okay, talk to me, Dad."*

Stan Blevins took the cue, continuing to smoke while he talked. "God, Calvin, it's wonderful to be back out here with you on Lake McDowell. Brings back so many memories. Those summers we used to come up here for our father-son fishing trips were some of the best days of my life. I remember teaching you how to cast. You caught on pretty quick, but at first you were every bit as clumsy as your birdman friend here," he said, jabbing his cigarette in Edgar's direction. "I still remember that first bass you landed . . . a baby striper not much bigger than the bait. The way you reacted I'd have sworn you'd reeled in Moby Dick. You didn't want to throw it back. You were so proud of that catch. You were convinced that it would be supper for you and me and your mother that evening. So we brought it back to the cabin along with my catch of the day, also not enough to feed one person as I recall. I remember your mother taking a photograph of the two of us, you standing there with that one puny fish on a long stringer, looking like you'd just conquered the world . . ."

Cal felt the tug of sentiment. He still had that photograph, a yellowing black-and-white Polaroid glued into the pages of one of his many photo albums.

". . . that night we ate fish," Stan Blevins continued, "and I told you that you were eating your own catch. I lied to you, Calvin. We ate frozen fish that night that your mother bought down at Lonnie's."

Cal thought about that. He couldn't remember whether he really thought he was eating his own catch back in the early 1950s. Anything was possible when you were a kid—Santa Claus, the Easter Bunny . . . even getting a full meal out of a two-ounce striped bass.

He listened to his father wax nostalgic about Cal's childhood and their time together up here on Loon Mountain. . . . their marathon hiking trips along the old Indian trails that led up to Eagle Summit, the highest point on the mountain from which you could view four states . . . Stan's unsuccessful attempts to teach young Cal how to water ski . . . Cal's first dog—Lasso—a border collie they had adopted from the North Georgia Humane Society . . . the many fishing excursions in Cal's father's boat, the aqua-and-white fifteen-foot WhiteHouse fiberglass craft with the 25-horsepower engine that appeared in many of Cal's album photos.

". . . and I'm sure you remember the time you hooked that snapping turtle, son. You got that thing on board and you started yelling your little lungs out because it went for you, snapping its jaws like some prehistoric beast. You almost jumped overboard as I recall. You were so scared you had turtle nightmares for weeks after that . . ."

Cal remembered all right. To this day, turtles still freaked him out, especially the snappers, though he knew it to be a silly phobia.

". . . Yesirree, Calvin, you sure picked a beautiful retirement spot. But then, where else would you go? We Blevins have been coming up here for three generations now. Sometimes I feel we're as much a part of these hills and this lake as the Cherokee. Too bad Sandra never appreciated the beauty of this place. Your wife's heart was always in the city. Same with Charley and Andrea . . .my grandchildren don't know what they're missing."

Stan Blevins paused to take another puff on his cigarette. Still the same brand, Cal thought—Marlboros in the crushproof box. "And I must tell you, Calvin, how proud I am of you. Director of Marketing!" Cal's father whistled, "I'm impressed! Only two steps away from President and CEO of Southwick Packaging. You really made something of your life. And you got out at the right time, too. Corporate America is flushing itself down the toilet. Things are very different from my day, when companies recognized good workers and promoted accordingly. No such thing as a career path anymore . . . it's everybody for themselves now."

Cal nodded in silent agreement.

"But I digress," Stan Blevins continued. "My purpose behind this visit is to let you know how much I love you, son. As I recall, I rarely said those words to you when I was alive . . ." He cleared his throat, spat over the side of the boat. "I'm also here to ease your fears about death, Calvin. I know you're especially terrified of stroking out the way I did. All I can say is don't worry about it. You're not going to pass over via a stroke. I know this to be true. I also know that death is nothing to be feared. It's not an end, it's a new beginning. I can honestly say that the past thirty-two years since my dying day have been wonderful. Marvelous. *Stupendous!* I've spent a lot of time with your mother, dancing . . .

"Which reminds me . . ." he reached into his coat pocket and pulled out a tarnished gold pocket watch, flipped open the cover. Cal recognized the antique watch, the family heirloom first owned by Cal's great grandfather, Morton Blevins. The watch disappeared shortly after Cal's father's death. ". . . I'm late!" Stan Blevins exclaimed. "I'm supposed to be hitting the dance floor with your mother in exactly four minutes. One thing I've learned is never keep a lady waiting who has dancing on her mind. I love you, son."

The cigarette smoke thickened around Stan Blevins, enveloping him, forming a funnel around him like a miniature tornado.

And then he was gone.

The day returned to its previous calm.

Cal just sat there, stunned and unable to move.

From the other side of the boat, Edgar said, "You hear that, Captain Cal? Was that a woon?"

12

CITRONELLA TEARS

"Talk to me, Daddy," Lauren implored. "You say Cal was talking to himself? Saying crazy things to you?"

Lauren and her father sat on the back deck, the darkness wrapped around them in a heavy curtain. Citronella candles flickered along the railing, casting jagged shadows, the waxy-lemon scent strong. Edgar had returned from the fishing trip in a frazzled state of mind. Something strange had happened out on the lake and Lauren was trying to get to the bottom of it. Whatever it was held Edgar in a near-catatonic vise grip.

She tried again. "Please, Daddy. I know it's hard, but tell me what happened. He didn't hurt you, did he?"

She watched him come back to life a bit. "No, no, no," he said, "Mr. Cal would *never* hurt me, Warren. He's my friend. He took me fishing, you know."

"Yes, I know. What happened to Mr. Blevins when you were out fishing, Daddy?"

She watched him take a sip of his iced tea, his hand shaky. He stared at the flame fluttering atop one of the candles. "Well," he said, as if in a trance, "it was spooky. Mr. Cal, he, uh . . . well, he said some weird things to me. But I don't think he was talking to me—"

"Who was he talking to?"

"I—I d-don't know. I think he thought somebody else

was in the boat with us."

"What'd he say?"

"He . . . he asked me if I was a g-ghost."

"A ghost?"

"Yes, yes, yes . . . a *ghost*. That's what he said. But I don't think he was talking to me." Edgar looked at her, his eyes haunted in the wavy candlelight.

Lauren knew from experience that she had to proceed carefully. She leaned over and rubbed his forearm. "I know this is difficult for you, Daddy, but I need to know what happened." She had a good mind to march next door and question Cal directly.

"I told you what happened, Warren. We fished but the fish didn't bite. Then Mr. Cal got a funny face and then he went crazy."

"Crazy how?"

"H—he asked me if I smelled smoke—"

"Smoke?"

"Yes, yes, yes. I was scared. I—I thought . . . the boat was on fire. And then Mr. Cal asked me if I heard any voices."

"Voices? You mean other than his own?"

"Yes, yes, yes! He . . . he kept looking at the steering wheel . . . like there was somebody there. He said it was in—*insane* . . . that's what he said. And then he said 'Y-you can't be real' or something like that." Edgar grew more agitated the more he explained. "And then . . . oh, god, Warren . . . then I messed everything up. I was worried about Captain Cal so I stood up to go help him. The boat tipped and one of Mr. Cal's fishing poles went over the side. I—I think he hates me now . . ."

Edgar's eyes pooled with tears. His face was slick with sweat.

"I don't believe Cal hates you, Daddy. In fact, I know he likes you very much—"

"No, no, no . . . Mr. Cal's fishing 'quipment. Cost him

money. My fault." Edgar's tears flowed freely now. His chest heaved, every word coming out in a wracking sob. "He's mad at me. He *hates* me, I just know it, Warren . . ."

She watched him wrap his arms around himself and curl into a protective ball in his patio chair. Lauren went to him, pulled him to his feet and hugged him to her. He trembled in her grasp.

". . . I mess up everything," he cried into her shoulder. "Everything I try to do."

Lauren ran her hand through her father's snowy hair, rocked him back and forth in her arms the way she had rocked her two nieces when they were toddlers. "Don't be so hard on yourself, Daddy," she said, his tears wetting her blouse. "We'll buy Cal a new fishing rod. Everything is going to be just fine."

They held each other in the flickering yellow light, Lauren consoling her father as he spilled his tears. She couldn't remember ever feeling this tired.

As she listened to Edgar weep and snivel, Lauren wondered just how much longer she could act as a mother figure for this misfortunate man-child.

13

JOHNNIE WALKER IS

A GOOD FRIEND OF MINE

Cal was rip-roaring-falling-down-smashmouth drunk.

He sat on the floor in his living room, back against the sofa, one hand wrapped around a half-empty bottle of Johnnie Walker Black, the other clutching a shot glass. On his right sat an open cooler, the Heineken bottles poking up through the ice like green sprouts on a spring Arctic tundra. Moby nuzzled Cal's left thigh, as though sensing his anguish. The Braves game on the television provided the room's only light. He watched Bobby Cox jawing with an umpire over a close call at first base. The sound was off but Cal could read lips and it wasn't pretty. On the stereo the Grateful Dead sang about touches of gray.

He poured another two fingers of scotch into the shot glass and threw it back, enjoying the burn as it went down. "Ahhhh—good stuff, Mobes." Another shot, followed by a beer chaser. Numbness spread through him. His head swirled pleasantly.

Drunk as he was, Cal couldn't obliterate what had happened out on the lake. No matter how much alcohol he consumed, he couldn't chase the oh-so-real image of his father sitting in the cockpit of Cal's boat in his dancing suit, the ever-present Marlboro tucked between nicotine-stained fingers, looking exactly as he had at age fifty-six, just before his massive stroke.

The fact that Edgar hadn't seen or heard anything both reassured and worried Cal—reassuring in that the encounter couldn't have been real, disconcerting because it lent credence to Cal's suspicions that he was suffering intense hallucinatory episodes. Earlier in the week he had seen the Cherokee fish hypnotist doing his thing in the cove; today he encountered his deceased father in the boat near the eastern shore. What next? Moby tap-dancing in a tutu? One of his guitars morphing into a singing cockroach?

For maybe the hundredth time, he thought about the stress factor: recent job loss . . . divorce . . . permanent move to a new mailing address—surely all three contributed to whatever was twisting his psyche into ravaged new shapes. Yes, he could easily settle on stress as an explanation. But then, Cal didn't really feel all that stressed out. In fact, since he'd come up here to Loon Mountain he felt downright good. Healthy. Relaxed. Enjoying his new leisurely-paced life like never before. So what gave with the visions?

His thoughts drifted into an area that terrified him: mental illness. Could he possibly have a brain tumor or some as yet undiagnosed neurological disorder that caused these delusions? Cal's heart flopped in his ribcage like a trapped animal. He had long been a borderline hypochondriac, imagining the worst possible outcome with each affliction and ache. Every upset stomach certainly meant intestinal cancer, every headache a malignant brain lesion. Each new age spot had to mean the onset of deadly melanoma, every heart palpitation the beginning of cardiac arrest. Cal disliked this about himself, but had written it off long ago as the side-effect of a deep imagination. Being creative was both a blessing and a curse.

Cal loaded up another shot of scotch, threw it back. Chugged half a beer. Moby peered up at him, questioning him with sad brown eyes.

"You're right, Mobes," he said, his words a slur. "I should slow down. Not a college kid anymore, am I?" Cal tossed the shot glass and watched it roll across the floor. He scratched Moby behind the ears with his left hand while he slurped beer with his right.

On the TV the Braves' players high-fived each other around the pitcher's mound. A win for Atlanta, 5-2 over the Phillies.

Cal let out a drunken *whoooop!* and did the tomahawk chop with the bottle of Johnnie Walker, scotch spilling down his arm and spraying across his lap. "GO BRAVES!" he roared, which chased Moby to the far side of the room. Cal tipped the bottle to his lips, took three glugging swallows of the numbing balm. He belched and looked at Moby, who was staring at him with what Cal perceived as disgust. "You're a fine one to judge," he said, watching Moby get up and leave the room. "Ah—you've always known when to avoid me," he said to the dog's disappearing hindquarters.

The CD changer on the stereo clicked. Shawn Mullins replaced the Dead. The room filled with fluid acoustic guitar and Mullins's cigarette-parched, whiskey-drenched vocals.

He grabbed the TV remote and restlessly clicked through the channels. Finally settled on Australian rules football. He watched one stout lad, blood streaming down his face, run with the ball up the sidelines for thirty yards or more before being gang-tackled by a horde of bandaged and bruised opponents. Crazed idiots! Cal thought as he tipped the bottle and drank.

Again his thoughts drifted to Sandra. He'd tried calling her earlier when he'd come in off the lake. Once again, no answer. Still no answering machine. Strange. Cal tried calling several other friends in Atlanta—his musician friends, Glenn and Albee—with the same result. The phone lines couldn't have been knocked out by bad weather. He'd just watched the Braves game and it was a clear, hot evening at Turner Field.

He went back to his encounter with his father. Stan Blevins looked and sounded like the real thing, had even reminisced about personal things that only Cal and his father would know. Cal also smelled the smoke. But there had been no physical contact, no tactile connection. Cal had been tempted to get up and go to his father, try to shake his hand. He bet that if he had, his father's image would immediately disappear in some Houdini-like illusion.

And what about that Indian fish hypnotist? Cal recently heard that the State of Georgia Fish and Game Commission just legalized noodling—fishing with your bare hands—but this went above and beyond that. This, too, had to be a product of Cal's fevered mind. But just to be sure, he was going to South Birdtown tomorrow afternoon to meet with Walter "Big Bear" Yanegwa. Maybe Walter Big Bear would set him straight, confirm Cal's fears that he was slip-sliding into madness. Cal prayed there was some other viable explanation. Besides, he was feeling too good right now to dwell on his imminent demise. Good scotch should not be wasted on negative thoughts.

He brought the bottle to his mouth and drained it. Belched again. Looked at the empty container with amazement. A whole fifth gone!

The CD changer shut off with a loud click. Cal debated whether to get up to put on more music, then decided he was too pie-eyed. Using the remote, he pumped up the volume on the television. Grabbed another Heineken from the cooler, twisted off the cap. The ice-cold beer soothed his throat as it went down.

The bone-cracking sounds of Australian Rules football filled the room.

14

LAUREN'S ELIXIR AT THE
HOG'S BREATH SALOON

They clomped up Cal's front steps, Lauren in the lead,
Edgar trailing close behind, flailing the new fishing rod
they had just purchased at Lonnie's. The sweet scent of
honeysuckle perfumed the air. Lauren sneezed. Edgar tried
to say, "Geshundeit" but it came out wrong. Flustered, he
muttered "Oh, fuggleshine!"

Lauren rapped at the door. Listened. No movement
from inside. Close to noon and not a peep, not even a bark
from Moby. She knocked again, harder this time, leaned
her head closer to the door. Same result. The house
remained quiet as a tomb. Odd. Any other day she could
hear Cal playing his guitar by now.

She tried the doorbell, the resounding gong obscenely
loud. Behind her she heard the *pffhhiiitt- pffhhiiitt* sound of
Edgar snapping the fishing rod, pretending to make casts
off the front stoop.

Maybe Cal wasn't home. Maybe he and the dog had
slipped out early this morning while she and Daddy were at
Lonnie's. But then, Cal's car was in the drive and his boat
was still moored at the dock out back.

She punched the doorbell again. This time she heard the
muffled thump of something hit the floor at the back of the
house. A loud complaining voice. Cal's voice.

"Oh, you did it now, Warren," Edgar said, pretending to

reel in a big fish from the front yard. "You woke up Mr. Cal. He's gonna be mad."

Lauren listened to the approaching footsteps. "Well, no grown man should sleep this late, in my opinion."

The door opened. "I heard that," Cal said, his voice a husky croak. "Ah, the Talbot clan!" he said, squinting. "At least you used the doorbell this time."

A wave of foul air slapped Lauren in the face, a stench like a seedy bar at last call. Cal slumped before her, hanging onto the doorknob as though his life depended on it. He looked sickly, like he had one foot in the grave—raccoonish dark circles under bloodshot eyes, puffy face sporting a spray of gray stubble, a patch of dried vomit imprinted across the Hog's Breath Saloon logo of his threadbare T-shirt.

"What's so important?" he said, his forearm shielding his face from the bright sun.

Lauren waved her hand in front of her face, warding off the stink. "*Phew!* You must have really tied one on last night, Cal Blevins."

"Thanks for the pep talk, *Mom*."

Cal's retort hurt her. But what did she expect? She didn't know this man. Not really. What right did she have barging in on him like this? To make comments about his personal life?

Cal weaved where he stood. On the verge of getting sick again.

She regretted coming here. "I'm sorry, Cal. I didn't mean to be judgmental. Are you okay?"

"Not really."

She thought about what Daddy had told her about his and Cal's fishing trip yesterday, the way Cal talked to himself, the way he acted like someone else was in the boat with them. And then there was the mysterious question Cal had posed to her: *Do you believe in the supernatural?* This man has more demons than I ever imagined, she thought as she zeroed in on his puke-stained shirt.

"Well," she said, "Daddy brought you something that might make you feel better. He has something to say to you, don't you, Daddy?"

"Yes, yes, yes!" Edgar chirped. He brought the new fishing rod to Cal, proudly presented it to him in outstretched hands, as though it were a magic saber. "I—I'm sorry I wost your st-stuff in the lake, Mr. Cal. *Real* sorry."

Lauren saw Cal's defensive posture soften, watched him struggle to focus on the fishing rod. "Lonnie told us you'd like this one," she said. "We bought you another reel, too, but Lonnie had to special order it. Said he should get it within a week."

Cal took the rod from Edgar, ran his hand down the length of it. "Aw, really, Edgar, you didn't have to do this."

"Yes he did," she said a bit too quickly. "Didn't you, Daddy?"

Edgar bobbed his head up and down enthusiastically.

Cal produced a weak smile. "Well . . . thank you. I'm touched."

Edgar grinned from ear to ear.

"The place is a mess," Cal said, "but you wanna come in?"

"Depends," Lauren said. "Do you have any air freshener? Smells like hog's breath in there."

Cal gave her a mock sneer. "I think I can scrounge up something, yeah."

He led them to the kitchen. As they passed the living room, Lauren glimpsed the floor littered with empty beer bottles, the scotch bottle laying on its side on the coffee table, the large amber stain down the side of the sofa. A plastic cooler was tipped over, the melting ice creating a dark wet spot on the carpet. The smell of stale malt and sickness overpowered her.

The kitchen was better, but not much. Dirty dishes piled in the sink. A trash can overflowing with more beer bottles, aluminum frozen dinner trays, discarded coffee filters. Half-full bottle of whiskey on the kitchen table. Beside it, a shot glass, smudged with fingerprints, and an ashtray containing the crushed-out butt of a thick cigar.

"What went on here last night? A bachelor party?" she blurted without thinking.

Cal leaned the fishing rod against the counter, busied himself making a pot of coffee. "I thought you weren't going to be judgmental," he said, his back to her and Edgar.

"I'm not," she said, pulling out a chair and joining Edgar at the table. "I'm just asking a simple question."

"Okay. Simple answer is I drank way too much. Sorry I didn't have time to clean up before the Welcome Wagon arrived. *Unannounced*, I might add."

His hands shook so that he had trouble dipping the coffee grounds out of the canister. Lauren hated to see anyone this way. This kind of morning-after sickness was one of many reasons she had sworn off alcohol. She watched him knock over the canister, spilling the dark grounds across the counter. He cursed the Almighty.

"Here, let me help you with that," she said, jumping up from her seat and going to him.

"No!" he barked. "I can get my own coffee."

She backed off, watching as he used his hands to scoop the coffee back into the can. His movements were jittery, tentative.

Lauren tried a different approach. "Where's Moby?"

"Don't know. I let him out earlier. Mobes loves to go exploring."

"And you don't go with him?"

"Are you kidding? That dog's like Marco Polo. I can't keep up with him."

He finished loading up the coffee maker and turned his head to one side, looking at the wall clock. "Oh *NO*!" he shrieked.

"What? What is it?"

He turned to face them. "I just remembered. I've got an appointment with someone over in South Birdtown."

"You mean the Cherokee village?"

"Yeah. Supposed to be there by—"

She heard him make a gurgling noise in his throat, then lurch toward the sink where he vomited onto the stack of soiled dishes. At the table, Edgar groaned, "Ooh, nasty!"

"You're not helping here, Daddy," she said, going to Cal, who was hunched over the sink, locked in spasms of dry heaves. "Cal," she said, gently rubbing his back, "you're not in any shape to go anywhere."

"I *have* to!" he blubbered. "Important."

"Why?"

"Because this guy . . . he's leaving tomorrow . . . going to the rez up in Carolina."

"Why is he important?" she said, dabbing his forehead with a wet cloth.

"Look," he said, breaking away from her. "You don't have to know all my business, okay?"

Lauren felt herself tense. She wrung the washcloth in her hands. "No need to get testy," she said. "I'm concerned about you, that's all."

They stared at each other for a long moment. Finally, Cal said, "I'm sorry. I'm coming off a real rough night and—"

"You have any milk in here?" she asked, going to the refrigerator.

"Milk?"

"Yeah . . . you know, that white liquid that comes out of cows?"

"Should be some in there, yeah. What are you—?"

"What about bananas? A jar of honey?" she asked, opening the refrigerator door and pulling out a jug of milk. She checked the expiration date, unscrewed the cap and sniffed.

"No," he said, watching her with a befuddled curiosity.

"No bananas or honey for me. Too sweet."

"Daddy, go next door and get me a couple of our bananas and the squeeze bottle of honey."

"What are you doing?" Cal asked, watching Edgar scurry out of the kitchen.

"I'm going to make you a magic potion guaranteed to chase that hangover of yours . . . my old home remedy. I call it Lauren's Elixir, but it's really just a banana milkshake drowned in honey. Works every time."

"But I—"

"No ifs, ands, or buts about it, mister," she said, nudging him out of the kitchen. "Go get in the shower and turn the water on as hot as you can stand it. And put on a clean shirt. You might think about donating that one you're wearing to science. Now go, go, go!"

Lauren watched Cal shuffle down the hallway to the bathroom. Heard the pipes groan and bang as the water flowed through the old plumbing. She went into cleaning overdrive, first going through the house opening windows, letting the place air out. Sticky humid air came rushing in, but at least it was fresh, a pleasing mixture of spruce and cedar and something vaguely aquatic. She found a can of air freshener under the sink and sprayed until it was empty, the house smelling like a field of lavender and lilac. Next she went through the living room, picking up beer bottles, hearing them clank as she deposited them in a plastic garbage bag. How much can one man drink? she thought. How much alcohol must any one person consume to drown their troubles? She could only imagine the magnitude of the demons that haunted Cal Blevins.

As she moved around the sofa, her toe stubbed something hard underneath. She got down on her knees and snaked her hand around, her fingers touching something cool and slick. She tugged, and it slid out from its hiding place. A small thrill raced through her as she realized it was a stack of three photo albums. She opened the leatherette cover of the one on top, the binding squeaking as though protesting this violation of privacy. The first page displayed four pictures of a very young Cal and his rosy-cheeked bride. The caption, in bold block lettering across the top, read: OUR WEDDING AT SACRED HEART CHURCH, ATLANTA, GEORGIA, JUNE 21, 1971. Lauren flipped through the pages. All wedding shots of the happy couple, Calvin and Sandra Blevins, and a myriad of their young friends and family members. Scrawled next to some of the pictures were personal witticisms, such as **Sandra never did like cake!** and **So begins the days of ball-and-chain servitude**. One page contained six pictures of Sandra, posing in her beautiful taffeta gown, her brunette hair piled atop her head in an elegant swirl, tiny ringlets escaping around her ears and brushing her shoulders. Next to a couple of them Cal had written: **The queen of my dreams** and **The most beautiful woman on the planet**. Cal's father appeared in several shots, decked out in a radiant cream-white long-tailed suit, a tailored cut that Lauren knew was an old-time fashion but couldn't put a name to. She knew it was Cal's father because next to one of the photos Cal had written: **Dad in his dancing togs**.

She opened the second album. This one seemed to be dedicated to Cal's children. Christmas pictures of the kids when they were small. Cal and Sandra, the proud parents beaming at them as they opened gifts near a Christmas tree. Lauren wondered who had taken the photographs. Her eyes went to the top of the first sleeve, saw the blocked inscription there: CHARLEY AND ANDIE IN THEIR BETTER DAYS. Better days? What's that all about? Lauren wondered. She quickly flipped through the pages, the children growing progressively older as she went. The photo gallery stopped when Charley—a serious-looking boy with dark hair and a milky white face marred by acne—appeared to be around fourteen, and Andrea looked about twelve. Andie, with her sandy blonde hair and round face, reminded Lauren of Cal while Charley more closely resembled his mother.

Lauren was about to dig into the third album when she heard Daddy returning. She heard the front door open, Daddy humming "Blackbird." She also heard the jangle of Moby's collar and his doggy nails clicking across the floor. Within seconds, the Lab was on her, licking her face and nearly knocking her over in his enthusiasm to greet her. Several bramble burrs clung to his black coat and he smelled of the lake.

"Hey, big guy," Lauren cooed, trying to scoot the photo albums back under the sofa while Moby continued his sloppy-kiss onslaught. "You won't tell Cal about this, will you?" she said, breaking free of him and pointing at the albums. "It'll be our little secret, okay?"

Moby just sat there on his hind quarters, tail swishing against the carpet.

"I got the stuff you wanted, Warren," Edgar said, entering the room.

She saw the bunch of bananas tucked under his left arm, the honey bottle in his right hand. "Thanks, Daddy. Take it into the kitchen. I'll be there in a sec."

"Moby wikes you."

"Yes, I believe he does," she said, plucking a couple of burrs from the dog's matted fur. "We had a lot of fun together yesterday, didn't we, boy?" She noticed that the squeeze bottle of honey Edgar held in his hand was missing the cap. A thick trail of the gooey golden liquid dribbled down the sides and coated his hand, dripped on the carpet. "Go on and get that stuff in the kitchen, Daddy. I'll be right there."

She got up off her knees, heard the buzz of an electric razor in the bathroom. Cal might be burdened by demons, she thought, but he has a sentimental streak. The knowledge of that made her smile. Cal Blevins was more family-oriented than he let on.

Lauren went to the kitchen, shaking her head as she

followed the trail of honey left by Edgar. She searched the cabinets for a blender, finding one in the small cupboard above the refrigerator. She knew from experience that every serious alcoholic had a blender.

"The birds are very vocal today, Daddy," she said, while slicing up two bananas. "Why don't you take Moby out on the deck and enjoy them."

"Okay," Edgar said. He was out of the kitchen in a flash, Moby chasing behind him in search of new adventure.

She was blending her banana-honey concoction when Cal walked in and sat at the table. He looked like a new man. Clean shaven. Skin freshly scrubbed and emitting a healthier glow. A pleasing herbal scent surrounding him, eyes a little clearer, more focused.

Lauren turned off the blender, poured half the contents into a plastic tumbler, pushed it in front of Cal. "Drink this," she commanded. "Guaranteed to bring you halfway back to humanity."

He looked at her for a long second, then grabbed the tumbler and guzzled the shake. He sat back and smacked his lips, said, "Not bad, not bad at all." Cal slid the empty glass back across the table, pointed at it, indicating he wanted more.

As Lauren refilled his glass, she said, "I want you to promise me something, Cal. The next time you get the urge to do something stupid like you did last night, I want you to come and get me. We'll talk or sing together or . . . I don't know . . . *chant* or something. Anything but self destruction. Will you do that for me?"

He sipped his shake, his eyes never leaving her. Finally he said, "You got it."

The way he was looking at her, as though studying her, made Lauren nervous. She busied herself with cleanup. "Are you starting to come back around?" she said as she cleaned the blender in the sink, her back to him.

"Yeah. I am. Your elixir is amazing."

Over the roar of running tap water, she heard Cal's chair scrape the floor, his footsteps approaching her. She sensed his presence as he stood behind her, could feel the heat of his body. She tensed, not knowing what was happening.

He touched her, his big hand gently squeezing her shoulder. She felt his fingers trace a feathery pattern down her back. He leaned into her, and she felt his warm breath on the back of her neck. "Thank you, Lauren," he whispered, his lips tickling the delicate skin under her jaw. She could smell his banana-honey scented breath, his masculine-sweet cologne.

His arms circled her waist and he kissed her cheek, chaste and innocent, but a kiss nonetheless. He thanked her again, and asked her if she wanted to accompany him on his trip to South Birdtown.

She wanted to tell him that she wanted that more than anything, but she couldn't find her voice.

15

NICOLE KIDMAN, JACK NICHOLSON, AND BLOOD FALLS

Cal felt better out here on the lake, the boat at full throttle, cool wind whipping his face, Lauren's elixir working its magic. They were en route to the Cheecheewah River, Lake McDowell's main feeder tributary that started up around Eagle Summit. South Birdtown was a couple of miles up the river, located on a wide lagoon known as Singing Waters.

Lauren sat in the seat next to him, looking hip and fashionable in her wide-brimmed Panama hat and oversized sunglasses. Cal sensed her looking at him and he chanced a glance at her. She gave him a timid smile, then looked away quickly, as though caught in an embarrassing thought.

Edgar sat on the port side, arm over the gunwale, slapping at the rushing wake with his hand. He wore one of Cal's old Atlanta Braves caps, the red white and blue hat of yesteryear. Cal had given it to Lauren's father with the hopes he would retire his ridiculous fishhook hat. The ploy worked. Edgar had taken to the baseball cap like a kid playing on his first Little League team.

Ever-vigilant watchdog, Moby, sat up front, occupying his usual spot on the bow, ears pinned back by the wind, eyes scanning the waters ahead.

Conversation was impossible with the roar of the outboards. Cal snuck another look at Lauren and thought about

"The Kiss." There had been nothing premeditated about it. Just something he felt compelled to do after the way she had taken care of him. He relived that moment, feeling her cradled in his arms, her long, lean body next to his, the heat radiating from her in a lilac-scented musk, her warm breath against his cheek.

He stole a glance at her impossibly long legs. Smooth pale thighs, elegantly tapered knees and ankles. He looked away, fighting an uncontrollable urge to touch her. Something about this woman stirred the long-dead embers of his internal fires. Something about Lauren Talbot pressed all of his hot buttons.

Cal had fully intended to make a solo trip to South Birdtown, maybe take Moby along. But then she showed up on his doorstep. Some unspoken exchange had passed between them, Cal coming to the realization that he didn't want to go to the Cherokee village without her, Lauren telling him with her eyes that she wanted to be with him.

They rounded Loon Island, passing the cove where Cal had seen the face-painted fish hypnotist. As they were loading up the boat earlier, Cal told Lauren about the strange encounter. He knew the revelation was chancy, since they didn't really know each other. But, miracle of miracles, she didn't look at him like he was a crazy man. There had been nothing judgmental in her expression as he related the story to her. Unburdened by his first disclosure, Cal decided to also tell her about seeing his long-dead father on the boat. Lauren had listened to the unlikely scenario without expression, but Cal could tell she was mulling something over as he talked. When he finished the story, she smiled at him. He asked her what she found so amusing and Lauren told him about Edgar's startled reaction to Cal's strange behavior during their fishing trip—talking to himself and smelling smoke. How Daddy was so worried about him. When Cal prodded Lauren as to what she thought about his two strange encounters out on the lake, she merely shrugged and said, "Our minds have minds of their own sometimes."

He cut the boat to starboard, heading for Sullivan Slot, the fast-running narrows that led to the largest section of Lake McDowell. He revved the outboards on approach, building up speed as they hit the whitewater, pushing the craft against the onrushing currents. Fishing was good here, but boating could be treacherous, with the jumble of smooth boulders and tangle of deadwood cluttering the way. Cal had been boating these waters and running the Slot since he was a kid, and he negotiated the run with ease.

They entered the main expanse of the lake, what locals called Upper Lake McDowell. The placid water spread out in front of them like a floor of highly-polished evergreen tile. A few small islands of lush foliage dotted the way. Half a dozen small boats cut white swaths across the glass-like surface. Cal heard the buzz of outboard motors, saw the water skiers doing their thing in the distance, their orange life vests and glittery skis reflecting brightly in the sun.

Entering this main part of the lake—a section the Cherokee referred to as *e-qua-di-do-di*, or Big Spoon—felt like opening the door from the inside of a cramped closet and entering a palatial room. Straight ahead loomed Tyler Ridge, the monolithic wall of red rock that towered above the lake. A waterfall cascaded off the top of the west end. From this distance, the tumbling water appeared as a twisted silver ribbon lowered into the lake.

Cal headed the boat toward a pair of wide cuts in the Ridge. These two divides had been carved out over the millennia by the incessant flow of two rivers—the Chee-cheewah and the smaller Winniehabba. As they approached the twin rivers, the water became choppy, the air saturated with a fine, cool mist. They entered the shade of Tyler Ridge and the temperature dropped several degrees. Cal ran the boat along the shoreline, about thirty yards from the imposing wall of red clay and sparkly granite, admiring the bucolic beauty.

He felt Lauren lean into him, the moist softness of her lips against his ear. "It's so gorgeous out here, Cal," she said. "Thank you for inviting me."

He nodded dumbly, the heat of her breath and lilt of her voice sending a sizzle through him.

They rounded a bend in the wall, passing the first cut and the mouth of the Winniehabba. From here, an excellent view of the falls opened up to them.

"Look!" Lauren said into his ear, "A rainbow!"

Cal looked to where she pointed. Sure enough, a dazzling rainbow arced across the falls, the reds and greens especially vibrant in the prismatic mist.

"The falls are breathtaking, Cal. Do they have a name?"

He turned to speak into her ear, and for a long moment they faced each other, their foreheads nearly touching. Cal could feel her sweet breath against his face, thought about leaning in and kissing her. Wanted to so badly. She tilted her head slightly as though in anticipation. But he started talking and she turned her ear to him. The moment was lost.

"The official name is Glory Falls. But the Cherokee have a different name for it."

"What's that?"

"Blood Falls."

"Why?"

"Because the blood of many Cherokee warriors was spilled there. White settlers forced many of them over the falls. Some on horseback, most shackled and thrown in, left to drown before they went over. All of them perished on the rocks below. It's said that the whirlpools below the falls ran blood-red for weeks at a time. Some of the village elders claim the spectacular red you see in the rainbows is the ghost blood from those who were murdered."

"How sad," Lauren said.

Suddenly, Edgar came to life, shouting, "Wook at that! A rainbow! It's so . . . awful!"

Lauren and Cal laughed together. "We see it, Daddy," she yelled over the noisy outboards. "But you mean *awesome*, right? Not awful."

"Yes, yes, yes! *Awful!*"

Lauren laughed again and Cal joined in. He relished the melodious sound of her joy.

Moby stared at them from his place on the prow, tilting his head, wondering what all the fuss was about.

Lauren squeezed Cal's hand, caressed his knuckle. Cal squeezed back. A warm glow spread through his chest.

Within minutes they entered the mouth of the Chee-cheewah River. Cal cut back the throttle. The river was deep but narrow, and he had to navigate carefully so he didn't slam his boat into one of the walls that rose so impossibly high on either side of them. A hawk wheeled overhead, gliding on the thermals, its head trained on the upper ridge, searching for prey along the tree line. Edgar spotted the large predator and began to call to it in some indecipherable whistle-chant that sounded suspiciously like his loon call. The hawk, however, was oblivious to the old man's greeting.

They made their way upriver. The cliff walls receded into flat terrain. Thick vegetation engulfed them. Ferns and wildflowers splashed patches of vivid greens and reds and yellows along the meandering banks. Huge poplars and oaks spread their leafy limbs over the river, creating a tunnel of striped shadows. A cool breeze carried a pleasing chlorophyll scent. The currents slowed to a steady gurgle. Cal cut the motors back to a quieter trolling speed.

Lauren spoke, her voice loud. "I'm not complaining, because this is beautiful country. But wouldn't it have been easier to take the car to the Cherokee village?"

"Only if you want to hike a couple of miles up a difficult trail. There aren't any roads leading to B-town.

Only horse trails."

"They don't have cars?"

"No. Just horses. And a few Vespa scooters. South Birdtown is a throwback to the old ways. Their only concessions to the modern world are cell phones and indoor plumbing . . . a television here and there. Oh, yeah . . . and motorized boats"

"So they have electricity?"

"Kind of. They run off gas-powered generators."

"So we're really out in God's country here." It rolled off her tongue as *Gawd's country.*

Cal shrugged. "This might even be too remote for God."

"You guys talk too much," Edgar intoned. "You're scarin' away the birds."

"Sorry, Daddy," Lauren said, laughing.

Cal loved Lauren's lilting, musical laugh. He was beguiled by its melodic sound the way Edgar was entranced by the loon's call.

They passed a couple of boats heading downriver to the lake, both lightweight aluminum boats with small, low-horsepower motors. Skippered by young Cherokee males wearing multicolored headbands and do-rags. The boats, with their simple engines, were whisper quiet as they puttered past. Cal waved to them. The Indians all waved back in unison, chattering rapidly in Cherokee.

"What are they saying?" Lauren asked him.

With a straight face Cal said, "They're talking about you, Lauren. Trying to figure out which Hollywood movie star you are."

This produced a wide, doubting smile. "Stop it!" she said, slapping his arm.

"I'm serious," he persisted. "Sounds like they reached a unanimous decision."

"Oh yeah? And just what did they decide, Cal?"

"They think you're Nicole Kidman."

She burst out laughing. "Cal Blevins, you are such a bloody scoundrel! Sweet, but a scoundrel nonetheless."

"See? You even talk like Nicole . . . Aussie all the way, mate!"

"You're really full of it."

"That's not all they said."

"Oh, please do tell, great Pinocchio nose," she said with measured sarcasm. "What else did they say?"

"They think I'm Jack Nicholson."

She lost it on that one, letting out great shrieks of laughter that caused the Indians on the two passing boats to stop their gibbering and stare at her.

"*You*? Jack Nicholson? Oh, that's priceless, Cal!"

Cal stared straight ahead, steered the boat upriver, big smile plastered on his face as he enjoyed the uplifting sounds of her laughter.

16

SINGING WATERS

They entered the large lagoon known as Singing Waters—the river access to South Birdtown. Cal cut the motors back to a low groan. Lauren felt like she had entered an alternate universe set in some prehistoric time. Tall trees laced with long strands of woody vines. Lilies and ferns draping the shoreline. Stonehenge-like boulders lining the lagoon. Watery chimes tinkling and clinking like a symphony of bells all around her.

Singing Waters was an environmental phenomenon created by centuries of wind and water erosion. Cal explained to her that over time, the erosion carved holes of varying sizes in the huge stones, creating a unique auditory experience. The plinking water sounds reminded Lauren of the New Age head shop she frequented in her undergraduate days—Capricorn Moon—a retail warehouse in Nashville that dedicated an entire showroom to wind chimes of all shapes and sizes and tonal pitches. Lauren remembered standing in the middle of the large room, overcome by a pleasurable dizziness as the chimes enveloped her in a magical acoustic cocoon. Singing Waters gave her the same vibe.

Off to their left were a pair of one-seat kayaks, each manned by elderly Cherokee males, both of whom had their paddles up out of the water and eyes closed.

"Hey!" Edgar shouted and pointed at the kayaks. "What are they doing? They wook d-d-dead!"

"Quiet!" Cal shushed him. "These are sacred waters. They're meditating."

Cal steered toward the far shore and the array of water craft moored there, a motley assortment of primitive dugout canoes and small motorized boats like the ones they had passed on the river. Lauren watched the corded muscles twisting in Cal's forearms as he brought the boat into shore, couldn't take her eyes off of his big hands working the wheel. She thought about their close encounter earlier today, when he had wrapped those arms around her from behind, when he had touched her with those hands. The quick peck on her cheek. His closeness. His manly scent. She replayed the scene in her mind and felt an unfamiliar wetness between her legs. She blushed. He was interested in her, no doubt about that. But why? Lauren knew she was a long way from Nicole Kidman, or any movie star for that matter. Cal's notion was ridiculous, and she knew on some level that he was just being playful with his comment. And yet, it was obvious to her that he was drawn to her. Maybe even *needed* her. Ever since Cal heard her sing, things had been different between them. And then, out on the river just twenty minutes ago he came within an inch of kissing her. But something had stopped him. What? His ex-wife Sandra? Too soon after his divorce? Lauren had given him all kinds of green-light signals, but maybe he had misread her. Or perhaps she had done the misreading.

They entered shallow water and Cal went to the rear of the boat to lift the motors, stomped back to the wheel and guided them toward the stretch of mossy gravel that served as the beach. Lauren scanned the shoreline. Three birch bark canoes in varying stages of completion sat in a wooden rack, curing in the sun, their ribbed interiors giving them the look of exoskeletons of some long-extinct fish. In the shade of the forest, several young Cherokee women painted bright designs on the hulls of larger dugout canoes—huge eyes and bird beaks and colorful feather patterns. Lauren caught a whiff of turpentine and freshly sanded wood. Two horses were tethered to a stout oak nearby. They twitched their tails and snorted, annoyed by pesky flies.

Lauren felt the scrape of gravel against the underside of the hull as Cal beached the boat.

They were greeted by a soft-spoken elderly man, who said something in Cherokee. The only part Lauren understood was Cal's name.

"Yeah," Cal said, "We're here to see Walter Yanegwa. Big Bear? He's expecting us."

"Ah . . . *a-se-hi di-gi-na-li*." (Yes, he welcomes his friends).

Lauren watched Cal exchange an elaborate handshake with the Indian that involved forearms and thumbs.

"We'd also like to see Izzie Kalanu if he's available," Cal said. "Izzie the Raven?"

The Indian cracked a wizened smile as he scanned the other occupants in the boat. "Izzie needs audience the way day needs sunlight," he said in broken English. "You want stories about birds? Our winged friends of Cherokee Nation?"

"Yes, yes, yes!" Edgar practically shouted, climbing out of the boat and splashing through the shallows. "Especially the woons! Yes, yes, yes . . . woons!"

Cal said, "This is Edgar Talbot, better known as Birdman. He has an unquenchable curiosity about loons."

"*A-si-yu*. Izzie will feel delight in seeing you."

Suddenly, the man's eyes widened in surprise as Edgar approached him, then flinched as Edgar threw his arms out at him. Edgar attempted to recreate the Cherokee handshake, which he turned into an awkward, spasmodic dance. The old Cherokee played along, laughing at the absurdity of it, which got Lauren and Cal laughing, too.

"And this," Cal said, taking Lauren by the hand and helping her out of the boat, "is Edgar's beautiful daughter, Lauren."

Lauren felt a tingle run up her arm through her fingers where they touched Cal's moist hand. "Nice to meet you," she said, getting her footing on the loose gravel.

Suddenly, Moby jumped off the bow and landed with a thud on the stony beach, began barking.

"Oh, I'm sorry, Mobes," Cal said, kneeling and scratching the dog behind his ears. "This here is Moby the Wonderdog. Hates to be left out. He's a little narcissistic, but we love him anyway."

The old Cherokee leaned over and let Moby sniff him. Instantly the Lab's tail started wagging.

"*A-si-yu*, Moby," the Indian said, raking his hand across his back. "He good dog, I can tell. Such fine fur . . . and black as a moonless night."

The old man straightened and tapped his chest. "*A-ya* Joseph Redhawk. Follow me. I will take you to the village now."

They hiked up a narrow trail that cut through thick vegetation. The path was carpeted with decaying leaves and pine needles and felt springy underfoot. Lauren breathed in the pleasant scent of lake fermentation and woodsy pollen. Birds chirped and cackled throughout the forest. Behind them, the chiming sounds of the water and pounding of hammers diminished and then died out altogether.

They came to a thick tree trunk that had been felled by lightning, and lay blocking the trail. Cal grabbed Lauren's hand to help her up and over. When Cal attempted to assist Edgar, Lauren's father just snorted "Oh *fuggleshine*," and waved him off, as though insulted. Lauren and Cal stood in the shade and exchanged glances with Joseph Redhawk as they watched Edgar labor to get over the log. Moby cleared it with an acrobatic leap, which only exasperated Edgar further.

They hiked up a steep incline and Lauren heard a dull syncopated thumping ahead, sounding not unlike the grinding machinery of a large manufacturing plant.

"What's that noise?" she asked Joseph Redhawk.

"The sound of my village," Joseph said without breaking stride. "Gas-powered generators—the heartbeat of South Birdtown."

Within five minutes they came to a clearing. South Birdtown spread out in front of them like a sepia-tone photograph in a dusty American history tome. Shacks with tarpaper roofs and lean-tos and crude tents made of animal hides. Several groups of scantily clad Cherokee congregated around open fires, cooking, eating, drinking. Lauren caught a whiff of something approximating barbecue—a very pleasant cooked meat smell—and felt her stomach grumble with hunger pangs.

Joseph Redhawk led them to Walter "Big Bear" Yanegwa's dwelling. Lauren noticed it was a cut above most of the other primitive structures, a one-room cabin with a rooftop cistern to provide running water, a color television hooked up to a small satellite dish, and a beat-up microwave. A rickety kitchen table and two chairs sat along one wall, a shabby sofa with an exposed spring along another.

Walter Yanegwa was an immense man. Lauren could easily see how he had acquired his tribal name of Big Bear. Massive, triangular head, like a bust sculpted from a solid block of bronze. Eyes that glinted red in the dim light, giving them a predatory look. Broad chest and muscular arms.

"I know you're busy so I'll get to the point," Cal said to Big Bear. "I understand you oversee all commercial fishing in the village."

The big Indian nodded. "*A-se-hi.*"

"And you still use the old dugout canoes."

Yanegwa nodded again. "Only not as much. Not good

use of resources. We catch more fish with our powerboats. We here in South Birdtown favor the old ways, but we do have good business sense. We go modern when it benefits us."

Lauren looked at the packed dirt floor beneath her feet and wondered about that. The modernism seemed to be slanted toward entertainment. Creature comforts took on a lower priority.

"But you do still send out the old canoes, correct?" Cal prodded.

"Only as backup to the *tsi-yu* with motors."

"What about your fishermen?

Big Bear gave Cal a questioning glance.

"I mean, do they ever paint their faces and wear the old animal hide vests when they go out for the daily catch?"

Walter Yanegwa looked surprised. "No, not for many years. Why do you ask?"

"Well, when I was a boy I attended summer camp here. I remember a show your people put on for the campers. They presented your fishermen in greasepaint and the kind of retro Native American clothing I describe. They were also in ancient-looking cutout canoes, much older than the ones we saw being made out on the beach."

"Very true. We once put on ceremonial shows to let the *yo-ne-ga* children see the traditional ways of the Cherokee. We have not done that for many years now. Not since the McDowell family sold the camps to a big corporation. The new owners refuse to pay us for our efforts. They say we should be proud enough to do it for free. They are not as generous as the McDowells."

"So it's all about capitalism, then."

Walter Yanegwa looked at Cal sternly. "We are a proud people, Mr. Blevins. But we are not stupid. The people who run those summer camps make much *a-di-la*. They very wealthy. We do not ask for much, but they refuse to pay. We need tourism dollars."

Lauren looked at Cal, who was mulling this over. Finally he said, "So then, there is absolutely no chance that I would have seen one of these throwback fishermen in an inlet out on the lake this week, correct?"

Big Bear looked dubious. "Did you?"

"Yeah, I did. East of Loon Island. But that's not all. The fisherman I saw also caught fish with his bare hands."

The big Cherokee looked away, remained quiet.

Cal continued. "This fisherman I saw did something to hypnotize the fish. Made them jump right into his hands."

A dark expression crossed Walter Yanegwa's face.

"What?" Cal implored. "Not possible?"

Big Bear spoke. "*Gi-ne-li*, all of us in the village know the tales of the master hand fishermen . . . the *a-su-hi-is*. Their exploits have grown to epic proportions. Did they really exist? Maybe. But one thing is certain. These fishermen do not exist today."

Cal sagged in disappointment. "So you're saying what I witnessed out there on the lake wasn't real?"

Walter Big Bear Yanegwa's eyes flitted from Cal to Lauren to Edgar, then back to Cal. His look was stern, analytical, as though sizing them up. Finally he said, "This lake holds many mysteries, Mr. Blevins. Over the years, I have heard many reports of strange happenings out on the water. Some of them make what you saw seem ordinary."

"Believe me," Cal said. "There was nothing ordinary about what I saw."

Big Bear nodded. "I understand. To give you better perspective on this, I shall tell you the story of FishHawk, the legendary hand fisher, one of the first *a-su-hi-is*. Some of our younger people think FishHawk was a myth. They scoff at his mention. But people in the village who are my age and older? We believe that FishHawk and others like him actually practiced their magic on these waters more than two-hundred years ago. We believe the *a-su-hi-is* really did hypnotize fish into their canoes. I will tell you the tale now, and you can arrive at your own conclusion, Mr. Blevins."

As the big Cherokee told them the story of FishHawk, Lauren felt as though she had been transported back in time and was riding with the master fisherman in his canoe.

17

THE LEGEND OF THE LOON

Cal felt dazed and bewildered as Walter Big Bear Yanegwa led them to Izzie the Raven's place. The bizarre tale of FishHawk seemed plausible the way Yanegwa told it. Yet it defied all logic. Had to be a Cherokee fable, pure and simple, Cal thought.

And yet he had witnessed a happening out on the lake that nearly matched Big Bear's description of FishHawk. It couldn't be mere coincidence.

So what exactly had Cal seen in that shallow inlet east of Loon Island earlier this week? A ghost? An apparition? Did he have a telepathic connection to Walter Yanegwa? Was he connected somehow to the collective psyche of the South Birdtown villagers? Or maybe he was tuned into the long-dead soul of FishHawk himself, channeled through some kind of complex image transference that only a Nobel-winning physicist could begin to explain.

But Cal feared the only reasonable explanation—that he was going crazy.

He hoped their meeting with Izzie Kalanu would give him some answers.

Izzie the Raven was a much younger man than Cal had anticipated. Cal reasoned that storytellers—the keepers of the people's history in Native American cultures—were the village elders, old as Methuselah and twice as wise. But Izzie Kalanu couldn't be much more than thirty-five. So much for preconceived stereotypes.

One glance at Izzie the Raven told him where Kalanu got his tribal name—long, lustrous ebony hair fell across bony shoulders, velvety strands shining purple-black in the late afternoon sun like the feathers of a crow. A snakeskin headband pulled the hair back off his face.

"Welcome," Izzie addressed them. "I have greatly anticipated your arrival."

They were congregated outside in a small clearing. Cal, Lauren, and Edgar sat on tree stumps. Moby lay at Cal's feet, panting. The clearing contained maybe forty stumps, all positioned with a good view of the ramshackle lean-to up front. Cherokee dreamcatchers of wood and feathers hung from the tin roof of the lean-to and were draped across the simple podium behind which Izzie stood. The South Birdtown version of a conference room, Cal thought.

"When Lonnie Whitefeather informed me you were coming today, I was filled with joy," Izzie said, standing at his crude pulpit. "The tales of my people explain the mysteries of this land. The Cherokee have a long and special relationship with birds who nest in this habitat. I will begin by explaining how this village came to be named South Birdtown—"

"Wait a minute," Lauren called out. "Sorry to interrupt, but I'm interested in hearing a little about you first. Can't know the story without first knowing the teller."

Izzie grinned, his face open and warm. "Absolutely. What would you like to know?"

"Well, I don't mean to get too personal, but aren't you a little young to be the village historian?"

Cal tried not to let his smile show. Uncanny the similar paths his and Lauren's minds traveled.

Izzie grabbed a walking stick—a smooth, dark-wood staff topped with an elaborately carved raven head—and approached Lauren. "I am often asked this question," he said, planting the stick in the dirt, as though anchoring himself in front of her. "How can one so young know all that went before? The answer is simple. I was schooled by one of our village's legendary scholars—Owl Who Sees Forever. It was just last year the loons escorted Owl to Lake Beyond, but his lessons live forever in my mind." Izzie took a seat on a stump near Cal and laid the walking stick across his lap. "I was groomed from a very young age to be the teller of tales. I come from a long line of storytellers. It is my calling to continue that tradition. If I break the tradition, I will be banished from the village, carried off in the dark of night by scavenger eagles. As you can see, it is a big responsibility."

Quite the rigid caste system, Cal thought. Scavenger eagles? Was Izzie talking about vultures?

Lauren said, "Did Owl Who Sees Forever also teach you English? You speak it flawlessly."

"Thank you, *gi-ne-li*. No, Owl did not teach me English. He knew only the Cherokee tongue. I studied languages at Duke University and earned a Masters degree in Linguistics."

"You hold a Masters degree?" Cal said, sounding a little more astonished than he intended.

Izzie stood, maintained a crooked smile as he scratched in the dirt with his staff. "Why does that surprise you? Several of us here in the village are quite well educated. We take advantage of generous Native American scholarships and casino money from the rez."

Cal said, "You have a Masters education and you elect to live *here*?"

Izzie's brows knitted in a frown. His sunny disposition melted into a glare. "What is wrong with *here*? This is my home," he said, waving his walking stick around the clearing. "My people have been part of this landscape for centuries. I feel comfortable here. This is where I belong.

This is where my education does the most good, schooling my fellow villagers. I would not feel comfortable living in your world, wearing synthetic clothes and working in a windowless cubicle for some soulless corporation, chasing after things that really do not matter."

Cal could certainly relate to that. "I'm sorry," he said, "I didn't mean to—"

Lauren cut him off, saying to Izzie, "You talk of ravens and loons and eagles, all in a spiritual sense. I find it fascinating that the Cherokee maintain an almost divine relationship with bird species."

"Oh, not all of the Cherokee Nation, ma'am," Izzie said, visibly relaxing, his eyes shining like polished black marbles. "Just those of our clan—the *Tsi-s-Qua*. We believe all of nature's winged creatures are our sisters and brothers ... our mothers and fathers ... our long-lost ancestors."

"How so?" Cal asked, curious.

"My people believe in reincarnation. When the Great Spirit calls us to Lake Beyond, we are guided from our earthly embodiment by Great Spirit messengers . . . birds. For us, this is almost always loons. After a short visit to Lake Beyond, we return as a bird. Usually as a loon."

"Why loons?" Lauren asked. "I mean, why not owls or hawks or even ravens?" she said, eyeing the carved raven-head knob of Izzie's cane.

Izzie beamed at Lauren, a teacher admiring his star student. "My forefathers developed an almost mystical relationship with the loons in these parts," he said. "Our first settlers worshiped these special creatures who travel through three planes of life—earth, wind, and water. Very unique, this power to travel through vastly different habitats. The Great Spirit has blessed very few creatures with this ability. Did you know that loons can dive underwater a hundred feet deep or more and stay down for minutes at a time?"

Edgar literally bolted from his stump and waved his hand like a grade school child trying to get the teacher's attention. "I knew that . . . yes, yes, yes I did! Woons can swim . . . yes, yes, yes they can!"

"My father knows all about loons," Lauren explained to Izzie.

Cal groaned. "Oh, he knows about loons all right. Edgar's loon calls have attracted some attention around the lake."

"Oh?" Izzie said to Edgar. "You can do a good loon call?"

This drew an exasperated sigh from Lauren. "Please don't encourage—"

As if on cue, Edgar launched into a screeching, cater-wauling loon call that flushed a covey of brown thrashers from the surrounding treetops. Moby, not to be outdone, got in the act with accompanying howls. Cal noticed several curious villagers gather on the fringes of the clearing, stretching their necks to see what the commotion was all about.

Izzie, Cal, and Lauren shared nervous laughs as Edgar and Moby finished up their feral act. After several long minutes, the clearing returned to its previous calm. Edgar returned to his seat on the stump. Moby curled around his feet.

"I'm truly sorry about that, Mr. Kalanu," Lauren said.

"No, do not worry about it," Izzie responded. "I enjoyed that. This man," he said, pointing his cane at Edgar, "is a loon lover, and as such, he is my family . . . my *tsi-da-na-lu*." He addressed Edgar directly. "Perhaps you would consider giving our villagers lessons in loon call techniques? The importance of the call has been lost on our youth in recent years."

Lauren cleared her throat. "Please don't give Daddy ideas."

Izzie looked at Edgar with a benevolent smile. "It is

clear that your father has been brushed by the wings of the Great Loon Spirit." Izzie turned back to Lauren. "Your father carries the song of the loon in his heart. He is blessed."

"You hear that, Daddy?" Lauren said. "Izzie the Raven thinks you're special."

"And I am sure your father also knows about the loon's keen intelligence," Izzie said, still looking at Edgar. "Contrary to mainstream beliefs, the loon is a sophisticated, intelligent creature. Popular culture has done a great disservice to the loon. A crazy person is called loony. A psychiatric ward is referred to as a loony bin. People use the term 'crazy as a loon' all the time, especially when talking about stupid people. I suppose that comes from the crying-laugh call of the loon that makes them sound a bit demented. But loons are far from crazy or stupid. It is a myth that offends us *Tsi-s-Qua* Cherokee."

Edgar jumped up from his stump and spread his arms, swayed from side to side as though flying. "Yes, yes, yes ... woons are not crazy. Not stupid. Woons are smart . . . yes, yes, yes!" As he continued moving in a small circle, Moby joined him, nipping close at his heels, thinking it was a game.

Izzie continued talking as he watched Edgar do his flying dance. "We developed ceremonial pageants built around the loon. Over time, it became a human-avian marriage. Over hundreds of years loons became our cycle of death and rebirth. We *Tsi-s-Qua* Cherokee look out for the loons. We protect them. And the loons, in their way, watch over us. They protect us from evil. They keep the crows and insects from destroying our crops. They direct big fish into our nets to help us keep our bellies full."

Cal thought about this. Was this spiritual reverence directed toward the loon exclusively a Cherokee thing? Did other Native American tribes also worship the loon? He inquired and Izzie responded.

"Because of their mournful song, many tribes think the loon is a guide to the netherworld. Early Inuit civilizations buried loon skulls in their graves as a means of carrying wisdom into the next life. Natives from the Faroe Islands thought the call of the red-throated loon flying overhead meant it was following a soul to heaven. The Ojibwa thought the loon call to be an omen of death. The Thompson River Indians of British Columbia thought the song of the loon was a prediction of rain. So, you can see the loon has played a significant role in other cultures, but we *Tsi-s-Qua* Cherokee are the only ones who weave the loon mystique so completely into our tribal customs."

Izzie the Raven continued with his oratory for another ten minutes. Cal noticed small groups of villagers quietly filing into the clearing and taking seats on stumps behind them. Something was about to happen, but what it was, Cal couldn't say.

Izzie finished his presentation and looked around at the gathering throng. To Cal and Lauren he said, "You have been a most appreciative audience." He pointed his walking stick at Edgar. "And this man sings the tune of the loon. He speaks their language. He *respects* them. And so I feel it is appropriate that you see one of our most cherished ceremonies. Very few people outside of South Birdtown have seen what you are about to. You should feel honored. You may not understand the things you are about to witness. All you need to know is that this ceremony is very special to us. We perform it once a week, much in the same way religions of the outside world observe their Sabbath. As in most sanctuaries, I must ask for complete quiet as we pay our respects to the Great Loon Spirit."

Izzie the Raven brought his walking stick high over his head, grasping it with both hands. Slowly he brought it down to his waist.

Cal heard a rustling behind him. He turned and saw that the villagers in attendance had gone into kneeling positions behind their tree stumps, heads bowed. Cal turned his attention back front, saw another Cherokee join Izzie. This villager was one of the elders, his face painted a garish white with purple wings slashed across both cheeks. A large black oyster shell strapped to his nose protruded like a silver-black beak. As the man moved, tiny bells laced into his tangled gray hair clinked. He lowered himself to the ground, sat cross-legged, and pulled a wooden flute from a buckskin pouch. He pursed his lips and began to blow into the instrument, producing a plaintive melody. As he played, he moved his head from side to side, the bells in his hair producing a tinkling counterpoint.

Izzie began to recite long passages in Cherokee, waving his stick in front of him slowly, seductively, like a master magician. Occasionally he paused, went silent, the villagers filling the voids with their chanting. All the while, the birdman flautist continued producing the haunting melody that drifted across the clearing.

Cal looked at Lauren, who shrugged her shoulders and bit her lower lip, as if to say, *I don't have a clue, but it's fascinating nonetheless.* Then he peered at Edgar where he sat with Moby. Both Lauren's father and the dog seemed to be completely entranced by the melancholy sound of the flute and the sweeping motion of Izzie's walking cane.

This went on for fifteen minutes. Then it all came to a halt. A complete and utter silence blanketed the clearing. Izzie brought the stick high above his head, all eyes focused there.

Cal heard the loons before he saw them, off in the distance, their mad calls distinct, coming closer, gaining in volume. He felt an odd tingle along the nape of his neck, the dizzying slant of vertigo.

And then he saw them, five loons in all, flying into the clearing in a perfect V pattern. The loons circled overhead, staying in their precise formation. The villagers began to cheer and shout excitedly, many of them standing on tree stumps and pointing skyward. The birdman flautist began playing again, the tempo much more lively than before, the melody happy and upbeat.

The birds swooped down into the clearing and roosted on Izzie's cane, lined up like ducks in a carnival shooting gallery, completely still and apparently awaiting their next instruction.

The flautist quit playing. He stood and slipped the flute back into its pouch. Izzie held the walking cane high above his head, holding it steady with both hands so as not to disturb the loons perched there.

The flautist began shaking his head from side to side, the bells in his hair catching the late afternoon sun in sparkling spangles as they jingled. He began chanting in Cherokee, the villagers joining in. Cal watched in amazement as the loons began swaying from side to side, in time with the chanting.

This cannot be happening, Cal thought. He glanced at Lauren, who, for the first time, looked more frightened than fascinated. A quick look at Edgar told Cal the old man was still held spellbound by the strange goings-on. Moby was on his feet, but seemingly just as paralyzed as Edgar.

And then the chanting stopped. Dead silence in the clearing. The loons sat five abreast on the cane above Izzie's head, their attention focused on the flute-playing shaman. From where Cal sat, the birds looked like the stuffed cloth birds Lonnie sold in his store. Completely lifeless they were. Not even a twitch of a wing or the dip of a beak.

Cal noticed the webbed feet of the loons, and wondered: How can they perch on the walking stick like that with webbed feet?

The flautist raised a hand and held it above his head, palm open. Incredibly, the loons began their raucous calls. Edgar joined in with his human version, Moby pitching in with his howling canine interpretation.

Just as the noise rose to a crescendo that hurt Cal's ears, the flautist circled his hand in the air slowly, five times. With each hand movement, a loon took flight. The villagers whooped and hollered as each loon departed the clearing.

Cal watched as the last of the loons cleared the treetops. He listened as their calls became faint, watching until the five specks on the horizon disappeared.

Had they returned to Lake Beyond?

Too bizarre, Cal thought as he tried to make sense of what had just happened.

Another look at Lauren told him she had no idea either.

18

PRACTICE MAKES PERFECT

Lauren yawned, checked the mantle clock above the fireplace in her living room. Almost midnight. She listened to Cal plucking his guitar where he sat in the old Adirondack rocker, the music soft and soothing. Daddy hunched over his card table, working a mammoth jigsaw puzzle, a panorama of a European castle hugging the side of a snow-covered mountain. He clucked his tongue and mumbled to himself as he snapped puzzle pieces in place.

Daddy's shenanigans on the return boat trip from South Birdtown had worn Lauren down. All the way back across the lake, he had chattered excitedly about the loon ceremony, repeating a strange mantra, "Woons on a walking-stick! Woons on a walking-stick!" like an insane parrot. Lauren loved her father dearly, but at one point, she had to restrain herself from pushing him overboard.

Daddy stayed ramped up on his "woon" rant through dinner and early evening. Lauren wasn't quite sure what they'd witnessed this afternoon in the Cherokee village, but Daddy saw it as a spiritual awakening. He could barely chew his food at dinner due to his excitement. He spoke of Izzie Kalanu with reverence, as though referring to a divine being. He babbled on about the flautist who had played Pied Piper to the loons. And about those loons … to Daddy, they were the true angel birds, messengers sent from heaven to deliver the word of Saint Peter.

Yes indeed, this has been one long day, Lauren thought, catching herself as she began to nod off.

"Aren't you getting tired, Daddy?" she ventured.

"No, no, no," Edgar said, head never turning away from the tabletop where he worked. "The angel birds give me energy . . . yes, yes, yes, they do!"

Lauren sighed. "It's way past your bedtime."

Edgar turned and glowered at her. "You can't tell me what to do! Don't forget that I changed your diapers, young lady . . . yes, yes, yes, I did. And they were messy things, too, don't ya know."

And now I'm returning the favor, Lauren thought sadly. She looked at Cal, imploring with her eyes for him to do something, to talk some sense into her obstinate father.

Cal stopped picking his guitar, said to Edgar, "Hey, Birdman, if I play 'Blackbird' for you, will you go to bed?"

Edgar scratched his head with one of the puzzle pieces, mulling over the offer. "Can I sing the verses by myself?"

Cal teased him by playing the intro to 'Blackbird.' "Do you know all the words, Edgar?"

"Yes, yes, yes . . . I do!" Edgar jumped up as though catapulted, nearly knocking over the table in his exuberance.

"You have every single word memorized?"

Lauren smiled, enjoying the way Cal played Daddy.

Edgar went and stood next to the rocker where Cal sat. "I'm not an idiot, you know, Mr. Cal. There aren't *that* many words."

Cal nodded. "I know, but you got stuck on the second verse last time we tried."

Edgar's face brightened. "I've been practicing, Mr. Cal . . . yes, yes, yes, I have! I'll do it right this time, I promise."

"And you'll go straight to bed after we do the song?"

"I promise. Scout's honor," he said, holding up two

fingers, his expression earnest, as though giving a blood oath.

"Then let's do it," Cal said, launching into the song for real, giving Lauren a sly wink.

Lauren watched with amusement as Daddy sang "Blackbird" to Cal's accompaniment, mostly off key. But he remembered every lyric, true to his promise.

"Very good, Birdman," Cal said when they finished. "That's the best you've done that song."

Edgar's grin stretched from one ear to the other. "Practice makes perfect."

"Yes it does, Daddy," Lauren said. "And now how about a little practice going to bed?"

Edgar went into sulk mode. He dropped down on the floor with an agility that belied his seventy-six years and went into a tantrum. He thrashed his arms, banged his head against the sofa, yelled, "Not fair! No, no, no . . . not fair at all!"

"You gave me your Scout's honor," Cal said. "Remember, the angel birds are watching."

Edgar transformed at the mention of the heavenly loons, his expression going from a sullen pout to serious. With a loud groan, he hoisted himself up off the floor. "You're right, Mr. Cal. I made a promise. The woons are watching me."

Edgar entered the hallway leading to the bedrooms, and Lauren said to his back, "Be sure to brush your teeth, Daddy."

From the hallway she heard, "Oh fuggleshine!" amongst a string of other indecipherable words. But then she heard the water running and the sounds of Daddy vigorously brushing his teeth. Shortly after, she heard him gargling.

Lauren said to Cal, "You handle Daddy so well. He listens to you."

"He listens to you, too," Cal said, strumming random

chords. "It's just that sometimes he gets his own ideas about what he's going to do, no matter what you tell him. Just like Moby when he was a pup."

She started to say something to Cal when Daddy burst back into the living room, a knowing look on his face. He pointed his finger at Lauren, the gesture accusing. "I know what you two are up to," he said, head swiveling between Lauren and Cal. "You want me to go to bed so you can play kissyface. I've seen the way you two moon at each other. I'm not stupid, you know . . . no, no, no, I'm not."

Lauren blanched, didn't dare look at Cal. *Moon at each other?* Had they been that obvious? "Whatever are you talking about, Daddy?"

"Oh, don't play coy with me, daughter dear. And you, Mr. Cal . . ." Edgar walked over to where Cal sat and put his hand on Cal's shoulder. "I only ask that your intentions toward my daughter are honorable—"

"Daddy!" Lauren admonished.

"—promise me that, Mr. Cal."

"Daddy, I don't think Cal has to—"

"Because Warren has been hurt before and I won't wet it happen again . . . no, no, no, I won't."

"All right, that's it!" Lauren stood, grabbed Daddy by the arm and dragged him away from Cal, who sat in the chair with his guitar across his lap, a befuddled look on his face. "Come on, Daddy, time to catch a few winks," she said, straining to pull him to the hallway and to his bedroom. "You're so tired you're talking nonsense." Edgar offered stout resistance, complaining that he wanted to finish his puzzle tonight.

After a bit of jostling, Lauren managed to get Daddy tucked into his bed. He was asleep almost as soon as his head hit the pillow. It brought back memories of twenty years ago, when she babysat her toddler nieces. Jenny and Michelle could be so charged up and hyper one minute, then dead asleep the next. Like a switch had been flipped.

Lauren stood at the edge of the bed, watching Daddy cradle his stuffed loon against his chest, listening as his breaths came longer and slower. She felt a rush of sentimentality, like sweet warm syrup poured over her heart. She bent and kissed his forehead, then turned out the light.

She returned to the living room and said to Cal in an apologetic tone, "I sure don't know what brought that on. Daddy's been in rare form all day today."

Cal smiled wearily. "I think it's nice the way he's so protective of you. He only wants the best for you, Lauren."

"I know," she said, feeling guilty. "It's just . . . how *embarrassing.*"

"Why should you feel embarrassed?"

"The things Daddy said. They were ridiculous."

"Were they? You mean you're not interested in playing kissyface with me?"

The comment caught Lauren off guard and she barked a nervous laugh. Hearing Cal verbalize her father's old-fashioned euphemism for fooling around struck her as funny. But it also put a charge into her, awakening something deep in her long-dormant libido. She chanced a look at him, noticed him staring at her, eyes wide, expectant. Something like an electrical charge passed between them, something primal, some force that was invisible yet palpable. Her pulse went into overdrive. Her mind raced, searching for the right thing to say. Finally she blurted, "I'd love to play kissyface with you . . ." Lauren dropped her voice into a deeper register, imitated her father's affected speech, ". . . but only if your intentions are honorable."

This brought hoots of laughter from Cal. He stood and approached her, laid his guitar on the end of the couch, leaned over in front of her, his smiling face inches from hers. She felt his warm breath against her face, smelled a faint scent of wintergreen.

He touched her cheek, whispered, "I guarantee you, Lauren Talbot, my intentions are most honorable."

Her heart thumped wildly against her ribs. Her exhaustion was gone, chased by the electricity of his closeness. She took in the contours of his face, his ruddy cheeks, his broad nose that bent slightly to the left, the sexy gray eyes that searched hers looking for an invitation. Full lips, wide mouth slightly open, part smile, part yearning.

The moment was so intimate, so incredibly erotic she thought she might self-combust right there on the couch.

He closed his eyes, dipped his head closer. His cheek knocked her glasses askew, and she fumbled them back into place with a soft giggle. He murmured a faint apology and tried again.

And against all of her rampaging instincts, Lauren leaned back away from him and said, "No, Cal!"

"But I thought—"

"Oh, I do," she said. "Just not here, okay?"

She took his hands in hers and stood from the couch, surprised that his palms were as damp as her own.

"Because of your father?"

"No. He'll be conked out for a while. I just want our first kissyface to be special. Not here on this smelly old sofa in a touristy rental cabin."

"Where then? My place?"

"Your sofa is older and smellier than mine."

"Yeah, but it's not in a touristy rental cabin."

Lauren laughed. "Come on," she said, tugging at his hand. "Let's go down to the dock. The stars are incredible this time of night."

In her eagerness, Lauren nearly tripped leading Cal down the flagstone steps to the water, maintaining a tenuous hold on Cal's hand as she stumbled down the three wood-slat steps onto the dock. Cal's boat rocked gently in its berth, the moon overhead painting a bright orange crescent across the windshield.

"You come here often?" Cal asked.

"Every night since Daddy and I got here," she said,

trying to control her runaway breathing.

"Naughty girl."

"Whaddaya mean?"

"You've been trespassing."

"So arrest me, then."

"I'd prefer to kiss you."

Lauren turned around, let Cal nudge her against a dock piling. She raked her hand across his chest. His lips brushed hers, the action tantalizingly slow and sensual. His tongue traced her upper lip. She responded to his fluttery kisses, opening her mouth, letting him in, feeling her knees buckle with each gentle probe of his tongue. She felt his hands slide down her back, his fingers teasing the sensitive knobs along her spine with deft feather touches. She leaned into him, feeling the heat radiate from him, the hard outdoorsy strength of his body against her.

Lauren was dizzy, slipping over the edge. It seemed like forever since she had been kissed. Without a doubt, she had never been kissed like this before. Cal was patient, tender, every touch awakening some long slumbering tactile memory, every kiss and whispered affection bringing out some heated response that had been too long in hibernation.

"Wow, Cal!" she said, leaning back, catching her breath, peering into his face. The moonlight reflected in his eyes like tiny twin fires. "You're a great kisser."

"I'm only as good as my partner."

"That's sweet."

"No, I mean that. You've got me so . . . ah—"

She put a forefinger to his lips. "Don't," she whispered. "Kiss me again. After all, Daddy says practice makes perfect."

Cal grinned. "Who am I to doubt Daddy?"

19

SASSY LASS AND THE PRAGMATIST

Cal and Lauren nestled into the cushions Cal had retrieved from the boat. They gazed at the broad night sky, quiet, reflective, taking in the winking stars above. Water slapped gently against the wooden pilings. Insects scratched out their nocturnal songs. Heavy humidity cloaked the dock in an earthy-sweet perfume of honey-suckle and lake mud and pine, a loamy fragrance Cal had always found pleasing.

Lauren leaned her head against his shoulder and he rubbed the nape of her neck.

"You think we're too old to go skinny-dipping?" she asked.

Cal stopped rubbing, gave her a look of astonishment. "Skinny-dipping? I didn't know you were such a wild woman."

"I'm a wild woman because I like to swim naked?" She laughed and nudged him in the ribs. "Really, Cal. You're such an old fuddy-dud. You ought to try it sometime. It's very liberating. Come on," she said, standing and pulling him by the arm, "give it a try."

"Naw," he said, remaining rooted to the cushions. "You go on. If I jumped in there naked half the fish in Lake McDowell would go belly-up from fright. It'd be worse than the red tide."

She giggled girlishly. "And I thought *I* had issues with *my* body!"

He scanned her long, smooth legs, boyish hips and thin waist, small breasts that poked through the thin fabric of her tank top. "Issues?" he said. "But you're gorgeous, Lauren."

She let go of his arm and gave him a quick kiss on the cheek. "You're a darling, Cal. I know I'm not pretty, but thanks for saying so."

"No, I mean it," he said, thinking that her rangy beauty was magnified tenfold by her inability to see it. "You, um, you *do* things to me. *Powerful* things."

He stared out over the lake, felt her looking at him. He wondered if he'd gone too far. Finally, her gaze became too much and he turned to her, was greeted by a huge smile, her teeth tiny pearls in the moonlight.

"That's the most honest, sweetest thing any man has ever said to me, Calvin Blevins." She hugged him, laid her head against his shoulder. "You do incredible things to me, too. So, how about it? Let's swim naked together. It'll be fun."

Cal wanted to, he really did. But he knew he hadn't aged well. His modesty had grown along with his waistline. He'd always felt there came a time in a person's life when they should not be seen in public without clothing. Cal was painfully aware his time had arrived. "Sorry, skinny-dipping isn't my thing, I'm afraid."

After a long moment she said, "You know, Cal, that Indian fish hypnotist you and Moby saw has nothing on you."

"What're you talking about?" he said, noticing the mischievous gleam in her eye.

"You said if you jumped into this lake naked, half the fish would go belly-up, right?"

"Well, yeah, but—"

"Think about it. It's a very efficient way to fish. You'd

be a folk hero in South Birdtown. I can see the headlines now: 'Loon Mountain Man Feeds Village by Skinny-Dipping.' You'd be the modern-day FishHawk."

Cal chuffed a laugh through his nose. "You're seriously weird, Lauren Talbot."

"That's why we get along so well," she said, poking him in his ample stomach.

Cal pulled her closer and they returned to their comfortable silence. He felt like he owned the world at that precise second, like the moon and stars and planets overhead were in perfect alignment for him.

It had taken all of Cal's willpower to break it off when their necking heated to the boiling point. Nothing more than kissing and a few well-placed gropes. No ripping off each other's clothes, no mindless animalistic coupling. He really *liked* this woman who had suddenly popped into his life, and he didn't want to jeopardize what they had going with a cheap and tawdry tumble. He'd wanted to, oh how he absolutely hungered for Lauren, this willowy bespectacled woman with the short-cropped cinnamon-colored hair and easy laugh, this gracious giving lady with the lilting Tennessee twang and impossibly long legs. Cal loved her bookish intellectualism, was attracted to her bohemian vagabond nature and offbeat sense of humor. And Cal knew she wanted him as well.

They had forced themselves to pull away from each other, both flushed and panting. Lauren had stumbled over an explanation, putting a spin on why it was best that they take it slow. They were both mature adults, she'd said. They had time to see where things went. No need to pretend they were a couple of horny teenagers and do something in haste they both might regret. Cal's instincts told him they wouldn't be able to hold it in check much longer. The attraction was just too powerful.

But in a vague way, he felt relief. Gnawing at the back of his conscience was the very real fear that he wouldn't be able to perform with Lauren. After all, until tonight it had been thirty-five years since he'd even kissed a woman other than Sandra. He had remained exceedingly loyal to his wife through all the ups and downs of those years.

Suddenly the sky above them lit up in a streak of light.

"Oh look, Cal," Lauren said, pointing, "a shooting star!"

Cal followed the path of the flash, watching it arc across the night sky and then burn out on its downward trajectory.

"That was spectacular!" Lauren exclaimed. "That's the first time I've ever seen one."

"They *are* something," Cal said, delighting in her enthusiasm. "You see them up here from time to time . . . well away from the city lights. You're supposed to make a wish, you know."

"I've heard that. Why?"

"Some ancient superstition about falling stars being a premonition of death to the king. Making a wish immediately after seeing one supposedly eliminates the threat."

"Well, we certainly don't want the king to die." She pulled away from Cal, clasped her hands together and bowed her head.

Cal said, "What are you doing? It looks like you're praying, not making a wish."

"Is there a difference?"

She turned to him and he saw the twinkling stars reflected in her glasses, the moonlight coloring her pale cheeks and glistening lips. He kissed her, felt the familiar stirring in his lap as she responded.

Cal said, "Have you really been coming down here every night?"

"Yeah, I have."

"Why?"

"I like to come down here after I get Daddy settled in for the night. It's a wonderful place to enjoy solitude. An

escape. I love Daddy dearly, but I need my own time . . .
my own space." She looked out over the lake, thinking.
"You know, quite often I put sleeping powder in Daddy's
apple sauce or his ice cream. I feel guilty about that.
Sometimes I think I'm the most selfish person on the
planet. Do you think that's wrong?"

He studied her thin profile, thinking about all the times
he had wished Edgar would take a hike so he could really
get to know this woman he was finding to be more
remarkable with each passing day. He wondered where this
burgeoning relationship would be now without Edgar
listening in on every conversation, wanting to participate in
everything they did.

"You have no reason to feel guilty or selfish.," he said.
"A lesser person would go crazy in your situation. I really
adore Edgar . . . your father makes me laugh and he's fun to
be around. He's an inspiration to everyone with his strength
and persistence. He's great, really, but his act would wear
down Job's patience. We all need our alone time."

"Gawd, Cal," she said, nestling back in under his arm,
laying her head against his shoulder, "you make me feel so
good about myself. You're so . . . *open* with me."

"You make it easy for me to open up."

Cal's heart thumped. He could feel Lauren's heartbeat
thudding against his side.

She whispered in his ear, "Since we're being so open, I
have a confession to make."

"What's that?"

"The main reason I've been coming down here every
night is hoping that a certain guitar player would join me."

Cal faced her, their noses practically touching.
"Really?"

She nodded. "You know that movie where the girl tells
the guy 'You had me at hello'?"

"Yeah, Renee Zellweger to Tom Cruise. The movie was
Jerry Maguire," he said, thinking: good movie, stupid line.

"Well, Cal, you had me with your first chord."

"Huh?"

"I've always had a weakness for guitar players. Especially good ones. I think I fell for you that first day, the first time I heard you playing your guitar."

"You're kidding."

"No, I'm not. I've really only had three serious relationships in my life, all with musicians."

Cal thought about this. "Your fiancé, Paul?" he ventured. The one who—?"

"Yes . . . a drummer. I should have known better. Should have stuck with guitar pickers. Drummers are about as stable as a kite in a hurricane. That's all I want to say about Paul Monroe. Bad mistake, that one."

"Okay."

"My other two, um . . . loves, were guitarists."

"From bands you sang with?"

"One band, yes. The second one I was more or less his groupie, sad to say."

"You, a *groupie*?"

"I've never been a nun, Cal. Especially in those days."

"No, I didn't mean it that way. What I mean is, you have a phenomenal voice. You should have been *fronting* bands, not skanking around backstage."

"Stop it, Cal. I wasn't a skank. I was in love. Or I thought I was."

"Regardless, you should have been front and center, singing your heart out."

"Oh, I sang with a few bands in high school and freshman year of college. Mostly country and blues bands. The last one—Sassy Lass—was pretty good. We played the club circuit around Nashville."

"The last one? You mean you haven't sung with another band since? That's been what? Twenty years?"

"Try thirty."

"Someone with your talent hasn't been in a band for

thirty years? That's a travesty."

"Not really. Two things happened that got me off the stage for good."

"Oh?"

"One night we were playing this dive where a lot of bikers hung out. A real rowdy place, the kind of roadhouse I was always a little scared to enter. After the second set I was accosted by two drunk rednecks. They took great delight in heckling me, calling me the Fifty Foot Woman. Said I reminded them of the monster in that hokey horror movie, *Attack of the Fifty Foot Woman*. A couple of trailer-trash losers. Followed me around during the break like retarded pit bull puppies. I let their comments get to me. Then the band went on for our third set and they continued to heckle me, yelling out 'Queen Kong' and 'Mrs. Igor' between songs. I started forgetting lyrics, losing my rhythm. Finally, Danny—the lead guitarist, my boyfriend— jumped off the stage and went after them. A huge bar fight broke out. Danny got a broken jaw for his chivalry. Half our equipment was destroyed. We eventually continued on as a band, but it was never the same. Especially for me. I started suffering episodes of performance anxiety. Bad ones. That night really shook me, Cal. I couldn't do it any-more."

"Yeah," Cal said, "I've been in some uncomfortable performing situations, too. It's not easy when you run into a few yahoos."

"And then there was Daddy," Lauren continued, "always giving me pep talks about the importance of an education. My grades were slipping while I sang in Sassy Lass. I nearly flunked out of Vanderbilt. I was a confirmed alcoholic and borderline drug addict. Daddy saved me from myself, convinced me that there wasn't any future in the music business. He said that an intelligent girl like me should be paving the way to a solid career rather than spending late nights getting trashed in honkytonks. I battled him a lot in those days. But of course he was right. And after the Fifty Foot Woman incident and the start of my performance phobias, I saw the wisdom of Daddy's advice. Sassy Lass and Danny Branton were history."

"So you don't sing anymore?"

"Oh, absolutely I do. I couldn't live without singing. It's as necessary to me as breathing. It's as necessary to me as your guitar playing is to you. I sound great in the shower, Cal, you should hear me wail."

"The shower?" Cal shook his head. "What a waste of blue chip talent."

"That's not the only place I sing. I'm also a valued member of the Friendship Baptist Church choir."

"You sing in the choir? You're not one of *those*, are you, Lauren?"

She eyed him suspiciously. "One of those *what*?"

"A holy roller Bible thumper."

"You're unbelievable, Cal! You think because I have fun singing with a good church choir that I'm some kind of . . . I don't know . . . religious zealot or something?"

"One doesn't know unless one asks."

"Well you can relax, okay? I don't belong to any right-wing Christian organizations. I don't tithe my paychecks to the church. I'm not even affiliated with any organized religion, Baptist or otherwise. If it wasn't for the choir, I wouldn't even attend church."

Cal smiled. "I can understand that."

"You can?" Lauren asked.

"Sure," Cal nodded, "You realize something that escapes so many people—you've discovered that organized religion has nothing to do with true faith."

"How in the world could you have possibly known that about me?"

Cal huffed a tiny chuckle. "You're more transparent than you might think, Lauren. I'm right, aren't I?"

She studied his face for a long moment, then smiled.

"Yes, you are," she said, looking away from him. "It took me a while, but I came to understand that organized religion is just another form of politics. Just another angle to control the masses through guilt and fear. Faith, on the other hand, is something completely different. True faith comes from the deepest part of our souls . . . you know . . . where music and love come from. Faith is what gives true believers the absolute conviction that no matter how much God tests us, everything will work out okay in the end. It's what's gotten me through my rough times with drugs and alcohol. True faith is what's getting me through with Daddy and his problems."

Lauren stopped talking and looked at him queerly, like she was trying to read his mind, see where he stood on this subject. She said, "I realize I'm talking too much, *preaching* too much—"

"No," he practically shouted, "this is great, Lauren. I feel exactly the same way."

"Really? You're not just saying that?"

"Honest. And as long as you're opening your closet to me, I have a confession to make."

"What's that?"

"I played my guitar at folk masses for a number of years. Sacred Heart Church in Atlanta."

"So you're Catholic, then?"

Cal smiled at her. "No more than you're a Baptist."

This brought on another round of kisses and hugs and whispered affections. Cal knew at that exact moment that he was crazy in love with Lauren Talbot. She had come into his life a week ago like a character plopped into one of his afternoon nap-dreams. Like some cosmic cartoonist had inked her into his sleeping imagination. An unreal vision come to life.

Lauren broke the silence. "I can't stop thinking about what we saw today over in South Birdtown? It was bizarre, wasn't it?"

"Well, it *was* a little out of the ordinary."

"*A little out of the ordinary?* A flute player got five loons to fly in over the clearing in perfect formation and land on Izzie's cane."

"Yeah," Cal mumbled. "And I'm still trying to figure out how birds with webbed feet could perch on that cane so comfortably."

"I hadn't thought of that, but you're right. That flute player was strange, too."

"Very. Those were eerie melodies he was playing. He's a tribal shaman. I saw a similar production when I was a boy at summer camp here . . . must have been fifty years ago now." Cal thought for a minute, then added, "Man, where does the time go?"

"And there was all that chanting," Lauren continued. "Like they were communicating with the loons. Then the ceremony ending with the birds flying off, like they had been given instructions or something. It was spooky, you ask me."

"Easy enough to train them to do that."

"Cal, you can't train loons. They're wild birds."

"They train wild animals every day. A good animal trainer can teach a grizzly bear to balance a ball on his nose and wrestle a man without hurting him. Circuses have elephants that do sophisticated tricks. Sea World trains killer whales to act on command. Seems like training loons to do what we saw today would be a cakewalk."

Lauren made a sound of exasperation. "Everything I've read about loons says they go out of their way to avoid human contact. I don't think training them would be all that simple. You're a diehard skeptic, aren't you?"

"I prefer the term pragmatist."

"A pragmatist, huh? Just how pragmatic were you about the Indian you saw hypnotizing fish? You didn't seem all that pragmatic when you told me about seeing your long-dead father in your boat, with whom, if I'm not mistaken, you had a long conversation. How do you explain those incidents?"

"I can't. Other than to think they were hallucinations caused by stress."

"You know what I think, Cal? I think Lake McDowell is a magical place. An *enchanted* place."

"Oh, I don't disagree with you there. This *is* a magical place. That's why I've been coming up here all these years. It's why I bought property here." He yawned. "It's getting late," he said. "Gotta be close to three o'clock. I've gotta go let Moby out. He's probably busting a gut."

He stood and pulled Lauren up by her hand.

"Yeah, I need to check on Daddy, too."

"Come on," Cal said, "I'll walk you home."

They walked up the flagstone steps. He kissed her goodnight at her front door—a passionate, lingering kiss, neither of them wanting to part—then trudged across her driveway to his house. He was almost to the shrubs that marked the boundary of his property when he heard her screams from inside her house.

Heard her front door slam open and Lauren shrieking, "CAL! OH MY GAWD, CAL! IT'S DADDY! HE'S GONE!"

20

THE DARK VISITOR

"Gone?" Cal said, meeting her on her front porch.

"Yes, vanished! Disappeared into the night! Daddy's bed is empty and his hiking boots are missing. He took his stuffed loon with him, too." Lauren waved her hands frantically. "He's never done this, Cal. He's pulled some crazy stunts but he's never left the house at night, especially not here. Daddy is scared to death of these woods after dark. He thinks there are boogeymen out there. Oh my gawd!"

"Try to relax," he said, taking her into his arms. "We'll find him, I promise."

"How can you say that?" She slapped his chest with her palms. "Daddy could be halfway to North Carolina by now. Or worse." An overwhelming sense of guilt crashed down on her. While she and Cal were necking under the stars, Daddy had slipped out. Tears rolled down her cheeks.

"What happened to your power of faith?" she heard him say.

She shrugged in his embrace, thinking how hollow her little soapbox oratory on the courage of faith rang at this moment. She could never forgive herself if something bad happened to Daddy.

Cal wiped a runaway tear from her cheek with his thumb and said, "We'll find him, sweetie. Keep the faith."

He rubbed her arms consolingly. "I'm going to get Moby. He isn't any bloodhound but he knows the trails through the woods around the lake. He'll be a good guide at night. Do you have a flashlight or lantern?"

She nodded again, feeling comforted by his take-charge attitude and the cocoon of his embrace. "Lantern."

"Does it work? You have fuel for it?"

"Yes."

"Good. I have a powerful flashlight. I want you to get your lantern and a piece of clothing Edgar has worn recently. Something to give Moby his scent. I'll be back shortly. Hang in there, kiddo."

"Thank you, Cal. Please hurry," she said, watching him disappear into the night.

She went to Edgar's room and found his fishing hat with all the dangly hooks fastened to the brim. Then she went to the storage room, grabbed the lantern, the can of kerosene and funnel, took everything into the kitchen. She set the lantern in the sink and unscrewed the fuel cap. Her hands shook as she inserted the funnel and poured, the kitchen filling with oily kerosene vapors. The digital clock on the microwave showed 2:37. Where could Daddy be at this ungodly hour of the morning? Lauren shuddered, tried not to think of possibilities.

Her legs wobbled as she took the lantern out to the front porch. She set the lamp on the glider and primed the pump, struck a long wooden kitchen match, fired up the lamp with a pop and a whoosh. Shadows danced around her as the wick sputtered, then finally caught. The porch area lit up like daytime, the lantern producing a hissing sound that seemed obscenely loud in the still of night.

She waited. Scanned the dark periphery of the porch. Time passed with excruciating slowness. Her mind concocted worst-case scenarios. With each glum thought, Lauren felt her fear ratcheting up a notch.

Her heart galloped.

She couldn't catch her breath.

Dizziness claimed her; a rush of nausea punched her in the stomach.

Her Dark Visitor was calling. Oh please, not now! she thought, trying to lock out the oncoming panic attack, using biofeedback methods taught to her by Dr. Phillips—*deep-breaths-in . . . hold-for-a-three-count . . . big-exhale . . . pleasant-thoughts . . . deep-breaths-in . . .*

But it was for naught. She couldn't talk herself down from the anxiety this time.

She dropped to the floor, gasping for air, a tightness gripping her chest with an iron fist.

The porch tilted crazily to one side, then back the other way, the dizziness making her sick.

Oh please, God, make this go away, her mind screamed. This is a bad one—a Dark Visitor of epic proportions.

Please! I don't want Cal to see me this way.

Her eyesight dimmed. She felt weak and shaky, on the verge of passing out. She tried to hold it off by opening her mouth wide and breathing in great breaths of air. But all she seemed to taste and smell were the gaseous fumes from the lantern.

This is it, she thought, as she lay there, cheek pressed against the cool wooden floor, the lantern hissing behind her like an enraged snake. I'm dying. Daddy has finally been the death of me. The Dark Visitor has come a-knocking one final time and I'm too weak to keep him out.

She felt cold. Utterly alone and afraid.

She shivered, a tremor running through her.

And then she blacked out.

The Dark Visitor had won another round.

* * *

She felt a tongue licking her cheek. She came awake.

Moby's jowly mouth came into blurry focus.

Cal's voice. "Hey, what happened? Are you okay?"

Moby kept lapping her face, coating her with his slobber. She was disoriented, sapped.

Cal pulled Moby away and kneeled down beside her. "Are you all right, Lauren?"

She struggled to sit up, felt around the floor for her glasses.

"Here you are," Cal said, perching them on her nose, wrapping the stems behind her ears. "What in the world happened? I was only gone five minutes."

Lauren began to regain her senses. She could feel the dampness of her sweat-soaked T-top and shorts. Her hands shook. Muscle spasms cramped her legs. She couldn't look Cal in the face. What to tell him? This had always been her luck with men she cared about. Things would be going along like something out of a Harlequin romance, and then Daddy would have a major episode. Or the Dark Visitor would make an untimely appearance. Or one of a million other things would go wrong sending her would-be suitor running for his life.

"Your eyes look funny." Cal's voice was sincere concern. "Did you have a seizure or something?"

"No!" she said a little too defensively. "Nothing like that. I—I was just overcome by the lantern fumes." She tried to get to her feet, but lost her balance, fell back down on her butt. She felt the burn of humiliation in her face.

"Look, sweetie," Cal said, "I think you'd better stay here while Moby and I—"

"No! Please don't leave me alone again! I *have* to go with you! It's *my* father who's lost out there. Just give me a minute and I'll be fine."

"Okay," he said, unsure. Cal helped her up and over to the glider. "You rest here for a bit while I go get you a glass of water." He looked down at the dog. "Moby, you stay and keep your Aunt Lauren company."

Moby wagged his bullwhip tail, licked Lauren's hand, sensing her hurt.

She watched Cal go into the house, felt Moby's soft warm mouth working over her hand. "You sure are a slobber bucket," she said, which only increased the whipping of the dog's tail.

Cal returned with a glass in one hand and a washcloth full of ice cubes in the other.

"Here, drink this," he said, handing her the glass, "then hold the ice against your face. It'll help."

She drank the water thirstily, met his gaze over the rim of the glass. This Cal Blevins was certainly a special man. Here she was, a panic attack basket case, her loony tune father running around lost in the woods somewhere, and this man was sticking it out. Cal Blevins was either a saint or the world's biggest fool. She laughed at the thought.

"What's so funny?" Cal asked, his face a mask of concern.

Lauren held the ice compress against her forehead. "I don't know . . . I guess it's better to laugh than cry."

"Atta girl!" Cal said, offering her an encouraging smile. "We'll get through this."

He rubbed the top of her head, his hand smoothing her close-cropped hair. His compassion was exquisite. Maybe Father Fate had finally smiled on her. Maybe at this late stage of her life, she had finally met a decent man. Was that too much to hope for?

"How are you doing?" he asked after watching her work the compress over her face for several minutes.

"Much better," she said, smiling at him, feeling her strength returning. "Thank you, Cal."

She handed him the empty glass and ice compress, stood. "Come on. Time's a wasting. Let's go find Daddy." Lauren bent to retrieve Edgar's fishing hat from the floor, put it down in front of Moby's nose. The Lab sniffed at it cautiously, wary of the sharp fishhooks.

"Are you sure you're up to it?"
"I've never been more sure of anything in my life, Cal."

* * *

Moby led the way, straining against his leash as he took them into the dark interior of the woods. Lauren pulled up the rear, trying to hold the lantern high but having trouble due to the weakness in her arms. She had hiked this trail before and knew it wound around to the lake, to a spot up the shoreline from their cabins. During daylight hours, this was a pleasant, scenic jaunt. But out here now, under cover of night, with the swinging lantern creating moving shadows and the sounds of nocturnal animals scampering through the underbrush, everything seemed more threatening and sinister. Tree trunks became gnarled monsters, their limbs swooping down from above as though trying to snatch them. The surface of boulders wore grotesque faces. Vines of kudzu took on the appearance of venomous snakes. Easy to see why Daddy was spooked by these woods after dark. Lauren tried to focus on Cal's broad back and the beam of his flashlight that danced along the trail in front of Moby.

Deep-breaths-in...hold-for-a-three-count ... big-exhale ... pleasant-thoughts ... deep-breaths-in...

She couldn't have a return engagement with the Dark Visitor out here. That would be devastating.

They made their way along the path, Moby's dog tags jingling as he pushed onward. She heard Cal huffing and puffing in front of her, struggling to keep Moby under control. Twice the dog stopped, snuffling at something along the ground, then led them off the trail, partway into the forest. Both times, false scents.

On they hiked. Smaller trails opened up on either side, their entrances gloomy and forbidding. The summer night air hung heavy with humidity, making breathing more difficult. Tiny dewdrops dotted the ground and surrounding foliage like diamond clusters.

And then they heard it.

The unmistakable laughing-cry call of a loon.

Moby came to an abrupt halt, on alert, listening for more.

Lauren heard a second loon call, up ahead, about a quarter of a mile or so. This one more raucous than the first.

"That's Daddy," she said, her hopes rising.

Another loon cry in the night.

"Yeah, I think you're right," Cal muttered. "That first one sounded like the real thing, but the second two . . . I'd know Edgar's mimicry anywhere."

A fourth loon call.

Moby erupted into a frenzy of barking, a feral blood-hound/wolf kind of howl that Cal said was unique to Labs. The wild, unbridled sound of it put a further sheen of strangeness on a night that had already spiraled out of control.

"Let's go find him!" she shouted over the barking.

Moby lifted his head and howled as he pulled Cal along. Lauren had to jog to keep up. They moved quickly down the trail, low-lying branches whipping at her legs. Twice she stumbled, nearly losing her grip on the lantern.

She heard another loon call. Closer now.

Feet thudded against the ground. Heavy panting. The swish of vegetation slapped aside.

Canine howls. Loon calls, real and otherwise.

This was like a dream, one of those otherworldly adventures Lauren experienced in her deepest REM sleep. But she could feel the early-morning dew on her arms, the scratches on her legs, the burn in her chest as she trotted behind Cal, and she knew this was real.

They rounded a bend and Lauren smelled the water. Moby led them off the main trail, into a small thicket. The going was slow as they kept getting tangled in the under-brush. Lauren heard the gentle lapping of waves nearby, then stepped in a boggy hole. She shrieked as her foot sunk into muddy cold water. The air took on a horrific smell, like rotten eggs and serious decay. They were entering the marsh, the small area of still, mucky swampland caused by the backwater currents of the Cheecheewah and Winnie-habba rivers.

They fought their way through the heavy growth, Cal cursing himself for not bringing something to help clear the way. A ground fog had rolled in, a fluffy shag carpet under the lantern's glow.

They heard the loon call again. Off to the right. Very close this time.

"Daddy? Is that you?" Lauren called out, her voice deadened by the thick vegetation and heavy air.

Another loon call. Moby headed in that direction, quiet now, head down, nose sniffing the tangled brush.

"Daddy?"

No answer. They crashed through the marsh for another few minutes, Lauren wondering if they would ever find their way back.

And then they emerged into a small clearing by the shore. The lake opened up to them and a fresh breeze blew away the rotten egg smell. In the pale moonlight, Lauren could see the ragged treetops of Loon Island across the water.

She heard something behind her, turned, held the lantern aloft for a better view. She saw Moby trying to nose his way through a curtain of tall cattails, his tail straight out as though he knew something was on the other side. She heard him whimpering and yammering, frustrated at not being able to break through. Cal stepped up and pushed through, shined his flashlight into the area.

"Edgar?" Lauren heard Cal say. "What are you doing out *here*? Are you okay?"

Lauren felt a ray of hope as she heard her father answer, "Hi, Mr. Cal. Please don't be mad at me. I'm doing a good thing . . . yes, yes, yes, I am."

Lauren's hope turned to trepidation as she stepped around Cal to have a look. She tried not to gasp as she peered in. Daddy sat on a pile of wet brush, his pants and hiking boots soaked through. His Braves baseball cap was perched on his head at an odd angle. He clutched his stuffed loon to his chest protectively. He sat with a kingly repose, his face bearing an expression of merciful contentment.

"Daddy, what in gawd's name are you doing? You had me so worried, I—"

"I'm sorry, Warren," he said. "I knew you would be upset, but I had this dream, see—"

"Dream? You haven't been sleepwalking again have you?"

"No, no, no . . . not sleepwalking. A dream. Told me to come out here. The Great Spirit told me right where to come."

"The Great Spirit?" Lauren said skeptically. She and Cal exchanged worried glances. "Why were you, um . . . told to come here?"

"Because mama woon was killed . . . yes, yes, yes, she was."

Lauren knew Daddy was confused. Doctor Spangler said his sleepwalking habit could return one day. Daddy had backslid. She felt a tug of desperation as she looked at him, sitting on his wet throne in this bog in the middle of nowhere at three o'clock in the morning, wispy fingers of fog wrapping around him.

Cal shook his head. "We're not following you, Edgar."

"I'll show you," Edgar said. He stood from the pile of brush and stepped to the side. "Shine the wight down here, Mr. Cal," he said, pointing down to where he had been sitting.

Cal did as he was told. Lauren stepped forward to see. It was a nest. In the nest were two eggs, olive green dusted with brown speckles.

"Oh, my gawd!" Lauren exclaimed. "Cal, those are loon eggs. I've seen them in Daddy's bird books."

"Yes, yes, yes . . . woon eggs! Mama woon was killed. I was sent here to protect her eggs. The Great Spirit told me all about it. In my dream."

Lauren and Cal stood stock still for a long moment. From somewhere nearby in the marsh came a loon cry.

Edgar answered.

"Oh, Daddy!" Lauren said finally. She sloshed through the muck and threw her arms around him, hugged him to her tightly.

Edgar warned her to be careful not to break the eggs.

21

BACK TO THE EGG

Cal awoke to the sound of rain pelting the roof. A crack of thunder shook the walls. The summer-long drought had ended dramatically.

He opened his eyes. The room came into focus. It wasn't his room. Or his bed.

The sheets smelled faintly of perfume, a sweet floral scent.

He sat up against the headboard, realized he was naked. He spied Lauren's walking shorts, tank top, and sports bra draped across a chair in the corner. His mud-caked sneakers were on the floor underneath the chair. The rest of his clothes were nowhere to be seen.

Last night? Oh no! he thought as he spied the pink pillowcases and frilly curtains, the vase of flowers and Lauren's watch on the night table. How did he get into her bed? Had Lauren slept with him? His mind was a drowsy jumble. He tried to reconstruct what had happened. Couldn't.

Mouthwatering smells of fresh-brewed coffee and sizzling bacon drifted into the room. His stomach grumbled. He leaned over and picked up Lauren's watch, amazed to see it was almost one in the afternoon. He heard footsteps coming down the hallway. Quickly he pulled the sheets up tight against his chin.

Lauren entered the room dressed in a powder blue terrycloth bathrobe, carrying a tray.

"Welcome to Talbot's Bed and Breakfast," she said cheerily, setting the tray at the bottom of the bed. "Best service of any B and B on the mountain."

She parked a hip on the bed near Cal. He breathed in her freshly scrubbed scent. Cal looked at the breakfast she had prepared for him—scrambled eggs, six strips of bacon, English muffin with strawberry jam, a bowl of assorted fruit, carafe of steaming coffee, tall glass of orange juice.

"To what do I owe this kind of hospitality?" he asked.

Lauren smiled down at him, her eyes bright and alert behind her wire rims. "You rescued Daddy for me, helped me get him back here last night. It's the least I can do."

She stroked him across the top of his head, her long fingers cool against his bald pate. Cal felt a stirring under the sheets.

"You got me through a major crisis," she said, fluffing the fringe of hair on the side of his head. "You were so calm and collected under pressure."

"Actually, I wasn't all that calm," he said, bits and pieces of the trek out to find Edgar coming back to him. Cal remembered almost losing it when Edgar refused to come home with them. The old man wanted to stay out there in the swamp, to roost on that nest like some kind of surrogate mother loon. Cal had raised his voice at Edgar, even threatened him. Finally, Lauren's father relented, but only if he could bring the two colorful eggs back with him. "Where is the Audubon oddity now?"

"Stop it, Cal," she said, a smile softening her face. "He's asleep in his bedroom. He had a long night last night."

"Yeah, didn't we all. Are you sure he's in there? Are you sure Birdman hasn't flown the coop again?"

"Oh, he won't be going anywhere. Not as long as he has those eggs where he can keep an eye on them. It's so cute, the way Daddy has the nest sitting on a TV tray next to his bed. While he sleeps, he puts his stuffed loon on top of the eggs."

"Yeah, *cute*. You do realize, Lauren, those chicks will never hatch out in Edgar's bedroom. You can't take them out of the wild like that. I would think they need warmth. They need the—I don't know—*presence* of the mother loon for nature to work its magic."

"Daddy thought of that. We set up a halogen lamp to shine on the nest. Keeps the eggs good and warm." Lauren looked down at the breakfast she had made for him. "Enough talk. You need to eat before this gets cold." She brought the tray to him, balanced it across his lap, poured him a cup of coffee, tucked a napkin between his chin and the top of the sheets.

Cal thought: Is this woman for real? *A halogen lamp shining on a nest of loon eggs?* What had he gotten himself into here? Was Lauren Talbot as bonkers as Edgar? Had the years of caring for her handicapped father turned her into the nut that had fallen close to the tree?

He took a sip of coffee, set the cup back on the saucer. Looked at her. "Last night . . . we didn't, uh—?"

"Make love?"

He cringed.

"Would you prefer I use a more crude expression?"

"No, I just—"

"The fact that you can't remember should answer that, Cal! No, we didn't do anything. I gave you my bed. I slept on the sofa."

Was she disappointed? Angry? Cal couldn't tell. Either way, he felt the need to explain. "It's just that ... everything seems so fuzzy from last night. Kind of like one of those dreams that's so vivid while you're having it, then you wake up and the details break into a million shattered pieces."

"Yeah," Lauren nodded, softening a bit. "It *was* pretty

weird. One minute we're making out under the stars like a couple of horntoad teenagers, the next we're off on a wild jaunt through the backwaters of Lake McDowell."

"And what do we find? Edgar perched on a loon's nest!" Cal shook his head in amazement. "Life as we've known it has gone over the edge." He picked up his fork and dug into the eggs.

She watched him eating. "Cal, how could Daddy possibly know where that nest was? That it was abandoned?"

"You tell me," he said, taking a bite of English muffin. "He's *your* father."

"Well, Daddy and I have walked that trail a few times, but we've never ventured into the marsh. And then there's the question of how he got there in the middle of the night all by himself. I mean, it was difficult enough for you and me. And we had light and Moby leading us."

"Edgar's a tough old bird, pardon the pun," Cal said, chewing his food.

"You don't find the whole thing odd,? I find it to be miraculous myself."

"Oh, I find it *very* odd. But miraculous? I don't know. Your father is tuned into a different frequency, Lauren."

"Yeah," she said, thinking. "Still, how could Daddy get himself all the way out there in the dark of night. It's got to be a mile or more to where we found him. And he was way off the beaten path. I think he was guided by a higher power."

He nearly choked on his breakfast. "You mean like a divine intervention?"

"Maybe," she said sheepishly. "It's either that or a severe sleepwalking episode."

Cal took a sip of his orange juice. "I'll put my money on sleepwalking."

She looked at him, long and hard, as though studying some alien species. Finally she stood, the box springs under the mattress making a popping sound as she removed her weight from the bed.

She said, "You were wrong about your body."

"What're you talking about?"

"You said that if you skinny-dipped in the lake all the fish would die of fright. You're so wrong about that. I think you're incredibly sexy when you're naked."

Cal stopped chewing and stared at her. "I thought we didn't—"

"We didn't," she said, walking toward the door. "But just because I'm a proper East Tennessee gal doesn't mean I can resist the temptation of taking a peek. Finish your breakfast. There's a robe in the closet you can wear. I'm going to check on Daddy."

"Where are my clothes?"

"In the dryer." She closed the door behind her.

Cal smiled as he listened to her footsteps recede down the hall.

Some woman, this Lauren Talbot, he thought. Maybe there was something to this divine intervention thing after all.

22

THE GREAT SPIRIT'S REQUEST

The rain continued, pummeling the roof with a ferocity that scared Lauren at times. The nasty weather canceled Cal's afternoon fishing trip, but he didn't seem to mind. Cal was in a guitar-playing mood and he had a captive audience.

They'd spent the day in her living room, playing music and singing, snacking on munchies. Edgar had sat at his puzzle table, hovering over his loon nest and blathering on about how pretty the two eggs were with the "spotlight" shining on them. Moby maintained a bored expression as he gazed through the rain-streaked picture window.

During the daylong songfest, Cal kept referring to his musician friends—Chuck, Glenn, and Albee—how he couldn't wait to get them together with Lauren, how his buddies would be slack-jawed amazed when they heard her sing. According to Cal, they were overdue for another pick-n-grin get-together.

"My buddy Albee Crenshaw could have made it big with a little luck," Cal told her. "The guy came out of the womb playing the guitar, I swear. I think maybe his mother was a jukebox."

Lauren laughed. "He's better than you?"

"Oh, Albee makes me sound like a *Gong Show* reject. The guy can play anything and everything. Flawlessly. He can hear a melody once and play it note for note. Albee has what they call an eidetic musical memory. A genius-level gift. Name just about any song, no matter how obscure, and Albee is off to the races, playing the tune like he just learned it that day. Great guitar player, but the man can't sing a lick. It's painful to listen to. But with you belting them out and us playing behind you—"

"Stop!" she said, cutting him off. "Please don't get any grand ideas. I'm not ready for anything like that. I love singing with you, but I'd prefer to keep it just the two of us right now. Okay?"

"Hey, what about me?" Edgar said from where he sat at his puzzle table. "I sing, too, y'know."

"Excuse *me*," Lauren said, looking at the bright halogen lamp with its gooseneck stem bent over the nest of loon eggs at Daddy's elbow, "make that the *three* of us."

She heard a whine of protest in Cal's voice as he said, "But you're an *incredible* singer, Lauren. You'll sweep my friends off their feet with your voice."

"I just don't want to be forced into something that will . . . make me uncomfortable."

"But you sing in the church choir."

"That's different. There are twenty-five of us up there in the choir. I can blend in and be anonymous."

"But you're too good to be anonymous," Cal protested. With your pipes, you should be front and center."

"Cal, listen to me. I discovered something about myself years ago. I didn't like it, but I've learned to accept it."

"What's that?"

"I'm not a performer."

"Not a performer? But you have an amazing gift. You're like Albee that way. I mean, millions of wannabe singers embarrass themselves in karaoke bars night after night. Most of them would give everything they own to be able to sing like you do."

Lauren shrugged. "What can I say? I'm not cut out to

be in the spotlight."

"What a waste."

"Maybe so. But it's *me*."

Cal studied her for a long time. Finally he said, "That's what got hold of you last night, isn't it? Anxiety?"

She nodded. "It's crippling at times."

Lauren really didn't want to go there, but the history of her panic attacks came pouring out as though her mouth had a will of its own. She told Cal about her Dark Visitor and the biofeedback therapy she'd undergone, the prescription medications she'd tried, even the four expensive trips to psychiatrist offices. Nothing she tried seemed to cure her of her dreaded disorder. This revealing of her inner self had a cleansing effect. In Cal she felt she had a confidant, a sensitive man who listened, a caring man who was tuned into her. And they'd known each other all of eight days. Incredible.

"What about your teaching?" he asked. "I would imagine facing a classroom of high school students could be a scary proposition ... one that could generate quite a bit of anxiety."

"You know it's funny, Cal. I've never had a problem in the classroom. And I've had some real delinquents over the years. It's just that—I don't know ... I just seem better able to handle that kind of stress. It reinforces my belief that teaching is what I was put on this earth to do. I don't think about it as much. You know that Nike commercial? I just *do* it."

"And singing is different?"

"Yes, it is. I'm too ... too—I don't know—*nervous*. I don't like being the center of attention on stage. I don't like all those eyes on me, all those people looking up at me with expectant stares that say: *Show me something! Entertain me!* It's too much pressure."

"But Glenn and Albee and Chuck would never judge you like that. I guarantee you they'll treat you like royalty."

"I'm sure I'll get along wonderfully with your musician friends. I just need some time is all. You and I are still getting to know each other. Let's not bring anyone else into the mix right now, okay?"

"You're right," Cal said with a sigh. "I'll give you all the time you need, sweetie. And I'll help you any way I can with your, um . . . Dark Visitor problem."

"Thank you," she said.

"Let's try another Patsy Cline song," he said, strumming a few country-sounding chords on his guitar. "I love the way you channel Patsy."

"Okay. How about 'I Fall to Pieces' or 'Crazy'?"

"You trying to tell me something, Lauren?"

"Yes, yes, yes," Edgar piped in, "Warren *is* crazy, Mr. Cal! Yes, yes, yes she is!"

Lauren saw Cal give her father a look of impatience as he said, "What are you flapping your lips about, Edgar? Last time I looked, you were the one pretending to be a mother loon. Some folks might think that to be a tad left of center."

"Don't be silly, Mr. Cal. I *know* I'm not a woon. I'm just making sure these eggs hatch. It's my duty, y'know."

"Who assigned you this, um . . . *duty*?"

"The Great S-Sp-Spirit."

"The Great Spirit, Daddy?" Lauren asked, thinking maybe their trip to South Birdtown had been too much for her father to handle.

"Yes, yes, yes," Edgar nodded. "The Great Spirit of the Cherokee . . . *God*."

Lauren looked at Cal, a swirl of emotions passing silently between them.

"You know," Edgar said, "I think the eggs are getting too dry." He pushed the gooseneck of the halogen lamp away from the nest of dried marsh reeds and crusted mud, bent over and gently poked at the two eggs. "My bird books say a woon nest must be kept damp at all times. Time for another bath, my eggy friends."

Edgar grabbed a spray bottle from under a heap of jigsaw puzzle boxes. Lauren watched her father spritz the nest, its walls collapsing as the caked dirt turned into a moist, muddy goop.

"Okay then," Cal said, grabbing his guitar. "Shall we take Patsy Cline from the top?"

"Which one are we doing?" she asked, eyes never leaving the mess Daddy was making on his puzzle table.

"Let's do 'I Fall To Pieces' . . . I love what you do with that song."

Cal played.

Lauren sang.

And Edgar continued fussing with his loon nest.

23

MOTHER MACY

Lauren snapped her book shut and stretched out on the couch. The hour was late. Cal had taken Moby home. She was alone with Daddy, who sat hunched over his table, quietly working a puzzle. Occasionally he stopped to utter a few words of endearment to the two loon eggs in the nest by his elbow.

Lauren feared her father had finally gone around the bend. She couldn't help but feel a pang of remorse as she observed him moving puzzle pieces around with his gnarled fingers, the way he kept touching the eggs in the sloppy, mud-caked nest. Daddy's stroke had accentuated his eccentric qualities, had brought his oddities to the surface. She had learned to accept his quirks during the years he had been in her care. But this loon business was something else entirely. Daddy wouldn't let the two colorful eggs out of his sight. He slept with a stuffed loon. He performed his loon calls nightly, thinking he was communicating with the Great Spirit. Yes, indeed ... around the bend. Lauren felt a piece of her life slipping away, and sadness filled her like the onset of some quick-striking disease.

She shifted her thoughts to happier things—to Cal Blevins—and wondered if he was thinking about her at this moment. Why did she let him go home? Cal had obviously wanted to stay, had wanted to spend the night with her as surely as she desired it. A faint trace of his cologne hung in the air, a masculine sandalwood scent. She could taste his kisses on her lips, could feel the scratchy softness of his mouth against hers, the comforting warmth of his strong embrace. Her skin still tingled from the tantalizing power of his touch.

She closed her eyes, her desire for Cal charging through her like a high-voltage current. Absently, she moved her hand to her left breast, began massaging her nipple through the thin fabric of her tank top. She wondered if Cal was thinking about her at that moment.

A young female voice brought her to a halt. "Naughty, naughty. You want your father to see you like that?"

Lauren's eyes shot open. She bolted upright on the couch, gasping at the vision standing before her.

Her long dead mother!

Macy Anne Talbot as Lauren remembered her, a youthful vibrant woman of thirty-six, just before her death.

"You had your chance with your new man, Lo," her mother said, addressing Lauren by her childhood nickname. "You need to be more aggressive. If you wait for a man to do something involving your best interests, you'll wait forever. You want something, go after it."

Macy Anne Talbot stood tall—all five-feet-ten-inches of her—a solid physical presence, a living, breathing human being. She wore the blue-checked cotton blouse and Capri pants Lauren remembered from childhood, the black leather Johansen shoes with the wedge heels and tie at the toe. There was the poofy bouffant hairdo Lauren remembered her mother taking such pains to achieve. Lauren flashed back to when she used to sit cross-legged on the floor of the master bathroom, watching Mom primp in front of the vanity mirror, setting her auburn hair in rollers the size of Coke cans. Her mother's makeup was just right, too—the frosted Natural Wonder lipstick and translucent foundation., the pale green eye shadow and heavy mascara that produced spiky eyelashes and the wide-eyed look that was so the rage in the Sixties. Macy Talbot looked like she'd just stepped from the pages of a 1965 Montgomery Ward catalog.

"Mother?" Lauren said, What? . . . how—?"

"Oh, don't get so dramatic, Lo. It's just me, here to give you some much needed advice."

"But I don't—"

"Yes, you *do*, dear. Your new friend Calvin really loves you, Lo. You had him naked in your bed last night. He wanted to sleep with you. For the life of me, I don't understand what you're waiting for. You and Cal Blevins were born to be together . . ."

Lauren sat open-mouthed, listening to her mother ramble in her sonorous voice. Macy had died when Lauren was twelve. It had been a sudden freakish accident, Lauren's mother struck down by a drunk driver in a grocery store parking lot, of all things. A scene lifted from the pages of a John Irving novel.

". . . I just wish I'd been around during your teen years to give you some guidance, Lo. I'm sure your love life wouldn't be such a mess now if I had . . ."

Lauren thought about Cal's encounter with his deceased father aboard his boat earlier this week. She wondered whether she and Cal weren't sharing some kind of telepathic hallucination, whether they weren't both heading down some rubber walled corridor toward the cuckoo's nest. This certainly had to be some kind of delusion, some kind of stress-induced hysteria. And yet, her mother's presence was just too real to be imagined. Real in the same sense that Cal had described his meeting with his father.

As Macy continued to offer her advice, Lauren looked around her at her father, who was still focused on his puzzle-solving, completely unaware of the presence of the gabby third party in the room. When Macy stopped jabbering long enough to catch her breath, Lauren questioned her.

"How is it that Daddy can't see or hear you, Mother?"

"Quiet, Warren!" Edgar snapped at her without looking up from the table. "You're messing with my focus."

Macy turned to look at Edgar, who bobbed his head and clucked his tongue, baffled by a puzzle piece that didn't fit anywhere. She turned back to Lauren. "Your father never paid much attention to me when I was alive. Why should he start now?"

Lauren felt the stirrings of a panic attack coming on, another unwanted appearance by the Dark Visitor. "So what're you telling me, Mother? That you're a ghost or something?"

Edgar lifted his head and peered at her. "Quit talking gibberish. I'm not your mother and I'm certainly not a ghost! You're scaring me, Warren."

I'm scaring *him*? Lauren thought. *The man who coddles loon eggs?*

She noticed her mother nervously fingering her wedding band. Macy shifted her weight from one leg to the other, unable to stand still. Whatever was going on here made Lauren's mother uncomfortable.

"No, not a ghost, dear," Macy said to Lauren. "I'm very much alive, very substantial. Go ahead," she said, extending her arm, "touch me."

Reluctantly, Lauren reached out and rubbed her mother's hand, felt the warmth radiating from her fingertips, the moist pads of her palms. She was real, all right. Or at least this vision standing before her possessed a perceptible tactile sense. "I—I don't understand," she said, feeling the Dark Visitor's grip squeezing her.

"It's complicated, Lo."

Nothing like understatement, Lauren thought, trying to catch her breath. She pulled her hand back and looked away. The walls were closing in on her.

"Are you okay, Lo?" Macy said, taking a seat next to her.

Lauren felt the cushions dip as her mother sat, could smell Miss Dior perfume and Herbal Essence shampoo wafting from her, scents that triggered more childhood memories. This has to be a dream, she thought, feeling the panic rise up through her sternum.

"There's no need to have one of your anxiety episodes now," Macy said in a consoling tone. "It's just you and me here. This should be a happy occasion. We haven't been together in, what? Thirty nine years, is it?" She caressed Lauren's cheek, the gesture tender and sincere. "Let's enjoy our time together, dear."

Amazingly, Macy's caress chased away the Dark Visitor. Magically, the heartfelt touch infused Lauren with wonderful memories of her mother's frequent displays of affection for her and her sister Claire. Macy Anne Talbot might have been an overly opinionated churl at times during her way-too-short life, but she had also been a loving, devoted mother, wanting nothing but the best for her and Claire.

"So what are you doing here, Mother?"

"I told you. To give you some advice about your love life. You're about to mess this thing up with Calvin. I can't permit that to happen."

"You can't *permit* it?" Lauren said with a laugh, thinking how preposterous this conversation was. "So, why now? I mean, where were you when Paul Monroe walked out on me? Where were you when I supposedly 'messed up' my other failed relationships?"

"Oh fuggleshine!" Edgar exclaimed. "I can't work when you're constantly babbling to yourself, Warren. You and Mr. Cal both talk to yourselves. You're both cuckoo," he said, circling an index finger around an ear, gesticulating the universal sign for craziness.

Macy smiled. "See how you upset your father, dear?

Just listen and let me do the talking. He can't hear me." She glanced at Edgar, who was still glaring at Lauren. "Yessiree! ... the egg man is in rare form tonight." She turned back to Lauren. "Where were we? Oh yes ... my whereabouts when things went south in your love life. I was, um ... *detained* with other things. I apologize for not being there for you, Lo. But this one with Calvin Blevins is so perfect that I couldn't sit back and watch you bungle it."

Lauren felt her anger rise, then realized the absurdity of her reaction. This woman who professed to be her mother was probably nothing more than a figment of Lauren's fatigued imagination.

"You and Cal Blevins are soul mates, Lo. I know that's a worn out cliché, but in this case, it fits. You're destined to be together."

Lauren started to say something, then stopped, gave her a look that said: "Oh, *please*—"

"It's true, Lauren," Macy said. "You don't really think you and Calvin meeting here at the lake was an accident, do you?"

Lauren shrugged, feeling something akin to déjà vu. Something about those words and the way her mother said them rang familiar, but she couldn't quite connect with the origins of it. Tiny goosebumps prickled up her arms.

"Well, I do, dear. I have a perspective on this that you haven't yet acquired. I've researched Calvin and his family. I know he comes from good Protestant work ethic stock. I've met his parents, and—"

"You're feeding me a line, Mother. Cal's parents are both dead."

"To you they are. To me, the Blevins are alive and well. They're good, salt-of-the-earth people, even if they do get a little carried away with their ballroom dancing. You should hear people talk about Stanley Blevins and his outrageous zoot suit. Stan's a little peculiar, but I've always admired that in a man, that ability to push ahead with their own agenda regardless of what others think. Your man Calvin inherited some of that independent spirit." Macy looked toward Edgar, who seemed to be on a roll now, clicking puzzle pieces into place at a rapid pace. "Your father was that way, too. Did his own thing and everybody else be damned. It's a pity what's happened to him," she said with a sigh. "I really admire you for taking care of him the way you have, Lo . . ."

Zoot suit? Stanley Blevins? Cal's parents' love for ballroom dancing? It was impossible that Lauren's mother could know these details. Lauren scrunched up her forehead, gave her mother a bewildered look.

"I told you, it's complicated," came Macy's evasive response.

"I'm an intelligent, open-minded woman, Mother. Try me."

Edgar mocked her in a squawky parrot voice, "*I'm an intelligent, open-minded woman, Mother. Try me . . . I'm an intelligent, open-minded woman, Mother. Try me . . . Awwkkk! Polly says Warren is crackers . . . Awwkkk! Polly says Warren is crackers . . .*"

"Shut up, Daddy! *Please!*"

"No, *you* shut up! You're scaring me, Warren."

Lauren glowered at her father. He wasn't helping her dilemma as she wrestled with this dream state or hypnotic trance or whatever she was experiencing here. Could it be that she really was talking to herself? Her *other* self? Was this possibly a psychotic breakdown? A coming out of multiple personalities? Possibly a mutation of the Dark Visitor?

"I loved your father so much," Macy said, staring at Edgar with a look of quiet longing. "He could be stubborn and obstinate and wrapped up in his own little worlds, but I loved him unconditionally. In fact, Edgar is the only man who ever affected me so profoundly. Your father cast spells over me, I swear, Lo. Charisma and passion flowed from

him like lava from an active volcano." Macy smiled
absently, shook her head in wonderment as she studied
Edgar, silently recalling some intimate detail of their
relationship. "And I still love him. I was always flattered
that he never remarried. But he should have. A wife would
have been good for him, especially when I left him with
two young daughters to raise. It's a shame that our time
together was cut short. But that's life, dear. Even if you live
to be a ripe old age, life's grand parade still zips by at warp
speed. You can't waste any of it. Not a second. You need to
grab your man Calvin and take him to bed with you. The
both of you need to quit doing this little mating dance
you've been doing and consummate your love for each
other."

"But I think he's still hung up on his wife."

"Sandra is his *ex* wife, dear. Yes, Calvin still has feelings for her, but they're officially divorced."

"How did you know Cal's wife's name is Sandra?"

Macy ignored the question. "You know, Lauren," she
said, reaching out to touch the side of her face, "you really
should let your hair grow out. Men like long hair on women
nowadays. I know Calvin does. Your shaved style makes
you look a little, dare I say it, *butch*."

"Gee, thanks for the vote of confidence, Mother."

"I'm just saying—"

"The last time I grew my hair out I looked like Mrs.
Bozo."

Edgar pushed back from the table. "Warren, for the
love of—"

A jagged flash of lightning zipped through the gray day,
followed by a monumental clap of thunder. The house
shook on its foundation. The lights in the living room
flickered.

"Oh fuggleshine," Edgar groaned.

Macy stood from the couch. "That's my cue," she said.
"I must leave now, Lo."

"No, wait! Just one more question. What's your take on Daddy's obsession with these loons here at the lake?"

Macy Anne Talbot stared at Edgar for a long time, turning something over in her mind. Finally she said, "Your father knows things, Lo."

"What's *that* supposed to mean?"

Another bolt of lightning followed closely by a rolling peal of thunder. Lauren watched her mother's image flicker along with the lights, then disappear as the living room plunged into darkness.

"I'm scared, Warren."

Lauren listened to the rain drumming the roof and thought: *You're not the only one, Daddy.*

24

LOONS IN LOVE

Cal watched the rain trickle down the kitchen window. Beyond the water-beaded glass, the morning hung like a soggy gray curtain. The weather dampened his already glum mood. Yet another day without his fishing fix.

Much more of this and the lake would rise up and wash them all off the mountain. Cal could envision the creatures in the forests around Lake McDowell pairing off and heading for the Ark. Surely Noah was at a higher elevation, working feverishly to get his mythical ship built before the entire mountain collapsed in a monstrous mudslide.

Cal sat at his kitchen table, nursing his third cup of coffee. Sleep had been elusive last night. The jagged bolts of lightning and rolling thunder kept him tossing and turning. But the storm, violent as it was, contributed only partly to his insomnia. Lauren Talbot was responsible for most of it. Thoughts of her flashed through his mind all night long. Her world-weary smile. Her incredible green eyes, wide and penetrating behind the lenses of her wire rims. Her long, lean body that was almost tomboyish, yet uniquely feminine. Her scent, like a garden of flowers after a spring rain. The way her face glowed with a spiritual light when she sang.

Yes, Cal had fallen hard for the quirky woman next door. She'd invaded his sleep, a sexy cat burglar who'd slipped into his dreams, stealing his subconscious with the nimble dexterity of a master thief. Cal remembered the dream, so vivid, so real: Lauren dressed in a sleek midnight-black leotard, her face blackened by charcoal. Entering his bedroom through the window, padding stealthily across the floor, flashes of lightning marking her progress toward his bed. A belt of climbing rope circled her thin waist, a pouch of lock-picking tools clinked at her hip. In Cal's dream she stopped at the foot of his bed, let the rope and tools drop to the floor, then peeled off her leotard and climbed under the sheets next to him. Her skin was warm, slippery as butter, her voice a husky whisper in his ear. She told him that his house was an easy mark, that he should spend some money to bolster his security. Crazy, but that's what she'd said. She massaged him with expert hands as she continued whispering. And just as he rode the wave of orgasm, a bellow of thunder shattered the dream. Cal awoke, alone, his sheets damp with sweat, his erection huge, throbbing with unfulfilled want.

Ridiculous? Without question. But that twisted erotic dream convinced Cal of one thing. He was crazy in love with Lauren Talbot. The gangly, bespectacled schoolmarm with the fuzzy head had stoked a fire in him. She had carefully arranged the emotional kindling and lit the match, then fanned the flames into a raging bonfire. Nothing intentional or mercenary on her part, Cal was sure of that. Lauren was just plain old Lauren, and he loved that about her. No pretensions, no real agenda that Cal could see, other than just enjoying his company and singing with him. So different from Sandra, yet so right for him.

But some things about her continued to nag him. He had big questions about her emotional stability. Her crushing anxiety attacks, her so-called Dark Visitor. Her reluctance to meet Cal's guitar-playing friends. The way she coddled her father through his most preposterous episodes. This loon egg business had taken things to new heights of absurdity. Sure, the old man had suffered a massive stroke, and deserved to be given some slack, but in many ways, Lauren enabled Edgar's outrageousness. She was the one who suggested using the halogen lamp as a makeshift incubator for the two eggs that Edgar obsessed over. Like father like daughter? Cal thought a lot about that. Did insanity swirl through the Talbot gene pool?

But then, the question of his own sanity remained, didn't it? *Cal* was the one who had seen a Cherokee fisherman hypnotizing fish into a dugout canoe. *He* was the one who'd had a conversation with his father's ghost. *He* was the one who'd taken Lauren and Edgar to South Birdtown to witness Izzie the Raven's bizarre loon ritual. So just who was the crazy one here? Before Lauren came into his life, Cal considered himself mind-numbingly normal. Since he had known her, all pretense of normalcy had taken flight. Cal felt like he might be slipping over the edge many times the past two weeks, like he was a participant in a waking dream where everything was just a little off. As if he'd been transported to another world where the laws of physics and the precepts of logic didn't apply. He knew Lauren was of a similar mind. They'd discussed this "weird enchantment" several times.

And then Cal thought: maybe that's what love is. Mutual insanity. Two people tuning in to each other so intensely that reality becomes a kaleidoscopic dream. Cal wasn't sure. It had been forty years or more since he had experienced anything like this. The last time he'd felt this kind of lunacy, he and Sandra had been living together in the tiny rental house in Tucker. Before the kids, before they'd legally tied the marital knot. He and Sandra were just kids themselves in those days, their shared world full of hope and promise. Their love for each other bloomed in a kind of naïve blush. His and his wife-to-be were definitely mutually insane back then. Cal tried to reconcile those feelings with the ones he had for Lauren now.

Couldn't do it. Different people, different circumstances. Different times. The only common ground was the mutual insanity, feelings that were wonderful and terrifying at the same time.

Cal knew he had to make his feelings known to Lauren. They had done the foreplay limbo long enough. It wouldn't be a down-on-one-knee kind of proclamation, nor would it be a gift of jewelry or a bouquet of flowers. That wasn't Cal's style, and he didn't think it was Lauren's either. But it had to be something memorable. Something romantic, perhaps a bit funny. Something that appropriately reflected the unique nature of their new relationship.

He sat, sipped his coffee, wracked his brain for ideas as he had for the past hour. Finally, he had it. So simple. So *obvious*. Cal would write a song for her.

You had me with your first chord he remembered her saying. *I've always had a weakness for guitar players,* she'd told him. *Especially good ones. I think I fell for you that first day, the first time I heard you playing your guitar.*

Yes, a song. Especially for Lauren. Then he would go next door and perform it for her, maybe decked out in some outlandish outfit to keep it from getting too dramatically serious. Or maybe he'd go over there naked, with just his guitar hiding his privates. *The nude troubadour* he thought, smiling.

His reverie was interrupted by Moby, who nudged him with his wet nose from under the table. Cal looked down at him, saw the Lab's sad, droopy eyes, and realized he forgot to feed him this morning.

"Sorry, partner," Cal said, rubbing the dog's velvety ears. "I'm so wrapped up in love, I forgot all about man's best friend. C'mon," he said, standing, "let's get you fixed up with some breakfast."

Moby was on full alert now, his nails tap-dancing across the kitchen tile as he followed Cal to the pantry. Cal dug out the bag of Kibbles n' Bits and measured two cups, poured it into Moby's bowl. The dog salivated as he sat on his haunches, waiting for Cal's command to eat. Cal smiled at Moby, whose eyes were now bright with anticipation, then made a sweeping motion with his arm, bringing his hand to his mouth. Moby lunged for the bowl, slamming it against the wall, spilling a trail of pellets across the floor. The Lab practically inhaled the food, snorting back mouthful after mouthful, smacking his jaws noisily with each chomp. Discipline and dining etiquette only went so far when Moby was hungry.

Cal went to the living room with his coffee, picked up his guitar and began composing his song for Lauren. He experimented with simple chord arrangements, humming a melody as he worked. After twenty minutes of doodling, he had it. Something sweet, but not too sappy. Something catchy without being cloying.

Now for the lyrics.

He put his guitar back in the stand and started jotting down some ideas, staying with things they'd experienced together the past couple of weeks. After twenty minutes, he had something he liked. He was especially fond of the chorus.

And we'll sing to the moon,
Like a couple of loons,
As we wing o'er the lake of dreams.
My song is my confession,
To you I'm professin'
My deep and abiding love.
Two loons in love, you and I
Together we'll fly,
Like shooting stars across the sky
I love you, Lauren
What more can I say?
I'll love you till our dying day
For we're two loons in love.

Excited, Cal picked up his guitar and tried singing the words. They dovetailed nicely with the melody he had written. He was pleased. He felt his pulse quicken as he thought about going next door to sing it to her. What would she think? Would she like it? Cal thought maybe it sounded too corny, like one of those corny sentimental Hallmark cards. But then he thought that would be just the kind of thing Lauren would appreciate.

Only one way to find out.

He put his guitar in the case and went to the hall closet, pulled his rain slicker off a hanger, threw on his Braves cap. No nude troubadour for him, just a straight performance. He thought the song too beautiful to ruin with nudity. Especially *his* nudity.

He closed the front door behind him, leaving a protesting Moby in the house. The day slapped him in the face like a wet blanket. His driveway and front yard were a swamp, little lakes forming everywhere. The rain pelted his slicker. His hand was slippery on the handle of the guitar case as he clomped through the soggy turf up to Lauren's front porch.

He tried opening the screen door, but it was locked tight. He knocked. Heard the raps echoing across the porch. Nothing. Knocked a second time, getting impatient as the cool rain dripped off the bill of his cap. Not a sound. She had to be home. He turned and looked at her minivan parked in the driveway, the crushed front end glistening in the rain. Surely she wouldn't be out hiking in this weather.

He was about to knock a third time when he heard footsteps. Heavy, awkward footsteps. Then he heard a muttering voice, the word *fuggleshine.*

The door opened slightly. Cal saw Edgar's eye peering cautiously through the crack. "Oh, hi, Mr. Cal. You wook wet."

Not for the first time, Cal was reminded of Elmer Fudd. He held back a laugh. "Yes, Birdman," he said, feeling the rain hit the back of his neck and trickle down his spine. "It's raining out here."

"Well, duh!" Edgar said, opening the door and walking out onto the porch. "What do you want?" he asked, hanging back in the shadows, tentative, as if frightened by Cal's presence.

"For starters, how about letting me come in. I'm getting drenched out here."

"No. Warren said I shouldn't wet anybody in."

"But you *know* me, Edgar. Where is Lauren?"

"She's in bed. Sick. Had a long night last night. Not much sleep."

Had a wong night wast night. Not much sweep. Edgar Fudd, Cal thought, unable to suppress a smile.

Edgar moved into the faint light. "What's so funny, Mr. Cal?"

"Nothing. Lauren's sick?"

"Yes, yes, yes . . . she is."

"What kind of sick?"

"Crazy sick."

"Crazy how?"

"Talking to herself. All night. Talking to her mother, too. My Macy passed on more'n thirty years ago, but Warren talks to her. My daughter's crazy sick . . . yes, yes, yes she is. Same as you, Mr. Cal. No offense, but you remember how you talked to your dead father out in your boat? Scared me, Mr. Cal. You and Warren are both crazy sick."

"Please let me in, Edgar." Cal rattled the screen door for effect. "I feel like a sponge out here."

"No. Warren said nobody comes in. Period."

"But I want to play a song for her. A special song. I wrote it just for her."

"Come back later. She needs her sleep. She's sick. Crazy sick . . . yes, yes, yes she is."

Come back wayter. She needs her sweep. Cal felt his

shirt sticking to his skin under the slicker, his shorts matted to his thighs. He shifted his weight and felt a squishy sensation in the soles of his sneakers. He was soaked, miserable, losing his patience. "Look, Edgar, I—"

"My name's Birdman, remember?"

"Yeah, I remember, but—"

"Excuse me, Mr. Cal. I have to get back to my woon eggs."

Edgar retreated back into the house. The door slammed. Cal heard the tumblers click as Edgar locked the door.

Cal swallowed back his anger.

Crazy sick. Yes indeed. That's exactly how he felt. Standing in the pouring rain with his guitar, waiting to play his goofy love song for Lauren who was in bed sick. *Crazy sick.* What had he been thinking? Cal stood there, cold and wet, feeling like a waterlogged fool.

Two loons in love. Winging o'er the lake of dreams.

Crazy sick.

Edgar's words mocked him as he sloshed his way home.

25

JOUSTING WITH BIRDMAN

Lauren felt like she'd been flattened by a tsunami. Would the rain ever quit?

She lounged on the couch, drinking her favorite herbal tea. She held the cup under her nose, breathed in the pleasing citrus scent, trying to clear her sinuses. Sounds were extraordinarily loud—the rain on the roof, the ticking of the wall clock, Daddy spritzing the loon nest again. The light from the halogen lamp hurt her eyes. The small living room held a faint boggy smell of Lake McDowell.

Almost one o'clock. She couldn't believe she'd slept past noon. But then, she knew she needed her rest after the past couple of days. Especially last night, when Lauren had wandered through a whirlwind of strange dreams and bizarre visions. Her most vivid memory was of her mother being here in this room, talking to Lauren, giving her advice. The encounter seemed too real to be a dream, yet too phantasmagoric to be real. She also remembered a few erotic trysts with Cal. Those *had* to be dreams.

Exhaustion sapped her. She'd spent a fitful night on this sofa, and felt drained by the sensory overload and wildness of her nocturnal adventures. Lauren smiled as she mused over what her therapist might conclude from her dream episodes. Doctor Leticia Phillips might even blush a few times if Lauren confided some of the juicy details.

Daddy's voice pulled her out of her reverie.

"What was that?"

"I said, Mr. Cal was here."

"What? When?"

"Couple hours ago."

"And you're just telling me now?"

"You just woke up."

"Well, what did he want, Daddy?"

"He had his guitar. Said he wanted to play a song for you. A *special* song. Said he wrote it just for you."

"And you didn't wake me up?"

"No, I didn't let him in."

"You talked to him out on the porch?"

"No. Didn't let him in."

"You—you left him out in the rain?"

"Yes, yes, yes ... I did. You told me nobody comes inside, yes, yes, yes ... you did."

"But I meant *strangers*, Daddy. Not Cal. And the porch isn't exactly inside."

"You didn't say that, Warren. You said, nobody comes inside while I'm asleep. *Period*! That's what you said."

"Oh, dear god!" Lauren said, setting her tea on the end table and throwing her blanket to the floor. "That poor man," she said, standing. "No telling what he thinks of us now."

"I just did what you said, Warren."

Lauren silently cursed her father's literal interpretations. "I know," she said, touching his shoulder as she brushed past him.

"Where are you going?" he asked.

"I'm going to get cleaned up. Then I'm going next door to see Cal. Thanks to you he may never talk to me again."

Lauren immediately regretted the words as she saw Daddy's face pucker into a pout. She hated when he pulled this hurt act on her. She was in no mood for it.

"I'm hungry! What about my wunch?" he said, the

demanding whine in his voice sharpening her anger.

"You've got two hands," she said. "Pull yourself away from those stupid loon eggs for five minutes and fix it yourself!"

* * *

A hot shower, fresh face of makeup, a change of clothes—Lauren felt reincarnated. She enjoyed the feel of crisp clean clothes against her scrubbed, lotion-softened skin. Her blouse and shorts smelled of the mountain spring fabric softener she used on their laundry. A dab of perfume behind both ears added a flowery scent to the mountain spring. She felt free and easy, unconstrained by bra or panties. Her nipples rubbed against the sheer fabric of her blouse, exciting her. The crotch of her cutoffs was tight, creating a pleasant friction there when she moved. She felt—dare she make such a bold proclamation—*sexy*. She was going next door with one thing in mind.

But then she hesitated as she checked herself in the bathroom mirror. She could almost hear her mother saying: *What in the world's gotten into you, Lo? Fifty-one years old and carrying on like a red light district streetwalker.* But then, wasn't it her mother who had pushed Lauren toward the idea of seducing Cal Blevins?

Cal had written a song for her, and Daddy left him out in the rain.

She would make it up to Cal, oh yes she would. And who cared whether her actions were questionable. Who cared if she was decked out like some middle-aged harlot. She wanted Cal Blevins. *All* of him. And she knew that Cal wanted her. Lauren's mother had been right about one thing—life was too short to dilly-dally around, to put off going for the things you wanted. What was it she had said? *Even if you live to be a ripe old age, life's grand parade still zips by at warp speed. You can't waste any of it. Not a second.*

Mother doesn't know me at all, she thought. But how could she? Macy hadn't been around when Lauren blossomed into womanhood. Her mother hadn't seen her in action during her rock band days. Mother wasn't alive during those years when Lauren would shack up with any musician or stage-door Johnny who'd have her, those drug-clouded nights after gigs when she found herself in many a stranger's bed. Mother's frame of reference didn't extend much past Lauren's thirteenth birthday.

She took a deep breath and turned from the mirror. It was time to go to Cal, to surrender herself to him once and for all.

Lauren walked back through the living room, looked at Daddy readjusting the lamp to a new position over the nest. A twinge of sadness ran through her as she watched him spritz the eggs yet again with his water bottle. "Gotta keep 'em wet, y'know," he said, purposely keeping his eyes trained on the soggy nest. "That's what the bird books say."

She apologized for snapping at him earlier, but he kept his head down, ignoring her. Realizing how much she had hurt him, Lauren apologized a second time, but he still wouldn't acknowledge her.

"Look, Daddy," she said, feeling her anger return, "there's no need to—"

"Just go, Warren," he said, his baggy eyes full of wounded pain. "Go and be with your kissyface boyfriend. See what I care."

They stared each other down for an eternal moment, Lauren's anger heating into simmering indignation. She was tired of his tantrums, of always making her feel guilty about wanting a life of her own. She was fed up with the way Daddy took her for granted, insisting that she be both daughter and mother for him. Lauren worked hard to keep him happy, and all he ever gave her in return was name-calling—insults like 'crazy' and 'weird.' And always so demanding of her. She was sick of it. If only she had the money to put him in a home. If only there was someone else who could take care of him.

If only . . . the story of Lauren's life.

She turned and went to the hall closet, grabbed her umbrella, took it out on the front porch and opened it up. She heard Daddy come up behind her. "I don't know when I'll be back," she said, placing her hand on the knob of the screen door. "You don't go anywhere, y'hear, Daddy?" She turned around to see him leaning against the doorframe, looking like an old basset hound who'd been throttled to within an inch of his life.

"Don't you *dare* give me orders, Warren!" he shouted, accenting each word with a thin blast from his squirt bottle. "Just go!" (*squirt, squirt*) . . .

He had changed the nozzle to produce a concentrated stream. The first couple of shots stung Lauren in the neck. Quickly she brought the umbrella around to shield her from his attack.

". . . go see mister kissyface Cal!" (*squirt-plop, squirt-plop, squirt-plop, squirt-plop*) . . .

Lauren jabbed the point of the umbrella at him in a parry and thrust that would have been embarrassing had she not been so angry. She screamed at him to stop, but Daddy kept firing away, frustrated that his shots weren't getting past the skin of the umbrella.

Then, finally, the water bottle was empty. She heard Daddy huffing and puffing, the dry swish of air through the nozzle. Then a clunk as the plastic bottle hit the floor and rolled.

Lauren pushed open the screen door, shoved the umbrella out in front of her, made her way into the gray rainy day.

She sidestepped puddles of muddy water on her way to Cal's place. The rain pelted the top of her umbrella. Behind her she heard Daddy yell: "I hate you, Warren!"

For the first time in days, Lauren was glad for the rain. It helped wash away her tears.

26

THE NESTING INSTINCTS OF LOONS

Cal drank beer and played his guitar, cycling through his favorite blues standards—John Lee Hooker, the Kings (B.B., Albert, and Freddie), T. Bone Walker, Stevie Ray Vaughn, Buddy Guy, Lightning Hopkins. The music he played matched his mood.

Edgy and raw.

Blue.

Lonely.

Needing human contact, he had tried calling Sandra again. Same result. No answer. No voice message. No Sandra.

His ex-wife continued to be AWOL. Weird. Not like Sandra at all.

Then again, he hadn't been able to reach any of his guitar-playing buddies, either. Hadn't, in fact, been able to contact anyone off the mountain since he'd been up here at the lake.

Was it possible that everyone from his life back in civilization had abandoned him? Could it be that he was slipping into a paranoid dementia?

Maybe Edgar's proclamation was spot on. Cal was crazy sick. Going nuts.

He had just finished singing a Howlin' Wolf tune when he heard the front door open and close. Moby was up and out of his dead sleep like a dog shot from a cannon.

He heard Lauren greet Moby, talking to him with that pseudo baby talk that Cal found endearing in a guilty pleasure sort of way.

Sneakers squeaked across the hallway floor followed by the *click, click, click* of Moby's nails.

"Hello Cal," she said, entering the living room. "I've missed you."

His heart caught in his throat. Tight frayed cutoffs emphasized her long, smooth legs. Her pink tank top was wet and clung to her small breasts. Large dark nipples poked through the thin material. The rain had smeared makeup across her face, but even in this drenched, disheveled condition, she looked sensational. Cal felt himself getting hard under the guitar parked on his lap.

"I—I've missed you, too," he said, starting to set the guitar aside and stand.

"No, please don't get up," she said, walking into the room and plopping on the sofa across from where he sat in the old maple-and-horsehair slatted chair. "I want you to play for me. I want you to play the song you wrote for me."

He smelled her wet hair and the heavy musk of her perfume. Shiny lip gloss lent her lips a soft fullness that invited lascivious thoughts.

"Your song?" he said, quite sure he didn't want to share it with her now. That mood had long since passed. Cal thought "Loons In Love" was perhaps the worst tune he'd ever written. She tilted her head and looked at him. "I apologize on Daddy's behalf. Communicating with him can be a real challenge. He shouldn't have treated you like he did."

"Yeah. Your father's not real high on my list of favorite people at the moment."

"He didn't mean anything personal by it." She spied the two empty beer bottles on the coffee table. "You're drinking again."

"Just a little something to take the edge off my cabin fever," he said, annoyed at having to justify his actions in his own house. "Where's Edgar now?"

"At home. We had a big fight."

"Home alone? Aren't you worried he'll pull one of his stunts?"

"Right about now, I couldn't care less what Daddy does. Look, it's just us, Cal. Let's enjoy this time we have alone together. I don't want to discuss Daddy right now, okay?"

"Yeah, sure."

"Please play my song for me."

"I—I'm not so sure I really like it that much anymore. I'm not sure *you* would like it."

"What, after a couple of hours, it's dropped off the American Bandstand Hit Parade?"

He laughed, appreciating her attempt to keep things light and playful. "I'm not sure it was ever on the Hit Parade," he said. "On the cornpone scale, it ranks real close to 'Muskrat Love.'"

She giggled. "Let me be the judge of that, okay?" she said, reaching over and touching his knee. "I don't care if it *is* 'Muskrat Love.' I want to hear it. No one has ever written a song for me before. It's sweet . . . a very romantic notion. Of *course* I'll like it."

Cal looked at her, hesitating. He honestly couldn't picture himself singing his hackneyed lyrics directly to her. But then he thought about the million-and-one other love songs he had learned to play over the years—*silly* love songs is how Paul McCartney self-deprecatingly referred to them. Taken alone, the lyrics of just about every love song did come across as trite and silly. But when you added a beautiful melody, something special happened. Something that reached deep into the human heart and pulled hope and compassion to the surface.

He saw the naked desire on Lauren's face, the longing

that shone in her eyes, the way she leaned forward in anticipation. Her eager body language reminded Cal of a little girl waiting to be told her favorite story. Looking at her now, he knew Lauren would like "Loons In Love," no matter how bad it was.

"Okay," he said, sliding his guitar back into position, "Here goes."

Cal started tentatively, then gained confidence as he saw her reaction. By the time he hit the first chorus, Lauren's face lit up like a thousand-watt spotlight. She swayed back and forth in time to the music, a beatific smile on her peach-painted mouth. When he strummed the final chord, Lauren jumped out of her chair and shrieked, threw her arms around his neck.

"Oh, Cal! That was so beautiful! I absolutely adore it! Loons in love! That's what we are! It's perfect!"

She smothered him with hugs and kisses. Cal tried to protect his precious Taylor guitar from the onslaught of Lauren's affections, but quickly gave up. What were a few nicks and dings when he was this happy. Cal Blevins was in love again, and nothing else mattered.

He felt her glasses pinching against his cheek and her moist breath in his ear as she kept repeating how much she loved him and how much he meant to her. Cal tried to tell her he felt the same way, but her mouth was on his before he could get the words out. Their teeth gnashed together. Their tongues explored each other's mouths. Lauren's hands were all over him. He felt her lift the guitar out of his lap and set it in the stand, her lips never leaving his.

And then Moby, feeling left out, jumped up on them. The extra weight and the dog's momentum sent the chair toppling backward. The three of them crashed to the floor amid screeches of laughter and barks of doggy glee. The slats of the chair dug into Cal's back. He felt a raw pain traverse his spine, but he didn't care. Lauren was on top, straddling him. Moby was to one side, tail whipping about furiously, his thick blunt head darting in and out, his long slobbery tongue licking at their faces.

The only thing missing is the white picket fence, Cal thought. It had been years since he'd felt this kind of domesticated bliss.

Slowly their passions ebbed. They lay on the floor, breathing heavily and snickering about what had just happened. They held on to each other, loosely now, confessing their love to each other. Moby finally got bored with all the mushy stuff and went to the kitchen, to see if by some miracle there was food in his bowl.

Cal said, "If I'd known a song did that to you, I would have written half a dozen."

"Oh, we're not through yet, my love," Lauren said, standing, pulling Cal to his feet.

He groaned as he stood, his hand going to the small of his back where there was a pinch of pain.

"Are you okay?" she asked.

"I'll live. Just a little twinge," he said, rubbing where it hurt. "What did you have in mind?"

"Well, first, I'm going to give you a luxurious back massage."

"What about second?"

"A *frontal* massage?" she said, winking at him.

"I like the way you think, sweetie."

"Yeah, and after that I'm going to show you just how much I love you. C'mon," she said, tugging at his hand, "I can't wait another second! Take me to your bed. *Please.*"

27

NEANDERTHALS DO THE LITTLE TANGO

They lay entwined in the damp sheets, spent, holding each other as though letting go might allow the other to vanish. Lauren wrapped herself in the cocoon of Cal's embrace, watching his chest rise and fall as he breathed.

"God, Cal. That was spectacular!" She ran her hand through his thick gray chest hair.

"Better than spectacular," he said to the ceiling. His face was scarlet, like he'd just run a record-setting marathon. "I don't think there's a word for what we just did."

Lauren propped herself up on an elbow, kissed the tip of his nose. "I can think of one or two."

"I know you can," he said. "I heard you shout a few during our, um . . . our little tango."

"Little *tango*? Cute, Cal."

"Don't you dare give me a hard time, missy!" he said, smiling. "At least my description is civilized. The things that tripped off your tongue shocked me, let me tell ya. And here I thought you were a right proper country gal."

Lauren laughed, enjoying the affectionate way he poked fun at her. "So you're complaining now?" she said, snaking her hand down his belly, under the sheets.

He flinched. "Ooh! Careful! I'm still..." His voice trailed off into a low moan.

She peppered his cheeks and neck with light, fluttery

kisses as she worked her hand under the sheets. "How's your back?"

"My back?"

"Yeah, you know, the one you hurt in our little Moby-instigated tumble? Our 'little tango' got a bit acrobatic. I thought maybe I hurt you."

He chuckled. "If you call what you did to me *hurt*, then consider me the world's most enthusiastic masochist!"

They laughed together. Lauren thought she had never loved a man more than she did Cal Blevins at this moment.

She said, "Not bad for a couple of old farts, were we?"

"Old? Right now I feel like a horny sixteen-year-old. Mercy, the things you do to me, lady."

"It's all your fault, mister man. When I'm with you I can't help myself."

Their conversation lapsed into a comfortable silence. Lauren pressed her naked body against his. She teased him with her hands and fingers, felt the heat from his slick body entering her. She listened to the raindrops plinking against the windows, tiny bells chiming through Cal's soft moans. She loved the way he responded to her touch, the power she had over him. He was hers to do with as she pleased.

As though in a trance, she climbed on top of him, straddling him, her knees lightly clenching his ribs. She moved her arm behind her and felt for him, guided him with her hand, her breath catching in her throat as he entered her. They rocked together, the squeaking of the box springs gaining in volume as their fire burned out of control. He thrust deeply, violently, and she rode him the way she once had ridden the mechanical bull in the Cowboy Palace during her nightclubbing days. Wild. Reckless. The little tango escalated into a body-thumping frenzy. Cal filled empty spaces inside her, completing her, his friction flooding places within her that had long been desiccated and dying.

They bucked and grunted, varying their rhythm—*fast-*

slow . . . fast-slow-slower . . . faster-fastest—knowing instinctively the proper pace at which to maximize the other's pleasure. She urged him on, filling the small bedroom with shouts of carnal encouragement. Lauren couldn't believe the things coming out of her mouth (if her students could only see the straight-laced Ms. Talbot now, she thought crazily). But it worked. Cal responded to her lusty coaxing in a big way.

She felt him reach behind her and grab her ass with his big hands.

Felt his body tense, go rigid.

Heard him groan, long and loud.

Time seemed to stop as Cal jerked spasmodically.

His reaction set her off. She shrieked as she exploded, felt the sweet warm nectar of her passion mixing with his. She shuddered—a release that went all the way to her toes—then collapsed on top of him.

After a while, when her breathing returned to normal, she pulled her head back, looked down into his eyes. Without her glasses, his face was blurred, but she could make out his ear-to-ear grin. "Did I make you happy?" she said.

"I think you know the answer to that."

"You make me *very* happy, Cal."

He smiled up at her. "You make me happy, too, sweetie. But if you don't get off me pretty soon I'll suffocate and that would make me very unhappy."

"Oops!" she said, laughing through her nose and flopping off of him. "Sorry, babe."

He took several deep breaths, then wrapped his arms around her and pulled her close.

Lauren felt a comforting sense of well being. She listened to the rain hitting the roof. Cal's bedside clock ticked in nearly perfect counterpoint to the raindrops. The choppy rhythm reminded her of a song, some reggae-influenced thing that she might have done with a band long ago.

After several long minutes, she said, "Cal?"

"Hmm?"

"When we first met, did you think it would turn out like this?"

"Like what? That I'd find myself in bed with a potty-mouth sex maniac?"

"Stop it! You know what I mean."

"Yeah, I do."

"And?"

He kissed her. She felt her furnace heating up again, could feel Cal getting hard against her hip. They groped each other with an urgency that would have been comical had they not been so turned on. Lauren whispered sweet intimations into his ear and he answered each with an amorous phrase of his own. They giggled like two kids first discovering the pleasures of the human body.

This man makes me completely crazy, she thought. We're old enough to be grandparents and here we are going for a triple play of white-hot sex.

Their foreplay was interrupted by a scratching at the door.

Moby.

Lauren felt Cal deflate next to her.

He brought his hands to his head and sighed. "Children and pets," he said with frustration. "Nature's perfect birth control! Mobes? Go to the living room and wait. We'll be there soon."

The scratching stopped. The dog let out several protesting whines. Then Lauren heard Moby padding down the hallway.

"Aw," she cooed sympathetically. "He's lonely."

"Nah, he's just bored. Normally, I would have let him out, but the weather is just too nasty." Cal sat up in the bed, fluffed up his pillow behind him. "Don't you think you should be getting back home to Edgar? I mean, I would love to stay in the sack with you forever, but aren't you worried about what your father might be up to?"

Lauren never wanted to leave the comfort and safety of Cal's bed, never wanted this Cinderella moment to end. But he was right. She gave him a sad look, her expression telling him she understood but was disappointed.

"He's a real burden to you," he said matter-of-factly. "Have you ever thought about putting him in a home?"

"You mean a *nursing* home?" she said, incredulous.

"No. A *retirement* home. A place where he can be with others his age . . . others with similar, uh . . . afflictions . . . interests. Other folks he could socialize with."

"Well, sure, I've thought about it. But I could never do that to Daddy. It would kill him. Literally. If I did that, I might as well just send him straight to the *funeral* home."

"So you keep him at home and pay for private care. That has to be expensive."

"Sure it is. It's tough to make ends meet sometimes. But we manage."

"I could help. I have some money."

"Oh, no, Cal. I could never ask you to do that. You're really sweet to offer, but—"

"Just hear me out, okay? I like your father. You know I do. Edgar can be a lot of fun and I usually enjoy being with him. But I've seen what he does to you. I've seen the way he drags you down, the way he's so demanding of you. You can't leave him alone for ten minutes without worrying about him. You can't go out anywhere without taking him with you. Your entire schedule revolves around his needs. You're in the prime years of your life, Lauren. You should be enjoying them. You shouldn't have to be shackled to Edgar . . ."

She listened as Cal explained that both she and Daddy would be much better off if he was living away from her. How the current arrangement was only stifling the both of them.

"You're enabling him, Lauren. He's manipulating you because he knows he can. Let me help. Please. I'll help you find a good eldercare facility for him. I'm sure we can find a good one in Chattanooga where you could visit him regularly."

Lauren knew it wasn't intentional, but Cal's directness wounded her. "I'm *enabling* him? Wow, Cal, you've got that tough-love thing down pat," she said, her voice wavering.

"Look, I'm just saying—"

"I know what you're saying. I'll think about it, okay? And thank you for the offer. It's very generous of you."

She scooted away from him, but he reached out and corralled her.

"Lauren. I've fallen insanely in love with you. Everything has happened so fast it's dizzying. It's the last thing I expected to happen. But it has and I feel wonderful and now I know you do, too. Believe me, I know real men aren't supposed to express their feelings openly like this, but I've always thought that was machismo nonsense ... nothing but male insecurity." He stopped talking and glanced around the room. "Listen to me," he said with a disappointed sigh, "I'm rambling like an obsessed teenager."

"You're not rambling, Cal," she said, stroking his arm. "You're a sensitive man and I think it's sweet the things you're saying to me. I love it that you tell me how you feel about me."

"So then you'll know that when I talk to you about Edgar and your relationship with him, it's because I care. I see your father forcing you to live his life to the point where you can't live your own. I can't stand to see you hurting the way you've been."

"That's nice," she said. "It means a lot to me, *really*."

"And frankly, I think your father is the source of your anxiety attacks."

"Yeah, my therapist has been telling me the same thing. I guess I've elected to ignore it."

A long silence ensued. A roll of thunder echoed across the lake. She heard Moby slurping water from his bowl in the kitchen. A stiff breeze slapped a sheet of rain against the window.

She knew he was right. But it didn't make it any easier. Every time she thought about letting someone else take care of Daddy, it felt too much like abandonment. But Cal was only trying to help her. He was looking out for her best interests.

He had a faraway look about him. She wondered what he was thinking.

"Does what I just confessed freak you out, Cal?"

"What?"

"The fact that I'm seeing a shrink? Does that bother you?"

He focused on her. Seemed return to the moment. "No. Why should it? Even in the best of times, it's tough being human."

She looked at him, at the unreadable, stoic expression on his face. Wondered if he might be judging her, whether he was contemplating the pros and cons of spending any more time with a crazy woman.

Then he surprised her by saying, "I've seen a psychiatrist a few times myself, Lauren."

"What?"

"It's true. And not just shrinks, but also enough family counselors to support a third-world nation."

"You're kidding. *You?*"

"Yeah. The head doctors and counseling sessions started right after my marriage began to slip."

Lauren thought about the photographs she had seen in Cal's albums, especially the ones of his children—Charley and Andrea—and the way Cal or someone had labeled them: *Charley and Andie in their better days.* She recalled the way the photographs had stopped around the age of puberty for both kids. She also remembered Cal telling her that their kids didn't communicate with him anymore, only their mother.

She decided to be as direct as he had been. "Did Charley and Andrea have anything to do with your marriage going on the rocks?"

He showed no surprise at her questioning. "Yeah. Our children definitely drove a wedge between Sandra and me."

"How so?"

He looked at her for a long time, but the longer she met his stare it seemed more like he was looking *through* her while he wrestled with something. She wondered whether she was prying too much, getting too personal too fast.

"What? What is it?" she said, noticing his eyes glisten with tears. "Talk to me, babe." She reached out and touched his leg, trying to comfort him.

"This is . . . this is hard for me, Lauren."

"You can talk to me about anything. I hope you know that."

He nodded, wiped at his eyes with the back of his hand. "Okay." He looked around the bedroom as he composed his thoughts. "I guess the best way is to come right out with it. Tell you point blank."

"Please do. I want to know."

"Okay, okay," he said with a nervous sigh. "It's like this. My son is gay." He looked at her expectantly, as though expecting this news to send her bolting for the door.

"I see," she said, seeing the carefully written line in Cal's photo album—*Charley and Andie in their better days*—scrolling past like a newspaper headline. "And this is a bad thing?"

"Of *course* it's a bad thing! Charley lives with a swishy hair stylist named Tony, who prefers to be called *Tootsie*, of all things. It's deplorable."

Lauren was shocked. The last thing she thought possible from this otherwise open-minded man was that he would be homophobic, and she told him so.

"I am *NOT* a homophobe!"

"Yes you are. It's like you consider your son a failure because he's not like you."

"No, you're not getting it, Lauren. *I* feel like the failure. I feel like some shortcoming in my parenting skills caused Charley to turn out the way he has."

Lauren couldn't believe what she was hearing. "Cal, do you honestly think Charley has any choice in who he is? You think he *chose* to follow the gay lifestyle because of something you did or did not do when he was a child?"

"Absolutely."

"No. You're wrong. Some things just *are*. That whole nature or nurture argument just doesn't hold water, in my opinion." She looked at him, seeing him suddenly in a new light. "What about your daughter?"

"Whaddaya mean?"

"You said you were estranged from both your children. What's your problem with your daughter?"

"It's more Andrea's problem with *me*. She's always been close with her brother. Andie's always supported Charley and his, um ... rather flamboyant lifestyle. When my son and I went our separate ways, Andie made this grand announcement that she was disowning me. She was all of sixteen at the time. My daughter's always been quite headstrong about causes. She's an active member of PETA and some Save the Whales organization. Andie lives in Florida and runs a greyhound rescue shelter. She's also quite active with an Everglades preservation movement. Always fighting for a cause, always looking out for the downtrodden. My daughter has a degree in Chemistry. Smart enough to maybe one day discover a cure for cancer or AIDS. But she's never used it. She's thrown away her education to be a champion for the down and out."

Lauren shook her head. "With all due respect, Cal,

you're a complete idiot! I have literally prayed for an opportunity to have children, but it never happened for me. Here you are with two you refuse to appreciate because they're, um . . . *different.* You push them away, reject them like they're ... I don't know ... like they're some assembly line products that didn't pass inspection. That thinking is so ignorant . . . so *Neanderthal.*"

"Neanderthal? You mean to tell me you wouldn't feel the same way if they were your children?"

"No, I wouldn't. I would love them no matter what. I would cherish them. I'd be proud of them for having the courage to be who they are, even though it's not the popular thing, or the most financially rewarding."

She rolled over and sat on the edge of the bed, reached down on the floor for her clothes.

"So now you're mad at me?" he said, watching her wiggle into her cutoffs.

"No, not mad. *Surprised* is a better description."

"Surprised?"

"Yeah. Surprised that a man as creative and talented and smart as you could be so stupid about your own flesh and blood."

"Ouch!" he said, watching her slip her tank top back on. "So you're going home?"

She turned and nodded at him. "Like you said, I need to see what Daddy is up to."

She bent over to strap her sandals on, then stood at the side of the bed, looking down at Cal.

"Please . . . don't look at me like that," he said.

"Like what?"

"Like I'm a, um . . . Neanderthal."

"You know, Cal, when you love someone, you take on the total package. You learn to accept the other's failings and you appreciate their good qualities. You love that person no matter what. It's unconditional. The reality of it is that we all have a little Neanderthal in us—you, me,

Daddy . . . *humanity*. It's an imperfect world. It's rare when anything lives up to our expectations. But you go on loving just the same. You go on appreciating that each day is a gift and every person in your life is important, even though they are flawed, even though we ourselves are flawed and confused and struggling to do the right thing. There is no guidebook to life, Cal. We're all just improvising."

He smiled at her, and she saw a new respect for her shining in his eyes. "In addition to being beautiful and sexy, you're also brilliant. I'll bet you're a great teacher, Lauren."

"Well, I can't deny that," she said, doing a do-si-do two-step twirl next to the bed, a short tongue-in-cheek dance step to lighten the mood.

He said, "Do you have to leave?"

"Yes, I do."

"Are you mad at me? Angry?"

"No," she said. "I love you, Mr. Neanderthal, even if you are terribly confused about your children." Lauren leaned over and kissed him. "I'll be back as soon as I can, but I have to check on Daddy. I need to get cleaned up, too."

She winked at him. "Even us Neanderthals need a shower once in a while."

28

MASTER SLAYER OF JIGSAW DEMONS

Lauren knew something was amiss as soon as she entered her enclosed porch. The front door stood wide open. A strange smell came from inside the house. A foul burnt plastic odor.

Dread assaulted her. She shook the rain off the umbrella and leaned it against the glider, took a deep breath to steel herself, then went in.

At the entrance to the living room she pulled up abruptly, looked at the scrawled crude letters on one wall in bright red Magic Marker.

I SORY LO

sory sory sory

I 🧡 *u*

Lauren felt something shift inside her, gears in her heart slipping a couple of cogs. She could tell Daddy had invested a lot of time and effort to get the letters and artwork as perfect as his shaky hands would permit.

Thousands of jigsaw puzzle pieces littered the floor. Scattered to and fro Lauren could see remnants of the cardboard puzzle boxes, ripped and shredded in long strips. Daddy's card table and chair were tipped over. The halogen lamp lay on its side, its beam casting an oval of light on the far wall. Lauren looked at that beam of light and the mess littering the floor. A sun setting over a battlefield, she thought. Daddy Talbot, the invincible warrior ... Edgar the Magnificent, master slayer of jigsaw demons.

She clomped through the mess, searching for the loons nest and eggs. No sign of them. A long red arrow etched low on the wall pointed into the hall. She followed it.

The stench was stronger here, the odor of burnt toast and over-fried food mixing with the noxious plastic smell. The bright red arrow continued down the wall of the hallway, pointing toward the kitchen. Lauren slowed her pace, not sure she wanted to see what awaited her there. She heard the clank of plates and the scraping of a chair. Heard Daddy humming softly. She recognized the tune: "I've Gotta Be Me" by Sammy Davis, Jr., the song Daddy resorted to when he was most depressed.

She stopped just outside the kitchen, listening to his out-of-key humming, trying to muster the courage to face him. For a fleeting second she thought about going back to get Cal. But she knew this was something she had to do on her own. As much as she needed Cal's strength right now, he would only complicate things.

Another deep breath, then she entered the kitchen. What she saw made the living room look tame. Lauren heard herself gasp. She felt her knees go weak and leaned against the doorframe for support.

She had entered a nightmare.

White streaks of flour covered the floor and countertops. Drawers and cupboards had been thrown open and every available pot and pan and cooking utensil was strewn around the kitchen in disarray, as if a besotted chef had been at work. The walls bled with more red Magic Marker scribbles and crude heart artwork similar to what Lauren had seen in the living room. She looked at the stove, cringing at the two frying pans, black as soot in an ancient chimney. The large casserole dish contained a crusted mound of something burnt beyond recognition. Bluish-yellow flames hissed from all four gas burners. The oven door leaned open, a wrapped loaf of sliced bread sending out reeking plumes of smoke from the melted plastic wrap.

Daddy smiled at her. "I fixed dinner for us, Warren, yes, yes, yes I did!"

Lauren tried not to show her shock as she checked out the kitchen table. Daddy had a plate of burnt food in front of him. Next to him was another place-setting for her, her plate heaped with blackened whatever-it-was. Apparently, Daddy had become frustrated trying to pick out the right eating utensils, so he had just dumped the entire contents of the silverware drawer in a big pile on the table.

"I wanted to do something s-sp-special," he stammered, "to show you how s-sorry I am. I shouldn't have talked to you the way I did, Warren. I don't h-hate you. I wuv you!"

She looked at him. Daddy had the Magic Marker in one hand, using it to bat one of the loon eggs back and forth on the table in front of him. She saw the remains of the nest on the floor next to his chair, reminding her of a pile of shredded wheat. He held the second egg in his other hand. The fingertips of both hands were stained crimson.

Lauren gathered the strength to go to the oven and, using two potholders, carefully extract the burning bread. "You most certainly did do something special here, Daddy," she said, throwing the smoldering mess in the sink and dousing it with water. As she turned off the stove burners, Cal's words came back to her: *He's a real burden to you. Have you ever thought about putting him in a home?*

"Come, sit," she heard Daddy say to her back. "Have dinner with me, Warren."

She turned, braced herself against the counter, not on solid ground with her emotions. Daddy had tried so hard to please her, so she really couldn't give in to her anger.

Lauren felt a draining sadness, a compassion for him that only fed her feelings of helplessness.

He had flour all over him, a small dusting of it across his nose and cheeks. A mime with makeup malfunction, she thought. Lauren didn't know whether to laugh or cry. She glanced at the two loon eggs—the way he was twirling them on the tabletop—then down at the destroyed nest.

"What happened here, Daddy?" she said, meeting his confused gaze.

"I-I cooked dinner . . . be-because I'm sorry."

She noticed the tears in his eyes, his lower lip quivering. "I appreciate that," she said, trying to keep her voice calm. "I mean, why did you ruin all your puzzles? Why did you trash the loon nest?"

"Because I'm bad, Warren. I *hate* being me!" he said petulantly, tears beginning to spill down his cheeks.

"You're not bad, Daddy. You're just—"

"YES, YES, YES, I AM!" he shouted, slapping his hands on the table, the loon eggs and his plate of charred mystery food bouncing with each slap.

"Please don't get upset," she said in a consoling tone. Lauren could see his childish tendencies surfacing and that things were about to get dicey. "No harm's been done. I forgive you. Completely."

"No you don't! You're just saying that!"

"Yes, I mean it. From the bottom of my heart."

"NO, NO, NO! You're telling a fib, Warren!" He grabbed a loon egg in each hand and held them out in front of him. "You called my w-w-woon eggs *stupid*! You hate me!"

"No, I—" she began, but was then rendered speechless as she watched him smash the egg in his left hand against his forehead with a loud *splat*, a yellowish, yolky syrup dripping down into his eyes, and across the bridge of his nose.

"STUPID, STUPID, STUPID!" he railed, then cracked

the egg in his right hand on top of his head.

He sat there, dazed, bits of eggshell in his hair, the goopy yellowish mess congealing with the flour on his face in little doughy patches. He looked at his outstretched hands, questioning, judging, *accusing*. And then he brought his hands to his face and began weeping.

"Oh, what have I d-d-done, Warren?" he sobbed, his shoulders trembling, his liver-spotted hands shaking noticeably. "I killed my woons! I killed my baby woons!"

Something broke open inside of Lauren, something deep and swift-running, like an underground spring flooding and crashing through a weak place in the limestone. She began crying, telling Daddy through her weeping jags that he hadn't killed anything, that they were just eggs and not real birds yet, telling him through her veil of tears that absolutely none of this was his fault. She went to him, threw her arms around him, feeling the hard slivers of shell cutting into her skin, the gummy yolk sticking to her clothes.

They cried together as Lauren tried to console him, all the while hearing Cal's voice as if he were standing there talking in her ear: *You're enabling him, Lauren. He's manipulating you because he knows he can.*

29

THREE-RING CIRCUS

Cal picked up the phone and punched in the area code, then the first three numbers of the exchange. His hands shook. Tension cramped his shoulders. He hesitated, just long enough to change his mind. This was a bad idea. Charles would never pick up anyway. One look at his caller ID and Charles would know it was the old man calling. Or worse, Charles's significant other, Tony—better known as Tootsie—would answer and give Cal a hard time.

He placed the receiver back in the cradle and sighed. Wondered why family matters had to be so maddeningly complex.

Cal had given a lot of thought to what Lauren said, about how she wanted children but it never happened for her. He remembered her saying: *Cal, I would fly to the moon in a leaky balloon for a healthy child of my own.* And he had shunned his own son and daughter. Why? He knew it wasn't for the reason Lauren sited—homophobia. Cal had nothing against the gay lifestyle. He embraced the myriad of diversity in people, genuinely felt that different races, creeds, and cultures added dimension to the world, added new colors to the palette of life. No, his problem with his children was that he thought he'd failed as a parent. Try as he had, he'd never been able to connect with Charles and Andrea as adults. It was a failing on his part, not theirs. It was a burden Cal had carried with him for years, one of the primary wedges that split apart his long marriage to Sandra.

Well, Cal, you had me with your first chord.

He smiled as he remembered Lauren's words. Cal had to see her, wanted to *be* with her. His longing for her was a palpable ache. He was an addict in need of a fix. Cal wanted to thank her for being so forthright with him, for reminding him how incredibly lucky he had been. Wanted to tell her again that he loved her and needed her. He looked through the rain-smeared window, saw that the murky daylight had darkened into coal-black night. The clock showed 9:20. Was it too late to go next door? Nah, he decided. When you're in love, time is irrelevant.

Something crashed against the front door, a loud thump that made him jump. Cal heard Moby's frenzied barks, the Lab throwing himself at the door, trying to get at whatever lurked on the other side.

Something wrong about this, he thought as he made his way to the utility room and grabbed the baseball bat. He crept through the living room, quieted Moby.

Listened. Nothing but his and Moby's breathing.

Probably another one of Edgar's peculiar entrances, Cal thought, but took no chances as he gripped the bat in his right hand and swung the door open with his left.

Moby darted out onto the wet stoop. A spray of fine mist slapped Cal in the face, momentarily blinding him. He tripped over Moby and took a tumble, his butt smacking the slick cement, the bat thunking off the stoop and rolling into the wet grass. He cursed, pulled himself up into a sitting position. Saw Moby nuzzling a soggy bundled newspaper.

Cal looked out across his flooded front yard, searching for a sign of the phantom paperboy. Couldn't see past the gloomy opaque curtain of night out to the street.

He wrestled the paper away from Moby. The crazy dog thought he'd found a new mega bone.

Cal ushered Moby inside and shut the front door, took the newspaper into the living room. Gingerly, he unrolled the paper, the wet newsprint smelling like a paper máché science project. The inside of the roll was dry, the lettering on the front page masthead bright and crisp.

LOON MOUNTAIN GAZETTE
News of Lake McDowell and Surrounding Areas

Cal stared at the familiar icon to the right of the masthead—a pair of loons in flight circling a mountain peak. He was immediately transported back to his youth. Cal remembered how he and his summer camp buddies used to fight over the comics section, each boy wanting to be the first to see the latest adventures of the Lone Ranger, Green Lantern, and Tarzan. He recalled how his mother once clipped coupons from this publication to save money on groceries at Lonnie's. How his father checked Artie the Angler's page to get fishing tips and keep up with the hottest fishing spots on the lake.

Only trouble was, the *Loon Mountain Gazette* had ceased publication thirty years ago. Cal checked the dateline, squinted his eyes at the small type font, saw today as the issue date. A creepy sensation crawled through his gut.

And then he spied the titles to two front-page articles and Cal felt all the oxygen sucked from his lungs.

Sandra Blevins Now Embraces Cell Phones

Charles Blevins to Marry Longtime Partner in Civil Ceremony

He began to read the first article about Sandra …

Sandra Blevins Now Embraces Cell Phones

In a bold reversal from her previous stance on the "evil and destructive" nature of cellular technology, Sandra M. Blevins of Dunwoody, Georgia has now embraced all things mobile by purchasing her first cell phone. "Yes, it's true," Ms. Blevins states emphatically, "I once blasted all the idiots running around with cell phones plastered against their ears, yakking away mindlessly. Now I've seen the light. Count me as a convert. I love the convenience of being able to reach anyone anywhere by just pressing a few buttons. It's funny, because my ex-husband always teased me about being a confirmed technophobe. Calvin said numerous times that the day I got a cell phone would mark the beginning of the end of days. So, I guess we now have the apocalypse to look forward to," Ms. Blevins said, laughing ...

Cal quit reading. He felt his heart slamming against his chest. How could this be? His wife as front-page news? In a defunct newspaper? For something as mundane as a cell phone purchase? Completely absurd.

Ludicrous.

Cal quickly scanned the byline. The author was listed as staff writer, Charlene Wolfe. The name meant nothing to him.

He went to the other article that had caught his eye, the one about his son Charles:

Charles Blevins to Marry Longtime Partner in Civil Ceremony

Anthony G. Martino of Boston, Massachusetts and Charles Andrew Blevins of Atlanta, Georgia have announced plans for a most unusual wedding. The two longtime partners will be married via a civil ceremony at Greene Park in the Boston suburb of Lexington on Saturday, September 15. What makes the ceremony unusual is the circus theme the two young men have settled on. The marriage vows will take place under a big-top tent with music supplied by a brass band. Jugglers, acrobats, clowns, white stallions, and even an elephant will round out the big-top entertainment. A Justice of the Peace dressed in full ringmaster regalia will marry them in the center ring. When asked about the unusual proceedings, Charles says, "It was Anthony's idea to go with a circus theme. My Tootsie-Tone is so creative!" ...

Cal quit reading. He needed a drink. A very strong drink. He headed to the kitchen to fix himself one.

About halfway there, he stopped, remembering what Lauren had told him while she nursed him through his hangover last week. *I want you to promise me something, Cal. The next time you get the urge to do something stupid like you did last night, I want you to come and get me. We'll talk or sing together or chant or something. Anything but self destruction.*

He ditched the drink idea, reversed direction and went to the hall closet for his poncho.

Cal had a promise to keep.

30

RIP VAN WINKLE AND CO-ED SHOWERS

Cal sloshed through the puddles, the raindrops pelting his poncho like sprays of buckshot. Would this dreadful rain never cease?

The door to Lauren's screened-in porch flapped open in the gusty wind. Cal walked up the steps into the dry womb of the porch, lowered the hood of his parka, shook himself off. He looked at Lauren's front door, seeing it as a dark and imposing roadblock. Suddenly the idea of coming here seemed absurd.

He put his ear to the door, listened, heard faint music. And something else. A brushing sound. Water sloshing. Lauren cleaning house this time of night?

He knocked, heard the brushing stop, the music shut off. Footsteps.

"Is that you, Cal?" Lauren's voice was muffled behind the door.

"No, it's not Cal. It's the Big Bad Wolf," he said, deepening his voice. "I'm here to eat you, my dear."

No laugh. Cal waited in silence for long seconds. Normally Lauren loved sexual double entendres. Normally she would bust a gut over that one.

"Lauren?" he said, finally. "Are you okay?"

He heard her fiddling with the lock. The door opened, spilling faint light out onto the porch.

"Oh, Cal. I'm so glad to see you."

"What's the matter?"

She tumbled into his arms. He could smell the biting scent of bleach on her, could feel tremors run through her body as she sobbed against his chest.

"What is it, Lauren? What's wrong?"

"It's Daddy. He went completely manic when I was over at your place."

"How so?"

"Come. I'll show you."

She led him into the living room. Cal couldn't believe what he saw. It looked like a twister had blown through.

Lauren removed her glasses, wiped her eyes and said, "Believe it or not, I've cleaned some of it up. You should have seen it when I first got home. Complete disaster."

Cal noticed the writing on the walls, the crude hearts drawn with what looked like red paint.

"What the . . .?"

"Oh, it gets worse, Cal. Much worse. Follow me."

She led him out into the main hallway. Much more wall scribbling here. A bucket of soapy water sat beneath a section where the red lettering was smeared. It looked like the wall was bleeding. A pile of pinkish rags and a scrub brush sat next to the bucket. The bristles of the brush were stained a dark scarlet.

They looked at each other. Cal said, "I hate to tell you this, but you won't get the walls clean that way."

"So I'm finding out. I can't afford to lose my damage deposit." She started crying again.

He hugged her to him and she clung tightly.

"It's all going to be okay, sweetie," he said. "Tomorrow morning I'll go to Lonnie's and get some paint. We'll have us a painting party. The place will look good as new when we're done."

"I swear, Cal," she said, her long face opening up in a contented smile, "you're my guardian angel. Every time I fall, you're there to pick me up."

"That's my retirement business . . . the guardian angel racket."

She laughed, an exhausted honk of a laugh.

He studied her. She looked drained and disheveled. Baggy dark circles under her eyes. A splotch of yellowish goop across her tank top. Eyeglasses smeared and sitting crooked on her nose. Tiny bits what looked like colored plastic embedded in her hair and stuck to the side of her face. Cal reached out and plucked a piece, felt its razor sharp edges between his fingers. "What's this?"

"Eggshell."

"Eggshell?" Cal thought about Edgar's loon eggs. "Oh no . . . Don't tell me—"

"Yep. Daddy went ballistic. He smashed both of them. Now he thinks he's a murderer."

"Where is he now?"

"Sleeping. I whipped up my best Rip Van Winkle potion for him. He should be out until morning."

She wrapped her arms around his waist.

He felt the cool, moist perspiration on her warm skin. "Tell me what happened, Lauren,"

"I will. But there's one more stop on this, um . . . this Better Homes and Garden tour. The kitchen. We'll talk there while I clean."

Cal was stunned by what he saw in the kitchen. He grabbed a sponge and helped Lauren clean while she told him about the little spat between her and her father that led to Edgar's binge of destruction. As Cal looked around at the damage, he thought: *Strange way to say you're sorry.* Cal felt a huge tug of sympathy for Lauren. She deserved better than this. But, at the same time, Cal felt compassion for Edgar Talbot. A tough situation all the way around.

* * *

An hour later they had the kitchen restored to some semblance of order and Cal knew all the particulars of what had transpired here. The most surprising thing was Edgar's annihilation of the two loon eggs. The way Edgar watched over those eggs made Cal believe the old man would try to see them through to hatchlings. So what had happened to change that? Surely Edgar Talbot had the strength to withstand a fight with his daughter. Then again, maybe not.

"A penny for your thoughts," Lauren told him.

"Just thinking about Edgar."

"What about him?"

"Oh, just how colorful he is. Never a dull moment with your father around."

"You're a master of understatement, Cal."

They were seated at the kitchen table, slaking their thirsts with glasses of iced tea.

"I love Daddy," she said, "I really do. But this episode has pushed me over the edge. I'm even starting to think about putting him in a retirement community. You know, your advice. And yet every time I think about it, I hate myself for it."

"You're beating yourself up over this, sweetie," he said, sliding his hand across the table and caressing her fingers. "The best thing for everyone involved is to put Edgar in a retirement home. A good one with top-drawer professional care. I told you I would help you with that and I meant it."

"Thank you, Cal. I really don't know what I'd do without you."

"You'd do the same things you're doing now. You just wouldn't have as much fun doing them."

Cal's attempt at lightness didn't change Lauren's down mood. She seemed preoccupied, a million miles away.

"What is it?" he said.

She pulled off her eyeglasses and cleaned the lenses with a Kleenex. "I've been thinking about us . . . this uh, *thing* we have going. Our, um . . . *situation*. We both know that Daddy and I have to go back home Saturday," she said, holding the frames up to the light, then polishing a little more. "I don't want to leave you, Cal."

"Then don't. Stay with me. You and Edgar. I have room."

Lauren inspected her glasses, then perched them back on the bridge of her nose. "If only it were that simple. School starts up again in a week. I have a career to get back to. I have lesson plans and course syllabuses to prepare, pre-registration meetings and parent-teacher appointments to keep. And you've convinced me I need to do something with Daddy. He certainly can't stay here. In some ways this mountain and lake are worse for him than the dull suburbs of Chattanooga."

"Well look," Cal said, "Chattanooga isn't another universe. It's what? Sixty miles from here? And my schedule is free and easy, so I'll come visit you as much as you want."

"Really?" she said doubtfully, then looked away. "I just have this feeling that things will change. That I'll get back to Chattanooga and discover this wonderful time we've spent together was just a dream. Or worse, that it was just a quick summer fling."

"You're over thinking things, Lauren."

"I'm sorry, Cal. I didn't mean to imply—"

"It's okay, sweetie. I understand."

"It's just that . . . well . . . you're newly divorced and I have Daddy to contend with and you and I have separate lives in different zip codes and—"

"Whoa! Hold on," he said. "Listen, things always work out when they're right. I'm a firm believer in that."

"And you think this thing we have going is right?"

"Absolutely. I *know* so. Don't you?"

"Yes. I do. I just don't know what this thing is."

Cal understood Lauren's insecurities, he really did. But he was beginning to lose his patience with this conversation. "Why do you feel the need to define our relationship? Why can't you just go with the flow and enjoy the time we have together?"

"I know, Cal. You're right. It's just that . . . well . . . I can't help but wonder about your feelings for your ex. You talk about her a lot."

There it was. Lauren finally came out with it. She had problems with Sandra. How to tell her that you couldn't completely shut down all emotional ties with someone after forty years. It wasn't a faucet you could turn on and off. His and Sandra's lives were so intertwined that even if he wanted to, Cal couldn't completely shut her out.

"Oh, gawd, I'm sorry, Cal. None of my business. I'm being Miss Nosy-Nose."

"That didn't stop you from looking through my photo albums, did it?"

Lauren sat looking at Cal, stunned. She opened her mouth to say something, but nothing came out.

"I know you went through my albums, Lauren."

Lauren's pale cheeks blushed a rosy pink. "Oh gawd. I'm so embarrassed."

"It's okay. I don't mind."

"You don't?"

"No. I'm flattered that you care so much. Besides, I have nothing to hide. I want you to know all about me, warts and all. What we have can't survive if we keep secrets from each other."

"You're right, Cal. But still … I'm sorry about my snooping."

"Forget about it. We're two loons in love, remember?"

That brought a relieved laugh. "How could I forget?" she said, wrapping her hands around his on the tabletop. "You really are a very special man. Putting up with me and all my baggage."

"That's what it's all about, I guess. Handling each other's baggage."

"I love you so much, Calvin Blevins," she said, leaning across the table and kissing him. "You're about the sweetest guy a gal could ever hope to meet."

"Hey, you know what?" he said, getting up from the table. "We're missing out on a great opportunity."

"How so?"

"You say Edgar's passed out until morning?"

"Hopefully . . . *probably.*"

"Well, you've got yolk and eggshell all over you. I was thinking a good hot shower would be just what the doctor ordered. Do you believe in co-ed showers?"

"Only if they lead to steamy sex."

He moved behind her. She remained seated at the table. He massaged her shoulders as he said, "That can be arranged."

"Let's go then," Lauren said, standing, taking him by the hand. "I'll soap your back first."

"We might not even get to the soap," Cal said, laughing.

"That's okay. Without my glasses, I can't tell the difference between a bar of soap and other things."

"That could be trouble," he said, watching her slide the shower curtain back and turn on the water. Cal smiled as he heard her humming their song, "Loons In Love."

31

PILLOW TALK

Lauren awoke in the middle of the night. She heard Cal snoring softly beside her. The bed smelled of soap and shampoo and the musky scent of spent sex.

She reached out, touched Cal's shoulder, snuggled up against him, the feel of his skin against hers liberating. Lauren still couldn't quite believe her good fortune, meeting a man like Cal Blevins on what was supposed to be a two-week getaway for her and Daddy. Little Miss Lonely-hearts, left-standing-alone-at-the-altar herself—Lauren Talbot—with a decent man! Would miracles ever cease?

Life with Cal here on Loon Mountain seemed like a fairy tale. *Enchanted* was the word she and Cal used most often to describe the ambiance of the mountain and Lake McDowell. She felt that same word—*enchanted*—also perfectly described their now-torrid relationship.

There was the music they made together. Lauren loved singing to Cal's accompaniment, loved harmonizing with him. She hadn't done any real singing in years, and her participation in what Cal referred to as his "pick-and-grin" sessions had lit a fire under her, threw her back into the music she had loved her entire life. And she could listen to Cal play for hours on end. The man performed aural magic on his guitars.

Yes, she was crazy about this man sleeping next to her.

But the fact remained: Lauren's life was back in Chatta-nooga, and she just knew that once she and Daddy returned home, the enchanted spell would be broken. Now that Cal Blevins had shown her how good life could be, did she really think she could live without him? She had given serious thought to retiring from teaching and coming back here to live out her days with Cal. But she still had Daddy's welfare to consider. That, and the fact she had known Cal a ridiculously short period of time. The situation seemed futile.

Cal stirred. His eyes opened. "Hi there," he said in a croaky whisper.

"Hi there, yourself," she said, touching the tip of his nose.

"Can't sleep?"

"No. Too much on my mind."

"You think way too much, Lauren."

"I know. It's a Talbot curse. One of many."

He yawned, rubbed her forearm. "So what is it that has you so preoccupied at this hour of the morning?"

"You. Me. Us . . . Daddy."

"Wow. That's quite a rogues gallery."

"I love you so much," she said. "I know it in my heart and soul even though I don't have a clue how it happened so fast."

"It happened fast because it was meant to," Cal whispered, then kissed her cheek.

"Cal?"

"Yes, sweetie?"

"Why did you come over to see me tonight?"

He emitted a snort, paused to think a second. "Because I have telepathic powers that told me Edgar went cuckoo and destroyed half your house and that you desperately needed my help?"

"Good try," Lauren said, laughing. "I mean, why did you *really* come over?"

"Well ... I guess because I was about to do something stupid."

"You mean like get drunk again?"

"Yeah."

"What made you want to get drunk?"

Cal told her about the odd newspaper delivery and the articles he saw about his wife and son. She listened to him questioning his sanity, asking how a defunct newspaper could come back to life and publish front-page articles about his own family. "I have to be going crazy, Lauren," he kept saying. "There's just no other way to explain it."

But she knew he wasn't crazy. He'd gone home to get the *Loon Mountain Gazette* to show her the proof. She had seen it with her own eyes, the articles about Cal's wife's newfound love of cell phones and his son's circus-themed wedding plans. No, Cal Blevins wasn't crazy. But something bizarre had sure been in the air the past two weeks.

Lauren thought about all the strange and puzzling events that had happened since she and Daddy had arrived here. Her own inexplicable encounter with her mother, which she hadn't told Cal about. Cal witnessing the Cherokee fish hypnotist at work ... Cal encountering his father's ghost, or whatever it was, out on his boat ... Daddy wandering out in the middle of the night, ending up down in the swamp, protecting an abandoned loon nest . . . the bizarre loon ritual at South Birdtown performed by a couple of Cherokee shamans. So many extraordinary happenings in search of an explanation.

"Hello . . . Earth to Lauren," she heard Cal say. "Something you're not telling me?"

"Well," she started, "you remember telling me about your encounter with your father out on your boat?"

"Of course. What, now you're going to tell me you don't believe me?"

"No, I believe you," she said, thinking that now was the time to share her weird experience with him. "I had a similar encounter. With my mother."

She thought he might respond with a snicker, but he didn't. Instead he said, "Tell me about it."

And she did. Lauren unburdened herself, telling Cal about her long-dead mother, Macy, and the way she had shown up in the living room during the worst of a thunderstorm. She related how Daddy wasn't aware of Macy's presence, just like Edgar had been oblivious of Cal's father out in the boat. She told Cal about how her mother claimed she had met Cal's dead parents, describing them as offbeat outcasts who wore exotic ballroom dancing clothes and seemed to live for hitting the dance floor. And Lauren's mother had described Cal's father's white zoot suit exactly as Cal had described it to her, complete with black silk dress shirt, broad white tie, and black-and-white two-toned patent leather shoes. And then there was Macy calling Cal's father by name—Stanley Blevins. Lauren's mother had even given her some bold advice—quit wasting time and go after Cal. Forget your genteel Southern Belle ways and make your intentions known. Nothing wrong in today's permissive society for the woman to be the aggressor.

"Well, at least she gave you some good advice," Cal said, giving her a dastardly smile and gently tweaking her nipple.

"Hey! Do that again and you'd better be ready for another little tango, buster."

"I'd love to," Cal said, "but my aging body says no. You've worn this old man out, sweetie."

"Hah! Old man?" Lauren snorted. "I know a few tricks guaranteed to work on tired old men."

"I don't doubt that for a second. You're insatiable, woman!"

"Just making up for lost time is all."

They lapsed into a silence, their communication reduced to light caresses and lazy kisses.

They lay there, entwined underneath the sheets, both

lost in their own thoughts. Finally, Cal said, "Wow! Listen to that."

"What?"

"Hear how quiet it is?"

"Yeah. What about it?"

"It stopped raining."

Lauren listened. The familiar drone of rain pelting the roof was conspicuously absent. The early morning had a peaceful stillness about it. "Finally. What's it been? Three days?"

"Four. But who's counting."

"I say this calls for a celebration."

"What kind of celebration?"

Lauren ran a hand up Cal's thigh, raked her fingers through his pubic hair.

Cal sighed. "I told you, sweetie. I don't think I can do it again so soon."

"You know what your problem is, Cal? You think too much," she said, turning Cal's words back around on him. "You just lay back and enjoy. I'll do the work."

"Mmmmnnn . . ." he moaned. "I wish it would quit raining more often."

32

A GATHERING OF LOONS

The sun made a glorious return appearance Thursday morning and Cal suggested they take advantage of the beautiful day, spend the afternoon out on the lake. Lauren's trashed walls could wait until tomorrow for a new coat of paint.

Lauren busied herself stocking the boat with food and drink while Cal prepped the fishing tackle and checked the fuel. He also made sure to load in his cheap nylon-string guitar, an ancient small bodied acoustic that had logged many hours out on the lake. It still played beautifully even though he'd worn a hole clear through the body below the plastic scratch guard and the humidity had stripped away patches of its original shellacked gloss down to bare wood.

While Cal and Lauren worked, Edgar stood at the far end of the dock, throwing a tennis ball out into the shallows for Moby to chase. Moby retrieved Edgar's feeble throws in tireless fashion, taking bounding leaps off the dock and slapping against the water in splashy belly flops. Cal stopped what he was doing to watch. Moby reminded him of a playful sea otter, the dog's slick coat shining in the bright sun like wet licorice. Each time the Lab brought the ball back to Edgar, his look seemed to challenge the old man, saying: *Can't you throw it any farther?* Cal smiled. He knew that look intimately. Moby could be a most demanding taskmaster.

When they were ready to depart, Lauren told Edgar to wear his life jacket. Edgar refused.

"No, no, no," he said, backing away from the vest in Lauren's outstretched hands, looking at it as though it was some kind of radioactive object. "I'm not wearing that, Warren! It pinches me."

"Yes you *are* wearing it, Daddy. You know you can't swim. Put it on. Just for my reassurance."

"No!" Edgar said petulantly, tugging at the bill of his Braves cap. "Mr. Cal doesn't make me wear one when we go out fishing, do you, Mr. Cal?"

Lauren and Edgar both looked at him. What could he say? Cal didn't like wearing life vests either. He shrugged his shoulders, gave Lauren the palms-up gesture of help-lessness.

"Cal! How can you not demand that Daddy wear one? What if something happens out there?"

They had been through this same argument earlier in the week, when they'd made the trip to South Birdtown. "Nothing happened when we boated to the village and nothing's going to happen today, okay?" Cal went to her and removed the life vest from her hands, tossed it under the bench seat. "Let's just enjoy this beautiful day, shall we?"

"Thank you, thank you, thank you, Mr. Cal."

Lauren gave a disgusted little huff and a sharp look at her father as she strapped on her own vest.

They headed out just before noon. Cal wanted to go first to Loon Island, the largest of the uninhabited scrub pine islands that dotted Lake McDowell like tiny emeralds laid out on aqua felt. Cal thought Loon Island to be the perfect picnic spot. Quiet. Secluded. Shaded. Just enough of a beach on one side to bring the boat in.

Cal skippered his boat out of their inlet. Lake McDowell had risen dramatically during the four days of heavy rains. He was astonished to see how many of the smaller islands were now completely submerged. All of the paved boat ramps were underwater.

The rains had spiced the air with a rejuvenating smell. Gone was the dead algae scent that clung to the lake during the long drought, replaced by the fresh ammonia-tinged smell of new rainfall. The rainstorms had also taken the suffocating edge off the humidity. Cal knew this was a preview of the cooler fall weather that would descend on Lake McDowell in a few weeks. He pushed the throttle to full, breathing in the fresh mountain air. After four long days of being cooped up indoors, he reveled in the sunny wide-open spaces and crisp air.

He felt Lauren's hands massaging his shoulders from behind. He turned to look at her and they exchanged smiles. The wind whipped the bright blue sun scarf that draped her neck. She bent to kiss him and he responded in kind. Her mouth was soft and moist, her tongue fluttery and teasing. Cal felt himself getting hard in his swimsuit. Amazing what a simple kiss from this woman did to him.

"Oh yuck!" Edgar proclaimed. "Get a room you two! That's disgusting!"

Cal and Lauren broke apart, laughing.

Moby began barking.

The afternoon was back on track, the life vest dispute forgotten.

Within ten minutes, Loon Island came into view. Tall loblolly pines and eastern hemlock crowded the tiny island. As they got closer, Cal could see a couple of eagle nests in the treetops. Patches of reds and golds were beginning to show through the lush greenery as nature began its transformation into fall.

Large boulders marked the near shoreline. Cal steered the boat in a wide swath, circling the island to the far side where a fifty-foot stretch of beach provided a safe landing point. The recent storms had put most of the beach underwater, but there was still enough shallows for Cal to bring them in safely. He secured the boat while Lauren and Edgar unloaded the supplies. Moby spotted a chipmunk and took off after it, chasing it into the shade of the thick forest.

There was just enough beach for Lauren to lay out a blanket under a squat scrub pine. Cal dug into the cooler and passed out drinks while Lauren handed out club sandwiches and spooned potato salad onto paper plates. From a sterno camping kit, she dished out steaming beans and franks.

"You think we lost Moby for good?" she asked, looking into the darkness of the dense woods.

Cal said, "Nah. One whiff of your world-famous baked beans and that dog will come running."

As if on cue, Moby came shooting out of the thick undergrowth like a black bullet, tongue lolling to one side, brown eyes bright and alert.

"Do I know this dog or what?" Cal said, trying to fend off Moby, who licked at his face with wet, sloppy kisses. Cal knew the only way to settle down the dog was to feed him. He dished out a mound of baked beans. The Lab practically devoured the paper plate in his mindless food lust.

"Great, Cal," Lauren said. "Now Moby will be farting all afternoon."

"That's okay. Moby's farts don't stink," Cal said, laughing. "Do they, boy?"

"I know better than that, Cal. Your dog ripped a couple the other night that could strip the paint off the walls. Hey! Maybe we could use Moby for the prep work before we repaint my walls."

"I think the lady is making fun of you, Moby, old boy. Are you going to take that from her?"

In response, Moby went to Lauren and began licking her face.

"See, Cal," Lauren said, trying to keep her sandwich

away from the dog, "Moby still loves me."

Cal watched the Lab washing Lauren's face with his tongue, knocking her glasses to the blanket in his aggressiveness.

"Moby! Behave yourself!" he commanded, and the dog obeyed, finding a spot at the far end of the blanket.

Cal noticed a strangely serious expression on Edgar's face, and said, "You're awful quiet today, Edgar. What gives?"

"Just thinkin'," Lauren's father said after swallowing a mouthful of potato salad.

"About what?"

"Wondering if we're gonna see any woons."

"I don't know, Edgar. Loons are mostly nocturnal."

"Nock-*what*?"

"It means they only come out at night, Daddy."

"No, no, no . . . they don't. We saw five of them at South Birdtown. It was daylight. Woons on a walking-stick, remember?"

Cal couldn't argue that. "I think what we saw there was a bit out of the ordinary, Edgar."

"No, no, no," the old man said, shaking his head vigorously. "They talked to me that day."

"Who? The Cherokee shamans?"

"No. The woons."

"What did they say to you, Daddy?"

"That they would be c-c-coming for me soon."

Cal laughed, but he noticed Lauren looking at her father strangely, a worry frown creasing her forehead.

"Coming for you to do what, Daddy?"

"To take me to Wake Beyond . . . yes, yes, yes."

Cal heaved a heavy sigh. "Edgar, that Lake Beyond business is malarkey. The Cherokee have been selling that nonsense to the tourists ever since I was a kid."

"No, no, no . . . you're wrong, Mr. Cal. I know things. I know some things you don't, yes, yes, yes I do!"

"Cal," Lauren said, her expression growing more stern, "this is getting kind of creepy. When my mother, ah . . . when she um, *visited* me, she told me that Daddy knows things. Said it just like that. *'Your father knows things, Lo.'* Those were her exact words."

"That could mean anything."

Lauren nodded. "That's true. But it could also mean *something*. Something specific."

"Come on, sweetie," Cal said. "You're thinking too much again."

"Maybe, yeah ..." she said, her gaze becoming more distant as she ate quietly.

Cal wanted to get the day back to a brighter place. He swallowed the last of his sandwich and wiped his mouth with a napkin. "What this picnic needs is a little music," he said, picking up his well-worn guitar and strumming a few chords. "Any requests?"

"Yes, yes, yes!" Edgar said, coming back to life. "Play 'Blackbird,' Mr. Cal."

"No, Daddy. I think Cal is probably sick of playing that song by now. I think it would be more appropriate—seeing as how we are on Loon Island—to play 'Loons In Love.' Whaddaya think, Cal?"

"Tell you what, Edgar," Cal said, going into the finger-picking intro of the song he'd written for Lauren, "I'll play 'Blackbird' right after I do Lauren's request. How's that?"

"Can I sing, Mr. Cal? Can I, can I, can I?"

"Absolutely you can sing, Edgar."

Cal sang "Loons In Love" with Lauren pitching in on harmony vocals. Edgar had never really learned the song so he stayed out of it. But when Cal launched into "Blackbird," Lauren's father got to his feet, announcing that he sang better standing up. He was still terribly off key, but the spirit was there. "Blackbird" worked on the old man like a healing tonic.

Before heading back out on the lake in the boat, Cal

played another half-dozen songs—a John Prine tune followed by "Norwegian Wood," the haunting Beatle ballad that had become a favorite for both Lauren and himself ... "Love Me Tender" by Elvis ... "Till There Was You" ... "If I Fell" ... a love song by Air Supply. Normally, Cal would have gagged on so much sugary sweetness, but something in him had changed. Lauren Talbot had changed him. He was a man possessed by the euphoria of new-found love, a man who now viewed "silly love songs" as not so silly anymore. He knew that he had never been happier than he was at that exact moment, sitting on a blanket on an island in the middle of the lake, playing music and singing with Lauren, stealing kisses and whispering confessions of his love to her between songs, Edgar making faces and snide comments about their public displays of affection. They sang and they laughed and they playfully cajoled each other. Life was grand. Cal felt like a king. He had a family again, something that had been missing from his life for many, many years.

* * *

They were drifting lazily just south of Big Spoon, fishing the deep whirlpools the locals referred to as blue holes, when Edgar spotted the loons. Cal looked to where Edgar pointed, and saw to his astonishment, five loons flying in a tight V formation above the trees on the main-land.

"Woons! Woons!" Edgar exclaimed. "They're coming our way!"

Cal looked at Lauren, and her frown told him she was thinking the same thing: Five loons flying in a close forma-tion, exactly as they had seen during the Cherokee ritual at South Birdtown. A flutter of apprehension ran through him.

They all stared at the approaching loons. Only Moby seemed to be oblivious, the dog busy gnawing on a bone in the sparse shade of the cockpit.

The loons flew in high over the lake, circling the boat once, twice, never veering from their precise formation. Edgar jumped up and began his hysterical loon call.

"Daddy, please sit down!" Lauren yelled. "You're rocking the boat."

But Edgar was not to be denied. He lumbered up on the bow, whooping and hollering, pumping his fist at the circling loons, urging them on. Moby leaped up on the bow and joined in. The boat tilted precariously. Cal shouted for Edgar to get back inside the boat, but his shouts were drowned out by the cacophony of loon calls and Moby's howls.

"Daddy! Get back in here right now!" Lauren screamed.

But Edgar was lost in the moment.

And then everything spiraled out of control. The loons, apparently spotting a school of fish, dove for the surface near the boat. Like five bullets shot from the ionosphere, each hit the water with a terrible velocity, then disappeared into the depths.

To Cal's horror, he watched Edgar leap off the bow in an awkward dive, Moby going in a split second after, both man and dog disappearing under a torrent of bubbles.

Cal sat there, stunned by what he had just witnessed, not sure if it was real or not. He saw Edgar's baseball cap pop up and circle round and round the periphery of the wake.

"Cal! Do something!" Lauren shouted. "Daddy can't swim! Oh my gawd, Cal! Daddy can't swim! Do something!"

Cal threw his fishing rod aside, unlaced his sneakers and kicked them off, then jumped in, swam toward the widening circle of froth, the water so cold he thought his heart might stop. He breast-stroked to the baseball cap, took a deep breath, then dove. The chill of the lake water paralyzed him momentarily, but down he went, the visibility getting cloudier the further he dove.

No sign of Edgar.

He suffered a momentary panic, became disoriented. This was one of the deepest sections of the lake and he didn't know if he had the lungs to reach the bottom. Darker and darker the depths became. Cal felt a pressure building in his ears, could hear his heartbeat thumping like cannon shots. Anxiety clouded his judgment, but he kept descending. Edgar had to be down on the bottom somewhere.

After what seemed an eternity, Cal hit the mucky bottom. He fumbled around blindly. Pulled up a clump of sawgrass. Ran his hands over large stones and mud slicks, feeling for body parts but finding none.

His lungs burned and his arms ached as he worked his way along the lake bottom. Cal knew he had maybe thirty seconds before he'd have to surface for air. Why oh why did Edgar Talbot have to be such an obstinate fool? How was it that Cal found himself in this predicament? Love, that's how. Love of a sensational woman. Unfortunately, Lauren's father came as a package deal. Cal alternately cursed and prayed for Edgar Talbot as he searched the murky lake bottom for him.

His hand found purchase on a rubber-soled shoe and he yanked it free of the mud. He held it close to his face. An old high-top sneaker, the kind Lonnie Whitefeather wore. But no sign of Edgar in the immediate vicinity. Cal's air was running out. He hoped and prayed that Edgar had come back up.

Cal swam toward the light, broke the surface gasping for air.

Lauren hung over the side of the boat, distressed. "Did you find anything, Cal? Oh sweet Jesus, tell me you did!"

Cal dogpaddled in place, shook his head no while he took in expansive lungfuls of air. He felt dizzy and scared. Lauren didn't help matters by shrieking repeatedly, "Oh gawd, oh gawd, oh gawd!"

Cal dove a second time, widening his search perimeter. The only thing he found on this dive was an old tire. He heard a large splash above him and he looked up toward the dim light. Lauren had joined the search.

After three more dives, Cal realized it was hopeless.

Lauren's father was a goner. Probably trapped in the rocky embrace of a blue hole and drowned.

Cal clung to the side of the boat and felt the bile rise in his throat.

33

THREE DAYS GONE

Lauren's grief depleted her. A shadowy weight pressed against her as she replayed Daddy's drowning accident, seeing him hit the water then disappear under the froth. Could she have done more to save him?

Third day now and no sign of his body. Lumpkin County Rescue had dragged the lake bottom repeatedly only to find cans and bottles, broken lures, and miles of snagged fishing line. The first two days, she and Cal watched divers search the area where Daddy had gone in, her hopes dashed each time a diver surfaced and shook his head negatively. Searchers covered a two-mile radius from where the accident occurred, knowing the lake's deep currents could have swept his body a good distance. They'd even risked diving a few of the deeper blue holes. Nothing. Not a stitch of Daddy's clothing. No sign of the watch he'd been wearing. Nothing resembling a human body part.

Daddy was gone. Vanished without a trace. How was that possible?

Lauren had cried herself out. She could produce no more tears. Today she'd had periods of wracking sobs where her shoulders hurt afterward, but her eyes remained dry. She hoped Daddy, wherever he was, understood that a loving daughter only had a finite number of tears.

Cal had been a godsend. He hadn't left her side the past

72 hours. He had been especially comforting that first night, as he'd held her and whispered reassurances into the wee hours. Lauren was so thankful for this sweet, caring man who genuinely loved her, a man she remembered thinking when they first met to be buffoonish. How wrong she had been. Cal Blevins had been a wonderful friend through all this, a compassionate partner. He comforted her, eased her pain. Helped her through her blackest mood swings. Cal always knew the right thing to say, when to inject a little humor and when to keep it serious. Lauren shuddered to think where she would be without him. Without Cal, Lauren knew she might have jumped into that blue hole, gone down where Daddy did and never come back up. It would have been so easy. Just slip over the side of Cal's boat and take a big breath of lake water. It would all be over, just like that. No more pain. No more loss. She would be with Daddy again. So easy. And yet, she knew she couldn't do that to her nieces. She couldn't do it to her sister, Claire.

And absolutely, she could not do it to Cal.

But she'd wanted to, oh yes she had. Lauren remembered how close she'd come yesterday afternoon when her grief had plummeted her to new lows. She was one involuntary muscle movement away from going over the side of that boat and ending it all. But a look from Cal stopped her. A gaze of adoration and unquestioning love. His look reminded her of how foolish she was acting, of how wrapped up in herself she'd been. Tragically stupid to kill yourself in such a dramatic way when you have a man like this in your life, dumb-dumb, she'd scolded herself.

Lauren tried once again to reach her sister by phone, but couldn't. Claire wasn't answering her home line or her cell phone. Lauren was beginning to think Cal's ancient Princess phone might be defective. Hadn't he been unable to contact his ex-wife? Hadn't Cal told her it was an old phone that only worked half the time?

Lauren had to get back to Chattanooga. At the very least she needed to get in touch with Claire. She needed Claire's help in getting Daddy's affairs in order almost as much as she needed her sister's emotional support. Even though she wanted to be with Cal, Lauren had decided against staying at the lake. There was nothing she could do here. She was just getting in the way of the search teams. And, truth be told, she couldn't take another day of the painfully loud dredging equipment or the stench of the equipment's diesel motors.

She wanted no part of this lake anymore, this evil body of water that had taken her father in such dramatic fashion. How could a place so beautiful be so deadly, she wondered. Lake McDowell was a *murderer*! Strangled Daddy with its watery arms. Swallowed him straight up like the whale swallowed up Jonah. Lauren had seen it with her own eyes. She needed to get away from here ... this lake, this mountain . . . it was all too much. She shuddered every time she thought about drowning in a lake. Such a cold, impersonal way to die. Nobody deserved that.

Home was calling her, and the pull was strong. She could stay busy back home. She had family members to notify, preparations for life without Daddy, not to mention the start of another school year.

"I'm coming with you, Lauren," Cal said.

"No, Cal. You need to stay here . . . just in case . . ."

"But I can be a lot of help to you in Chattanooga, sweetie. You're in no shape to be dealing with lawyers and insurance companies and funeral directors. Let me take care of that for you."

"I appreciate it, Cal. I really do. But as much as I love you and as much as I value your support, you're not immediate family. A lot of this is legal stuff that only immediate family can touch. This is something me and my sister Claire have to deal with."

"You talk a lot about your sister," Cal said, snuggling in

closer to her on his couch. "Claire sounds very special."

"Oh, she is. We've always been close. Even when we were kids. Claire was always the strong one. This news about Daddy ... it'll tear her up, but she'll soldier on, the way she always has. Claire has this remarkable way of getting through things. I wish I had some of her moxie." Lauren peeked up under Cal's arm, into his face. "I just want it to all be over, Cal. There are times when I think I'll be okay, and then ..." She didn't need to finish the sentence. "But it's kind of weird. Today I've started remembering all kinds of happy moments I've shared with Daddy. The happy memories are what's with me today, and I'm thankful for that."

"Yeah," Cal said, "I remember when my father died. For the longest time I thought of him as a saint."

Lauren stared out the living room window, speaking as if recalling a vivid dream. "I remember Daddy teaching me how to ride an adult bike. That's the thing that's always stayed with me. I was always such a klutz, being so tall and awkward, I could never keep my balance on a bike. I was hell on training wheels, Cal, but my girlfriends had all ditched their training wheels long before and yet here was gawky Lauren, still depending on her helper wheels. I was the biggest girl, and also the biggest wimp. It was embarrassing. Humiliating. Daddy saw my friends making fun of me, and he vowed to teach me balance on a two-wheeler. He worked with me and worked with me, week after long week, each night after he got home from work. I was a terrible student. Alone, I would have killed myself. But with Daddy's guiding hands, I learned to ride that bike. I knew he would never let me fall. He was always there to catch me. That's what kept me going through the years of Daddy's illness, the fact that he never gave up on me when I was a little girl. How could I possibly abandon Daddy when he'd done so much for me?"

She focused on Cal, seeing what he thought of all this.

"I know this must sound incredibly stupid to you, Cal, but I think Daddy's always given me my sense of balance. Now that he's . . . now that he's not here, I'm feeling very out of balance. Dumb, isn't it?" Her voice trembled. She teetered on the edge of another dry cry.

"No, it's not dumb at all," Cal said, pulling her closer.

"Yes it is," Lauren sniffled. "It's such a lame, common little story. And Daddy was anything but common. It just seems like my most powerful memory of my father should be something more than ordinary bike-riding lessons. My memories of Daddy should be *monumental*."

Cal thought for a long moment, then said, "It's those lame, common little stories that define us all, Lauren. The sum is greater than the parts. Those lame, common little stories all add up to make your father monumental in memory."

She looked at him brightly, rubbed his forearm.

He said to her, "Do you really have to go now?"

She wrapped her arms around his neck and kissed his cheek. "Yes. I should leave while there's still enough daylight. It's just for a couple of days, Cal. Then we'll be together again. We'll talk a couple of times a day ... that is, if that lousy phone of yours works."

"Please, just stay tonight and go back early tomorrow morning."

"No, Cal. I have to go this afternoon. It's just a ... I don't know . . . just a feeling I have."

"A feeling?"

"Yeah, you know. Like a strong reason. A motivation."

"I'm going to miss you like crazy, Lauren. A few days will be an eternity."

"I know. But we'll make it. You've taught me that. Together we can make it through anything."

"God, I love you so much, Lauren Talbot. I'll be counting the minutes."

"As will I."

They kissed. Lauren pulled her head back, looked at Cal, laced her fingers in his, and said, "The sooner I go the sooner we'll be back together. Will you come next door with me while I pack?"

"Sure."

As Cal watched Lauren placing articles of clothing in a small suitcase atop her bed, he said, "Just promise me one thing."

"What's that?" she said.

"That you'll be careful. I couldn't bear the thought of anything happening to you."

Lauren smiled. "You're starting to sound like me."

"I just worry about you, sweetie."

"I know. You're so adorable, but don't worry. I'm fine, *really*. I'm getting stronger every day."

A half hour later she was behind the wheel of her minivan, driving away from her rental cabin and Lake McDowell. Driving away from all that had turned her life topsy-turvy the past couple of weeks. Driving away from a man who had taught her strength and companionship, a man who had given her back her laughter. She kept her eyes on the rearview mirror, Cal's waving image getting smaller and smaller until all she could see was his hand above the dust cloud that billowed out behind the vehicle. She laughed. He looked like one of those ridiculous bobble-head dolls, with his hand waving like it was on a spring.

And then she felt a wetness on her cheek, could feel a solitary tear drip onto her lap.

34

ASCENT TO EAGLE SUMMIT

Somehow Cal made it through the night alone. He thought constantly about Lauren. Tried calling her no less than a dozen times. The calls all seemed to get cut off before he could get a connection. Twice he'd picked up to make a call and the line was completely dead. Lauren had been after him about replacing the balky phone, but he just hadn't done it yet.

And then there was Cal's guilt. He hadn't expressed it to Lauren, but Cal felt responsible for Edgar's death. After all, he was the one who had been slack about letting the old man go without a life preserver when they were out in the boat. If Edgar had been wearing a safety vest, he never would have been able to dive after the loons. If Lauren's father had been wearing the vest he would still be alive. Cal knew he should have insisted on it, especially since he knew the old man couldn't swim. His idiotic short-sightedness had taken another human being's life, and he didn't think he would ever get over it.

Cal's guilt and worries about Lauren led him to wrestle with old demons. He knew he still had half a bottle of Johnnie Walker and a six pack of Heineken in the house. Late in the evening, he had become so desperate that he lined up the bottles on the kitchen counter to admire their artistic flair. How pathetic is this? he'd thought, as he sat there, moon-eyed and lusting for a drink. Finally, after hearing Lauren's voice chastise him for his near misstep, he gathered up all the bottles and poured the contents off his deck, watching with a warped fascination as the alcohol stained the flagstone steps below.

Cal was never so glad to see morning. His fitful sleep had brought intense chilling nightmares that featured snapping turtles and loons with teeth like piranha coming out of the lake to eat him. And in his dreams he had found Edgar, or at least his leg. Cal dreamed repeatedly of latching onto the drowning man's leg as the powerful current of a blue hole was sucking him under. Every time Cal got his hand around Edgar's ankle his hand would slip, and he was left holding Edgar's sneaker while the old man disappeared into some nether-region of the lake. Every time, same outcome.

Cal made coffee and then checked his phone. Still out of commission. Well, he'd pick up a new phone when he went to Lonnie's to get paint this morning. He decided painting Lauren's walls was a good way to pass the time and keep his mind occupied with something productive. He had to keep busy. The loneliness was eating him up. Cal had never known loneliness like this, not even during his trial separations from Sandra. This solitude produced a hollow ache inside him, a sore empty place just under his breastbone.

Moby was also down in the dumps. He missed Lauren and her father, and the dog sensed Cal's sadness. Normally, Moby loved to wrestle with Cal on the living room floor, but Cal's attempts to engage the black Lab resulted in a halfhearted tussle that saw them both just going through the motions.

The phone rang and Cal jumped, the sound loud and foreign.

"Hello?"

"Hi, Cal." The sound of Lauren saying his name sent a fire through him.

"Hi, sweetie! God, I've been going crazy around here without you!"

"I know."

"You *know*?"

"Yes. I know because I've been going crazy myself..."

Cal listened to her talk, an excited babble of words that made him pause. She sounded different somehow. Like she was high on something. He also realized that Lauren hadn't mentioned anything about Chattanooga—nothing about hooking up with her sister Claire ... nothing about being back home or attending to her father's arrangements.

"Lauren, are you all right?"

"Except for missing you, I'm wonderful."

"Are you taking care of Edgar's business?"

"Claire is organizing a memorial service for Daddy. She took charge the way I knew she would. She's a real trooper, my sister."

"But what if they, um . . . what if, um . . ."

"Find Daddy's body? They won't, Cal."

This didn't sound like the Lauren Talbot who had left here not twenty-four hours ago. "How can you be so sure he won't turn up? It's only been four days."

"I just know, okay? I know Daddy's gone and I'm fine with it now. That's why I'm calling you. It's time for you and Moby to come join me."

"Join you? You mean in Chattanooga?"

"No, Cal. Not Chattanooga."

Cal waited for more, but Lauren kept silent. "Uh—I'm not following this."

"Listen to me, Cal. Get in your car and drive up to Eagle Summit."

"Eagle Summit? But that's the top of Loon Mountain!"

"Exactly. It's so beautiful here. Did you know you can see four states from here?"

"You mean you're up there? Right now? You're not in Chattanooga?"

"That's right. And I'm waiting for you, Cal. You and Moby."

Cal sputtered something, then said, "I'm really not understanding this."

"Do you love me, Cal?"

"Of course, but—"

"Do you trust me?"

"Absolutely, I do."

"Then get in your car and come see me. I'm standing right now in the most beautiful place. I want to share it with you and Moby."

"Okay, if you say so," he muttered. "Give me a half hour or so."

"I'll meet you at the sign. Then I'll bring you to this incredible place."

* * *

The sign Lauren referred to was the billboard entrance to Eagle Summit, the small county-managed park that sat on the highest point of Loon Mountain. Hiking paths cut through most of the wooded acreage. Three lookout stations clung precariously to the sides of the steep cliffs overlooking the magnificent panoramic view. Each station had a set of telescopic binoculars the tourists could rent by the minute.

Cal parked under the sign. Got out of the car and looked around. Moby followed, sniffing around the edges of the lot, then finally finding a comfortable spot for a good pee.

There were a few other cars in the large dusty lot. He saw Lauren's Caravan parked next to a pickup truck, but she was nowhere to be seen. Cal looked up at the huge billboard that cast shade over half the lot.

WELCOME TO EAGLE SUMMIT
YOUR BIRDS-EYE VIEW OF THE WORLD
Elevation: 4752 feet

The sign had changed very little since the last time he'd been up here. Cal had always been impressed by the billboard's artwork, with the magnificent bald eagle, wings fully extended, coming in for a landing. Cal stared at the painting, admiring its three-dimensional lifelike qualities. The sky was perfectly rendered in the background, the lake appearing as a silver slab far below. He was about to look away when something caught his eye. Something in the powder blue sky ... in the distance ... small and barely noticeable. Cal moved in for a closer look at the sign. Felt his breath catch in his throat as he made out the tiny objects.

Five loons flying in a tight V formation. He'd never noticed them before.

"I'm glad you came."

Lauren's voice. But where was she? Cal glanced around the parking lot, saw Moby with his head tilted sideways, also trying to discern where the voice was coming from.

"I'm right here, guys," Lauren said, stepping out from behind one of the billboard's support posts.

She looked more beautiful than ever. Cal would even say radiant. Soft afternoon sunlight gave her face a mild glow. Her eyes were bright and curious behind her delicate wireframes. Moby took off running after her, nearly bowling her over with his exuberance.

Cal went to her and kissed her, held her in his arms, professed his love for her while trying to fend off Moby.

"You're going to love this place, Cal."

"But what about Chattanooga?" he said, his confusion increasing. "What about taking care of your father's business? What are we doing *here*, sweetie?"

Lauren gave him a beatific smile. "So many questions," she said. "Shortly you will have answers. Soon you will understand everything that's happened to us the past few weeks."

"How? When? This is nuts, Lauren."

"No, it isn't. It all makes perfect sense. You'll see."

Considering all the craziness that had transpired since Lauren and Edgar Talbot came into his life, Cal figured he'd just go along with it, see where it went. Lauren seemed different—calm and peaceful, a poised student of Zen practicing her Buddhist meditation. Not at all the creative, neurotic, angst-ridden woman Cal had come to know and love. She seemed very sure that Eagle Summit was where they needed to be, not Chattanooga. Lauren had a plan and wanted him to follow along. Her assured demeanor sold him on it. That, and something else. A tiny voice inside of him was telling him that Lauren was onto something special. Something inevitable.

He watched her bend down and grab Moby by the collar, then say to him, "Take my hand. I'm going to show you an incredible place. If you think Lake McDowell is enchanted, wait till you visit this place. We'll be able to live our dreams every day."

Cal stood there dumbfounded, trying to make sense of it all. He felt Lauren lace her fingers in his. She then escorted him and Moby across the threshold beneath the sign.

A bright light swallowed them up and Cal was struck by an overwhelming sense of joy. His entire being inflated with goodness and compassion. He felt a powerful sense of love and empathy for all of humankind. He sobbed with happiness, then laughed as he heard Moby yip three times. Cal knew those yips to be fun yips. Moby was off on a new adventure.

They seemed to float forever, the three of them. And through it all, Cal never let go of Lauren's hand.

She was right. It all made perfect sense.

Epilogue

Atlanta, Georgia

Sandra Blevins heard her cell phone chirp as she pulled into her driveway. She flipped it open and answered.

"Sandra?"

"Yes?"

"Hi. It's Claire."

Sandra was drawing a blank. "Claire?"

"Yes, Claire Hicks. You know . . . from the accident?"

"Oh, yes. Hi, Claire," she said, pulling the car into the garage and shutting off the motor. "You'll have to excuse me. It's been a long day."

"I understand. Are you doing any better?"

"Just taking things day to day. I'm surviving. Cal's been gone for what? Three weeks now? It feels like three years."

"I know what you mean. I still can't believe my sister's gone. You would have liked Lauren, I just know it. My world is so empty without her."

"I would have liked to have known her, from what you've told me."

Sandra unlocked the door to the kitchen and hung her keys on the rack.

"I'm not really calling to launch another pity party, Sandra. I actually have some great news!"

"I could use a bit of that right now."

"It's my father. Edgar. He's come out of his coma and

he's talking. Not making a whole lot of sense, but he's communicating with us. We're in his hospital room with him now."

"Oh, Claire, that's wonderful!"

"Yes, the doctors told us that since he didn't come out of the coma after the first two weeks, then we could possibly be looking at a permanent vegetative state. Daddy wasn't all that strong before the car accident, what with his stroke and all. Of course, this doesn't bring back my Lo-Lo or your ex-husband, but it is something good after all the bad we've been through."

Sandra went into the living room and kicked off her shoes, put her feet up on the sofa. "I'm so happy for you, Claire."

As Claire Hicks rambled on about her father's improved health, Sandra thought about the catastrophic event three weeks ago that had brought them together. Cal had been driving back to the lake after a late Sunday night dinner here at the house. Cal was tired, but refused to stay over, insisting he had to get back up to the lake house that night. On the way north, Cal and Moby literally ran into Lauren and Edgar Talbot, who were driving south, coming from Chattanooga to visit Claire in Atlanta. They met in a violent head-on car crash. Lauren, Cal, and the dog went instantly. The old man, Edgar, was found still alive at the crash site, but there wasn't much hope for his survival.

Sandra had met Claire that tragic night at the scene of the accident. Broken glass glittering red and blue in the swirling emergency lights. Police radios squawking. The smell of gasoline. Blood spilled across the narrow two-lane country road like oil slicks. The utterly despondent feel of death and dying. Sandra Blevins and Claire Hicks gravitated toward one another that long night, seeking each other out, supporting each other through the horrendous ordeal. Sandra had always found it difficult to make new friends, but with Claire, the friendship had been a natural. The two women hit it off. Sandra even attended Lauren's funeral while Claire accompanied her to Cal's. Sandra had also been by the hospital to check on Edgar Talbot a few times. They had been through so much together the past few weeks, Sandra and Claire. They had leaned on each other and did their best to make it through. Claire even told Sandra last week that she had lost a sister, but felt like she had gained another one in the process.

"Sandra, are you still there?"

"Oh, yeah, sorry."

"I was just saying that from what you've told me about Cal I think he and my sister would have really hit it off. Too bad they never had the chance. Wait a minute . . . Daddy's trying to tell me something. What is it, Daddy?"

Sandra could hear a man's voice in the background, but couldn't make out the words.

"Did you hear that, Sandra?"

"No. What?"

"Daddy just told us that Cal and Lauren have already met. He claims he can hear them singing together."

"Oh yeah? Ask him what song they're singing."

Sandra heard Claire ask the old man the question, then heard Edgar's garbled response.

"What's he saying, Claire?"

"He keeps saying something about woons in wuv. Doesn't make much sense. It's going to take Daddy a while to get his speech back to any degree, but we're just pleased as punch that he's talking. It's a miracle, really."

Just before hanging up with Claire, Sandra heard something that sounded like a bird call. It brought to mind the madcap laughing cry of the loons that she and Cal used to hear up at the lake.

"Claire?" she asked. "Is that your father?"

"Yes, dear god. He's making some kind of goofy bird call and insisting we call him Birdman. He's very confused, but he seems happy. Daddy's going to wake up the entire hospital. Here comes an orderly. I have to go, Sandra. I'll call you tomorrow."

THE END

Acknowledgments

By no means is a book a solo effort. So many people to thank and a limited space to do so. First and foremost, a big shout-out goes to my fellow members of The Fictioneers writer's group, Krishna Avva, Sherry Haney, and Tracy Rud, who were there with me from the first word, offering many insightful suggestions for story improvement. Same goes for Jack Massa, who, among many other valuable editorial contributions, schooled me in the art of the prologue. Pam Anderson (no not *that* Pam Anderson!) kept me honest on the landscape of the North Georgia mountains and made sure my characters didn't stray from who they really were. Christy Welsh also chipped in with great advice about character and plot and some useful tidbits about the music. And thanks to Julie Chinander for her sharp editorial eye and friendship.

Then there are two beacons in the literary community who keep me inspired. Jedwin Smith—author of two of my all-time favorite memoirs, *FATAL TREASURE* and *OUR BROTHER'S KEEPER*—is my mentor, always encouraging me and giving me hope. And bookseller extraordinaire, George Scott (no not *that* George Scott!), with whom I could talk books 24-7 if only time would permit. I swear, George could sell a book to a blind illiterate!

Canadian photographer, Linda Davidson, provided the graphic vision behind the book. Her cover shots are stunning and possess the perfect mix of surrealistic dark whimsy that such a story deserves. I looked though the work of hundreds of photographers before stumbling upon several of Linda's galleries. I knew immediately that her pics were the perfect visuals for this novel. Travelers on the same artistic train? Destiny? Yep, I think so.

Lastly there are those kindred souls who keep this bizarre carnival known as life interesting. Jeff Chinander, my band mate in The Jeffs, keeps me inspired on the music side of things. Simply put, Jeff is a genius with a guitar in his hands. Rock on, bro! And my mother, Mary, who instilled in me at a very young age, a love of story and reading. Thanks, Mom, this is all your fault! (smile…). My brother Wayne, the athlete of the family, is a veritable one-man wrecking crew on the tennis courts. Wayne has taught me a lot about competitiveness, and toughing it out even when the game seems lost. My wife Cheryl, so beautiful in a myriad of ways and fellow creative soul. She can do things with pottery that you have to see to believe. My son Ira, just getting started with his professional life, will some-day be known far and wide for his grand architectural visions. Ira also has more guitars than I do, which makes him A-OK in my book.

And finally, we come to my father, Campbell Paul Dennis, the model for the Edgar Talbot character and initial inspiration behind my writing *THE WISDOM OF LOONS*. From him, I got my drive and ambition. He gave me every-thing a son could ever hope for, and he was always my biggest hero. Sadly, he passed away January 23, 2009, just before publication. The loons have escorted him to Lake Beyond, so I know he is in a wonderful place and in the loving hands of The Great Spirit. I miss you, Dad. The world is a lonelier place without you. This book is for you!

Jeff Dennis
Atlanta, Georgia
February, 2009

Author Notes on LOONS

THE WISDOM OF LOONS began as a writing exercise in which I wanted to accomplish two goals: 1) to write a story featuring a character based on my father, and 2) to produce a short novel with just a handful of characters after penning five huge doorstop novels with casts of thousands.

When I started work on *LOONS*, all I had was the Edgar Talbot character. Edgar embodies my father on so many levels: longtime stroke survivor, intelligent and strong-willed, stubborn, opinionated, charismatic and enigmatic, standoffish, yet a man with a huge heart who would do anything for those he loved. Perhaps the closest similarity between the Edgar Talbot character and my father is a shared obsession with jigsaw puzzles. That part of the story was my dad all the way. My father, post-stroke, was completely fixated on jigsaw puzzles. He was oblivious of them before his stroke, but after, he couldn't get enough of them. It was as if his illness had rearranged his brain to think more graphically, to see puzzle pieces as tiny stories within a bigger story. Puzzles became his creative outlet and his central point of communication. As with Edgar Talbot, jigsaw puzzles tamed my father's restless nature.

Gradually, the Cal Blevins and Lauren Talbot characters came to me, Lauren first, as I needed a caregiver for Edgar. The Lauren character needed to be complex and multidimensional. She needed to be able to show extreme love and patience for her father, yet at the same time, she had to realistically demonstrate her frustration and helplessness over her difficult situation. That's when the Cal Blevins character was born. A new romantic partner for Lauren would give her someone with which she could verbalize her frustrations. But how to get Lauren and Cal together? And what would be the bond that kept them together?

The answer was music. Both characters share a passion for music and an unflagging respect for those who do it well. Both are gifted musicians. And when they sing together, magic happens.

Coming up with a locale was a bit easier. Lake McDowell is fictional, though it is based on several lakes in the North Georgia mountains. I needed an aquatic setting to incorporate the loon mythology into the story. Many of you sharp readers probably know that loons are not indigenous to Georgia. I did this by design. All through the story I planted subtle clues that things are not what they seem, that something is a little out of kilter. The inclusion of loons on Lake McDowell is one of the subtler clues.

Much of the Cherokee lore is accurate, especially the language. Of course, all Native American tribes communicate verbally, but the Cherokee are the only major tribe known to have an alphabet and written language. I borrowed quite liberally from Cherokee writings to come up with authentic dialogue. In fact, Cherokee comes from a Creek word "Chelokee" meaning "people of a different speech." And while pockets of Cherokee people still remain scattered throughout North Georgia, South Birdtown is a fictional place. My version of South Birdtown and its inhabitants is based on the Oconaluftee Indian Village in western North Carolina, on the Cherokee reservation there on the Qualla Boundary. There you will find those who still practice "the old ways."

The loon mythology that I weaved into the story comes from my longtime fascination with Native American relationships with the animal kingdom. The Cherokee, along with many other tribes, revered the eagle, and used the regal bird in their ceremonies leading up to war. The Cherokee also believed that the hummingbird brought them tobacco, which they thought had strong medicinal qualities.

The rabbit was seen as the bringer of trickery and deceit. The water spider with black downy hair and red stripes was the bringer of fire. The traditional Cherokee also had a special regard for the owl and the cougar. The owl and cougar were the honored ones in some versions of the Creation story as they were the only two living things that were able to stay awake for the Seven Nights of Creation. This makes the owl and cougar sacred, as were many other nocturnal animals. It was this sense of nocturnal spiritualism that led me to the loons. So, although there is no real proof that loons played a spiritual role in the lives of the ancient Cherokee, it certainly isn't much of a stretch. It *is* known that loons played big roles in other Indian cultures. As I mention in the novel, the early Inuit civilizations buried loon skulls in their graves as a means of carrying wisdom into the next life. Natives from the Faroe Islands thought the call of the red-throated loon flying overhead meant it was following a soul to heaven. The Ojibwa thought the loon call to be an omen of death. The Thompson River Indians of British Columbia thought the song of the loon was a prediction of rain.

And for those wondering about the Fish Hypnotist—I'll never tell. What happens on Lake McDowell stays on Lake McDowell!

Lastly, an explanation of the short story that follows— "When Mighty Methuselah Falls." My father suffered a massive stroke in 1984. Because of his strength and courage, he survived. For years I thought about writing a nonfiction piece about that experience, but I just couldn't do it justice. So, a few years ago, I decided to write a story based on what happened. It is fiction, but thinly veiled. Of all the short stories I have written, this one is my most personal, and comes closest to the truth. I include it here because the Edgar Talbot character in *THE WISDOM OF LOONS* is based on my father, post-stroke. "Methuselah" is a fictional snapshot of my father leading up to his stroke.

The differences are that my dad had his stroke at age 57 while the character in the story is some twenty years older, and my father was nowhere near the fitness nut that I depict in the story. I think it is a nice bookend to the novel. Hope you enjoy it.

— J.D. —

WHEN MIGHTY METHUSELAH FALLS

Jeff Dennis © 2009

The phone on my desk rang, cutting through the news-room buzz. I grumbled, not wanting to pull myself away from work on my current column. The clock on the bullpen wall told me my deadline was mere hours away, and so far, I only had the opening two paragraphs nailed.

The phone kept ringing, persistently, annoyingly. In my line of work, the telephone was both blessing and curse. Against my better judgment, I picked up. You never knew when one of your sources might be calling with a good lead.

"Jerry Dahlbeck," I answered, eyes never leaving my computer monitor.

"Jerry, this is Mom," my mother said quietly. I heard concern in her voice. Immediately my guard went up. She and Dad were living in a Phoenix retirement community and she rarely, if ever, called me here at work in Atlanta.

"What is it Ma? Something wrong?"

"I'm sorry to bother you, Jer. I know you're busy, but—"

There was a hesitancy in her voice I had never heard before. Alarm bells clanged in my head.

"—there's been an accident. It's your father. He's, uh…"

"Dad?" I said, pushing away from my keyboard and gripping the phone tighter. "Accident? What happened?"

"He's had a stroke, Jerry. A nasty one. It's not good. Not good at all."

"*What?*" A sick feeling came over me. I struggled to process this dark information, this jagged bolt of lightning from out of the blue. "Is he—?"

"He's barely hanging on. The prognosis isn't good. It's minute to minute. The doctors tell me he had more than seventy percent blockage of his carotid arteries. Would have killed a lesser man, is what Dr. Getty told me."

My mind shifted from controlled-and-focused work mode to complete chaos. My father was in his late-seventies now, a time in life when these catastrophic life-enders were more prone to strike. That part of the equation made some sense. The part that didn't make sense was how a man like Dad, who prided himself on his peak physical condition, could fall prey to a deadly stroke. The concept was completely incongruous to me. He was an obsessive fitness nut. I had long kidded him about being the eternal jock. Just three weeks ago he called me to brag that he had won the seniors bracket in a prestigious Phoenix tennis tournament. He'd told me the trophy was so big he had to build a new shelf in the den to hold it. This latest victory had put yet another athletic feather in his cap. Most amateur athletes half Dad's age could only dream of the number of awards that Peter Dahlbeck had amassed for his sporting prowess during his sixties and seventies. Dad at death's door? It didn't make any rational sense.

"How are you holding up, Ma?" I said, trying to order my thoughts. "Are you okay?"

"I could lie and say that I am. Look, Jer, I know you're really busy and I hate to impose—"

"Don't be ridiculous. I'll be on the next plane out there."

"Thank you, hon. This is a tough thing to face alone."

"Have you talked to Barb and Louise yet?" I said, referring to my younger sisters.

"Yes. Barbara took it in stride, but Louise? . . . well, you know how Lou is. They'll both be here tonight."

"Don't you worry yourself, Ma. Everything's going to be all right," I said, not believing my words. In a deep, recessed corner of my mind, I was irked that she had called my sisters before she had phoned me. Especially Louise, my flighty youngest sister, a woman without an internal compass who was prone to wild mood swings, and had adopted more personas and bed partners than Madonna. Lovely Lou had missed the past five years of family get-togethers, including all five Christmases and two weddings, one of which was mine. I knew my annoyance at my mother's calling order was irrational and petty, especially considering what was at stake. "I'll be there with you soon," I told her. "I love you."

"Be careful, Jerry. I need you here in one piece."

* * *

After rushing home and throwing a few clothes into a suitcase, I caught a 4:15 flight to Phoenix. I tried to watch the movie, some middle-of-the-road yawner about a woman with relationship problems. Even the gorgeous Sandra Bullock couldn't save this one. Normally Sandra was the perfect stimulant for me, but too many other things were vying for my attention. The long flight gave me way too much time to think.

Something that kept running through my mind was the irony at work here. One of my columns last week dealt with health and aging in America. I had written it in response to Dad's tennis tournament victory. I had long ruminated on my father's incredible string of athletic conquests during his golden years, and thought a story about him would appeal to my North Georgia readership. The column compared my less-than-stellar health habits and physical conditioning with those of my father. All very tongue-in-cheek and self-deprecating, but with serious journalistic underpinnings. The point of the column was to illustrate what an exceptional physical specimen my father had been through his later years, and that with the right mindset and self-discipline, a person's senior years didn't have to be nursing homes, wheelchairs, and clinical depression. It proved to be a nice change from my usual hard-hitting, in-your-face reporting on rampant corruption in Atlanta city government, crooked politicians, greedy corporate executives, and the ongoing ruination of the Georgia environment. My columns usually dealt with the dark underbelly of capitalism and politics and big business. But this new, lighter approach seemed to strike a chord with my readers. My employer, *The Atlanta Journal-Constitution*, had never received so much positive mail for one of my pieces. I thought perhaps this new style in my twice-weekly column and the enthusiastic reaction from my readership would help my push for national syndication, something I had been aggressively campaigning for the past few years.

The column was entitled "The Mighty Methuselah," which is what I had dubbed Dad. I thought the Methuselah reference to be particularly apt after reviewing all the press clippings Dad had sent me over the past twenty years, articles that described his impressive athletic achievements. Methuselah is a Biblical character from the Book of Genesis who was purported to have lived to the ripe old age of 969 years, finally succumbing in the Year of the Deluge. According to the Bible, Methuselah had fathered a son, Lamech, when he was 187 years of age. Son Lamech, while living a long and robust life himself, fathered Noah when he was 182, and lived to be 777 years old, which was impressive, but paled in comparison to father Methuselah's amazing feat of longevity. Being a lapsed Catholic, I had to laugh at religious scholars who took this metaphorical family seriously. But the representation certainly worked for my column. I had cast my father as Methuselah and myself as Lamech. The piece worked well, and I was proud of it. But now, sitting here in the cramped aisle seat of this long flight, I felt that maybe the column had jinxed my father. Maybe through some strange twist of fate, I had orchestrated my father's stroke by committing certain

words to newsprint. I was superstitious that way. Most
reporters I knew were.

I had my laptop open, reading the column again, trying
to spot anything that might have tipped God that maybe
now was the time to arrange for the demise of Peter M.
Dahlbeck.

> . . . *and at seventy-eight years young, he is more
> spry and energetic than most men half his age.
> Winning the Phoenix Seniors Amateur Grand Slam
> tennis tournament last week was just his latest
> conquest in a long line of athletic accomplishments.
> Two years ago he finished third out of a field of 364
> cyclists in the Maricopa County Cross-Country
> Jamboree, a grueling bicycle race that covers fifty
> miles of blazing desert and hilly trails. Only a
> broken chain on the home stretch prevented him
> from winning it all. Dad made up for it last year,
> however, winning the event going away. When
> asked to what he attributed his win, Mighty
> Methuselah responded: "A bicycle with a durable
> chain!" And last year, my wondrous Methuselah
> competed for the first time in the Scottsdale Seniors
> Iron Man Triathlon, in which participants swim a
> thousand meters, cycle forty miles, and run 8 miles.
> How did Pops do? Yep, you guessed it. He won. The
> second-place finisher was fifteen years his junior.*
>
> *When asked about his golden-years successes,
> Methuselah Dahlbeck answers, "It's simple, really.
> I've been happily married for fifty-five years to the
> most wonderful woman on the planet, I don't drink
> or smoke, and I follow the Jack LaLanne fitness
> regimen. I've got a complete library of the Jack
> LaLanne training videos, which I follow down to the
> last detail. I have long idolized Mr. LaLanne, and
> he has served as my only real role model through*

the years. He's an old fart now and I figure if this relic can do it, a young stud like myself shouldn't have any problems. And per Mr. LaLanne's advice, I gobble down a slew of vitamins and herbal supplements, too numerous to mention here. But the bottom line is, I hate to lose. At anything. My motto? Think young and refuse to lose."

I looked up from my laptop. There's one competition we're all sure to lose eventually, Dad, I thought. No way could my father outswim, out-cycle, and outrun the Grim Reaper forever. None of us could, I thought forlornly. I shook my head, trying to chase the depressing thoughts, and went back to my reading.

. . . while I, on the other hand—the underachieving Lamech to Dad's Mighty Methuselah—become winded walking up a flight of stairs. At the relatively youthful age of forty-nine, I have a sedentary job and little interest in working up a sweat for sport. My pursuits tend to be cerebral in nature. My second wife tried to get me interested in power walking. The third day out, I pulled a hamstring and declared myself unfit to continue. I ended up placing myself on the disabled list for a month while nursing the injury back to health. By the time I was reluctantly ready to return to action, my wife had taken up with a young, virile aerobics instructor.

And while Dad is seemingly blessed with good genes, I seem to have inherited every negative genetic acorn in the Dahlbeck family tree. I can count the number of hairs remaining on my head while Methuselah has a healthy mop of salt-streaked dark brown hair that hasn't shown the first hint of receding. My metabolism moves at freeze-frame speed: I can look at a cheeseburger and put on five pounds while Dad can chow down at an all-you-can-eat Shoney's buffet and not gain an ounce. My blood pressure hovers near the top of the Richter scale and my liver produces cholesterol at nearly the same rate the television networks churn out bad shows. My vision has always been far-sighted, and I wear eyeglasses so thick that the pupils of my eyes look like planets in a galaxy far, far away. Methuselah Dahlbeck just started wearing light reading glasses three years ago on his seventy-fifth birthday. My upper torso is becoming Frankensteinish from all the pre-cancerous moles I've had surgically removed, the result of overzealous sun worship in my youth. Dad, on the other hand, spends hours working out under the hot Arizona sun, and maintains an all-over bronze glow that makes him a candidate for a Senior Living cover model.

And so I must concede. There is no way I can keep up with Mighty Methuselah, for I am Lamech, the weak-willed, feeble-boned understudy to the master athlete. While Methuselah has dedicated an entire den in his Phoenix home to his trophies and plaques and ribbons and medals awarded for his sporting deeds, I have but a single trophy that sits on the mantel over my fireplace, a solitary icon that represents my one "athletic" achievement. The figure on the glossy gold prize is that of a football player with his arm cocked to pass the ball. The inscription reads: "1971 State Champions, Georgia High School Division AAA." I had been a member of that powerhouse Valdosta Wildcats football team. It had been legendary head coach Wright Bazemore's final year and he had led us to a 13-0 record during a dream season in which we outscored our opponents 629-137. My position? Team Statistician. Ah, how humbling life can be, hovering in the shadows of greatness . . .

I felt the presence of someone standing in the aisle, looking over my shoulder. I turned my head and glanced up, saw an obese man bursting out of an expensive suit.

"Say, aren't you Jerry Dahlbeck?" he inquired. "The writer for the Atlanta paper?"

This kind of invasion of privacy had always bothered me. I knew many writers who felt the same way. We all wanted to be hugely famous and have millions of readers cherish our words and stories, but we didn't want them bothering us personally. We wanted fame and fortune, but only if it came anonymously.

"That would be me," I said reluctantly

"I thought so," he beamed, "I recognized you back in the terminal at Hartsfield. You look just like your photo they publish at the top of your columns—"

I thought: Most people look like their photographs, my friend.

"—man oh man, I just love your work," he gushed, taking the empty seat across the aisle from me. "I'm Carl Moncrief, Junior," he said, extending a pudgy hand my way.

"Nice to meet you, Carl," I said, hesitating before finally taking his moist hand in mine.

"I'm a huge fan. And my wife Sarah is an even bigger fan, let me tell ya. On Tuesdays and Fridays, when we get the paper, Sarah reads your column first, even before she turns to the comics."

"Well, thank you, Carl. Tell your wife I'm very flattered."

"Oh, she'd just die if she knew I was on a plane talking to you. Say, would you mind doing me a favor and giving me your autograph? I'd be most appreciative."

I told him I'd be honored and pulled a sheet of my letterhead out of my briefcase, began to write out a personal inscription to Carl and Sarah Moncrief.

While I thought and scribbled, Carl Moncrief droned on in my ear. "The wife and I just loved your column last week, the one about your father? King Jock Methuselah? You know, the one about how your old man makes you feel inadequate and all."

I looked up from my writing. "That wasn't really the point of—"

"It really made me come to grips with the relationship I have with my own father," Moncrief said, cutting me off. "I'm sure you've heard of Moncrief Plastics. My father, Carl Senior, he started up the company from nothing forty-some-odd years ago. Today we're a Fortune 500 company. My father is known as the vision, brains, and ambition behind the success of the business. I'm seen as the son with the silver pacifier in his mouth who became Director of National Sales through nepotism. I've had a tough time dealing with that. But your column, it made me see that we're all individuals. We can all excel at something, even if it's not the same thing our parents have succeeded at. I've turned into a pretty good sales manager, even though I'll never found a multi-million-dollar company the way my dad did. You have become an award-winning journalist but could never win a marathon the way your father has . . ."

I stopped writing and smiled at Moncrief, silently thanking him as he continued to talk. This well-intentioned stranger had interpreted my column in a completely different way than I had intended, and yet he was right on the money. And, most importantly for my hyperactive ego, he had remembered the part about my winning two Georgia Press Association awards for investigative journalism. The almighty Pulitzer was still a distant dream for me, but I was grateful that someone had remembered my smaller accomplishments. God bless Carl Moncrief, Junior. He was indeed a true fan.

"So what does your father have planned next?" he

asked me, and suddenly I felt a cold tremor run through me. "Is Mighty Methuselah going to scale Mount Everest? Maybe hang glide off the North Rim of the Grand Canyon? Something equally spectacular? I mean, how can he possibly follow up what he's already done?"

The chill I felt made me shiver as I thought about Dad's current state. I didn't want to be rude to this kindly man, but I also couldn't continue this conversation. I finished my lengthy inscription to the Moncriefs, signed my name with a flair, and handed the sheet of paper to him. While Moncrief read my words, I said simply, "I think Methuselah Dahlbeck is facing his greatest challenge yet."

"What's that?"

"Survival."

"Huh?" Moncrief said, looking up at me, a confused expression dogging his pasty face. "You mean he's going to be on that *Survivor* TV show?"

"Uh, no, not hardly," I said, aghast. "Look, I don't mean any disrespect here," I said as calmly as possible, "but I planned to get some work done on this flight, so if you don't mind . . ."

"Oh, sure," Moncrief said, struggling to get up out of his seat. "I understand. Thanks for your time, Mr. Dahlbeck." He admired the inscribed letterhead like it was the Holy Grail. "The wife is going to flip over this. Keep up the great work." He shook my hand again, and then he was gone, disappearing into the First-Class section at the front of the plane.

* * *

Dad was in Intensive Care at Phoenix Memorial Hospital. I've always dreaded hospitals, with their ether/ammonia smells and air of wounded mortality and caravans of white-suited professionals running to and fro with Godlike importance. No surprise to me that Phoenix

Memorial was no different.

Upon arriving, I thought the nurse had taken me to the wrong room, so unrecognizable was my father. Mighty Methuselah had been reduced to a drooling, desiccated shell of the man he had been when I last saw him. As I stood at the foot of his bed observing him, I couldn't get over how emaciated and pale he looked. He was hooked up to a respirator and an IV line dripped life-sustaining fluids into his left arm. Electrodes ran from his chest to a phalanx of scary-looking diagnostic machines that beeped and clicked from the corner of the room. Dad's eyes were open, staring vacantly at the ceiling overhead, seeing nothing, registering nothing, his expression a blank mask. I thought about the last time I'd seen him. Last Christmas it was. He had been so jovial and full of life then. So *healthy*. Mom had given him a pair of top-of-the-line Reebok running shoes. I remembered how his eyes had shone with gratitude as he opened the gift, how his voice bubbled with excitement as he described the way he would break them in during his training for a late-January marathon he was planning to enter. Now he lay here like an inanimate stone, unconnected to anything mortal, floating in an unnamed purgatory somewhere between this world and the next. He was like one of those zombies from a B-grade horror movie, one of the great undead who completely lacks conscious experience and a working soul. But this wasn't a movie, I had to remind myself. This was real life. This was my father.

I moved around to the side of the bed, alarmed to see Dad's eyes tracking my movement. It was eerie, the way only his eyes followed me while the rest of his body remained rigid. I groped for his right hand, thinking that maybe I could reach him through my touch. His hand was cool and sandpapery, his grip limp and unresponsive. I shuddered.

"Hi, Pops," I whispered. "It's me, Jerry. I'm here for

you, Dad." I tried to muster a smile. His usually expressive eyes were dead, their adobe hue reminding me more of twin tombstones than earthy windows to his soul. I was shocked to realize that he didn't know me. Not even a flutter of recognition. He was looking through me as though I was transparent.

"Hi, Jer. Didn't expect to see you again until the holidays."

I turned to see my sister Barbara enter the room. Considering the circumstances, she looked great, and I told her so as we embraced, hanging on a little longer than we normally would under less drastic conditions. We exchanged a few social pleasantries about airline flights and families, then fell silent. Barb, the middle child, had always been the pillar of strength among us Dahlbeck siblings. For as long as I could remember, she had cruised through life as though she had discovered some divine secret about inner peace. Compared to Louise and me, Barb had her life together. While I had failed at marriage three times and Louise had never married, Barb was still hitched to her high school sweetheart, Ronald Taylor, a very nice guy who made a lucrative living as a master electrician. The Taylors lived in San Antonio and had raised four beautiful children. Barb was the quintessential modern housewife, organizing the Taylor household in such an efficient manner that I had to wonder whether she had gained matriarchal experience in a previous life. Their two oldest children, my nieces Brandy and Tiffany, were now attending University of Texas, while the two youngest, Bradley and Jonathan, were in their junior and senior years of high school. Barb was the heart and soul of the Taylor clan, and I had long been envious of her togetherness. When I mentioned this to Barb, she would counter in her usual humble way that she envied me my career successes. The grass is always greener, as they say. Barb's gracious humility and nurturing selflessness were qualities that made her a superstar wife and mother. She was like Mom that way.

"Is Mom here?" I asked Barb after a time.

"Yeah, she's downstairs in the cafeteria grabbing a bite to eat. With Lou."

"Louise is already here?"

Barb nodded. "Lou got in earlier today, before I did."

"How is she doing?" I asked, not looking forward to another encounter with my volatile and unpredictable sister. The last time I had seen Louise was almost six years ago at a family reunion picnic. She had gotten rip-roaring drunk and caused a scene by climbing up on one of the picnic tables and proclaiming the entire family to be "capitalist pigs" and "fornicating heathens" among other unflattering accusations. She finished it off by dropping her jeans and mooning us, then climbed into her beat-up Escort and motored off into the sunset, all of us just looking at each other in stunned silence. Dad had checked out on her emotionally after that incident. That's why Louise's presence here surprised me.

"Lou did not handle this well at all," Barb said, looking past me at our father lying in the bed, his eyes now closed. "She really freaked out when she first saw him."

"I guess that's understandable," I said, not believing I was sticking up for Louise. "I had a rough moment or two myself when I first walked in."

"Yeah, but at least you have your emotions under control, Jerry. Lou went into her histrionic act, windmilling her arms around dramatically, wailing in despair. Melo-dramatic to the extreme as usual. A doctor and a couple of nurses came in and told her she had to leave, that she was disturbing the patients. It was pretty embarrassing really. Even for Lou."

"Glad I missed it," I said, thinking how much more stressful Louise's presence made this already emotionally wrenching situation. "What's she been up to the past few years, Barb? Did you catch up with her much?"

"Yeah, she's taken up surfing and lives under a pier on Venice Beach. Best I can tell she's been dating a guy who fancies himself as a preacher for the homeless who live on the beach. She makes money by panhandling and working as an assistant for some of the street performers there."

"Louise sure sets her sights high, doesn't she?"

Barb nodded. "Well, we both know Lou's always danced to the beat of her own drummer, Jer."

"She's got her own percussion section, who're you kidding!"

That brought a smile from Barb.

I looked down at the bed containing the lumpy form that was my father, and I pointed at him. "Has he, um . . . said anything . . . communicated anything to you yet?"

"No. But the doctors are hopeful. One of them told us earlier that most stroke survivors make at least a partial recovery within the first seventy-two hours."

"How did it happen?"

"He collapsed in the shower after a workout. Mom said she heard a tremendous crash in their bathroom, like one of the walls was coming down or something. She rushed in to find him slumped against the wall, unconscious, his hair all lathered up with shampoo."

"Jesus. Poor bastard."

"Yeah. Methuselah has finally fallen, hasn't he, Jer?" She looked at me, and I noticed her cheeks were shiny with tears. "I didn't have a chance to e-mail you, but I loved your Methuselah column."

"You don't think it jinxed Dad?"

"Don't be ridiculous, Jerry. The only thing that jinxed Dad was Father Time." She put her arm around my waist and hugged me close. "I'm glad you're here, big brother of mine."

* * *

The vigil had moved into its third day. Nothing much had transpired except some verbal jousting between me and Louise. Yesterday had been the worst. We had gotten into it in one of the hospital waiting areas amidst the stares of other frazzled people waiting to see their loved ones. I had grown tired of handling Louise with kid gloves and had started in with my "tough love" act. Intense stress does that to me, brings out my fatherly instincts. Lou snapped at me, and when Louise snaps, everyone in the near vicinity would be best to run for cover.

"Who the hell are you to tell me how to live my life?" she'd yelled at me after I had mistakenly given her my opinions about a 42-year-old woman taking up surfing, living on a beach, and falling in with a man half her age who proclaimed to be a 'messiah of the sands.' "I mean, it's not like you've done much of anything with your life either, mister know-it-all! How many divorces you been through? Six? Seven?"

"Three, but who's counting?"

"And no kids either. No one to carry on the precious Dahlbeck name."

That one hurt. My sterility problem was the underlying cause of my first divorce. Louise knew it and used it as a weapon whenever she could. I was defenseless against it, and so kept quiet.

"No," she said, fire in her eyes, "your entire world is that stupid column of yours. You're so wrapped up in yourself and that bird-cage-liner newspaper you work for that you don't even realize there's a big beautiful world out there waiting to be discovered. I'm *living* my life. You're just existing, Jerry. You don't have a clue."

Her attack on my career got to me. I had let loose with an emotional barrage, to which Louise responded with some vulgar invective of her own. Then she stormed out of the waiting room and slammed the door behind her. I was left acknowledging accusatory stares of several parents who embraced their young children protectively. They looked at me as though I was a serial killer or something, and I was consumed with embarrassment. My heart raced madly. My blood pressure was out of sight. I thought about Lou's beach attire—revealing surfer tank top, clam digger pants, cheap rubber sandals, wildly colored hippie headband—and I thought about her self-centered, arrogant attitude toward me and the rest of our family. I knew somewhere in my heart there existed a love for my youngest sister, but at that moment I was sure that I hated her.

The stress of Dad's illness was getting to us all.

But Barb had stepped in and worked her compassionate magic on Lou. Barbara had always been good at controlling Louise, and I was glad of that. And so, here on the third day after Dad's stroke, things were stable. Still uncertain, but tolerable.

Mom and I had gone to lunch at a steak restaurant while Barb and Louise watched over Dad. Today's lunch was like meals had been the first two days: silent affairs at which we nibbled nervously while privately ruminating about Mighty Methuselah Dahlbeck. It was difficult for me to comprehend that at any moment, God could tap my father on the shoulder and say "Come with me." As I watched my mother pick at her spinach salad across the table from me, I knew her thoughts were running parallel to mine. I thought about all that Dad had done for me over the years, all that he meant to me, and I tried not to get choked up. He had slaved in a South Georgia textile mill for forty-five years, working his way up to a shift foreman position, scrimping and saving to put me through University of Georgia's School of Journalism, then to put Barbara through two years of nursing school. He'd always preached to us that education was the ticket out of millwork and the factories. Dad had no formal education past high school, but he was a wise old owl in the ways of common sense.

Many memories of my father were humorous: Dad backing our boat trailer too far down the ramp at Lake Lanier, swamping our new ski boat when I was eight; Dad taking my Cub Scout den on a camping trip when I was ten, warning us about deadly snakes and straying too far from camp, then getting lost in the woods himself and contacting a serious case of poison oak to add to the humiliation. Then there was Dad's embarrassing attempt to teach me about the birds and the bees when I was twelve. I smiled every time I reconstructed that conversation. Being a reserved man, Dad had resorted to the use of a clunky metaphor to explain the basics of the sexual act. He described it as explorers with flashlights going into caves to search for golden eggs. It was an activity known as spelunking, he'd said, and that it was a fun but serious proposition. Of course, I was already wise to the mysteries of sex through Billy Janson's older brother's girly magazines, which we consumed with a fevered, wide-eyed passion unique to hormonally-crazed boys teetering on the edge of puberty. I knew about the dark and mysterious things my father spoke of, and then some, but I didn't let him know that. I found his approach much too entertaining, watching him turn beet-red and squirm in his chair while relating this ludicrous fable to me. The only thing I didn't understand at the time was the term 'spelunking,' which I looked up immediately following our discussion. My friends and I got a kick out of it, and began referring to The Dirty Deed as spelunking, giggling every time the word tripped off our tongues.

Then there were the touching moments with my father at center stage. When I was very young, I was diagnosed with poor vision complicated by a depth perception problem. I remember having to go through vision therapy each night, placing a patch over my good eye while looking at two-dimensional black-and-white photographs, thereby strengthening my weak eye and sharpening my depth perception. My eye doctor also prescribed Little League Baseball as part of my therapy, the theory being that hitting and catching a baseball would help me with motion perception. I wasn't much of a baseball player. I had a little speed and so I could play the outfield okay, but I was a disaster at the plate. I couldn't pick up the ball coming out of the pitcher's hand, and to make matters worse, I was terrified standing in the batter's box. Consequently, I usually struck out. A moral victory for me was hitting a weak foul ball. But one game, with my father in attendance, I actually connected with one, hitting it over the shocked left fielder's head, and I made it all the way to third with a standup triple. The entire way around the bases I heard Dad screaming, "THAT'S MY SON! THAT'S MY SON! GO JERRY GO! RUN, RUN, RUN!" He had almost tumbled out of the bleachers he was so excited. I remember pulling up at third and then searching the stands for Dad through the fogged lenses of my glasses. I'll never forget the look of pride on his face. Dad had always been the serious jock in the Dahlbeck family, but for one shining moment, I was his equal, and his congratulatory glance and thumbs-up hand gesture acknowledged me as such.

And then there was perhaps the defining moment in my relationship with my father. It was February of 1972 and I had just started second semester of my Freshman year at Georgia. The Vietnam War was raging on and Washington had just performed the annual draft lottery, in which any male born in 1953 and deemed physically capable of serving the country received a lottery number. It was my bad luck that this was to be the first year when student deferments could not be exercised to keep young men from eligibility. So my enrollment at University of Georgia did nothing to protect me from the draft. My number was 105 and rumor had it that all men holding numbers through 125 would be called for induction into the military.

This draft lottery was an event that opened my eyes to

what a crapshoot life could be. I had been following the war for a year or two, and had come to the conclusion that we had no business being in Southeast Asia. I started researching areas that were sympathetic to U.S. draft resisters, certain cities in Canada and Sweden. I was nervous about broaching the subject of my possible flight with Dad, a man who had served proudly during World War II. But my father had surprised me. Methuselah had never been mightier than he was the night we discussed it. He'd told me, "Jerry, if this was either of the great World Wars, or even the Korean War, I'd disown you in shame. But this crap in Nam is all wrong. It's doing nothing but killing a lot of innocent boys and lining the pockets of defense contractors and politicians. Your mother and I would hate to see you go, Jer, we'd miss you terribly and worry about you. But we'd also understand. That said, you have my full support in whatever you decide to do, Son." Dad became a superhero in my eyes that winter night all those years ago.

"Earth to Jerry . . ." My mother's voice cut through my recollections.

"Sorry, Ma. I was just reminiscing about Dad."

"I know you were. I could see it in your eyes. I've been doing a lot of the same."

"This has got to be tearing you up, Ma. How could this have happened?"

"We all get old and frail eventually, Jerry. Even your father."

"But Dad is in such tip-top shape."

Mom frowned. "Well, he is and he isn't."

"How do you mean?" I asked.

"Your father hates doctors, Jer. He calls them 'white-coated yuppie extortionists.' He claims he knows far more about his own body than any Harvard or Johns Hopkins educated physician could ever hope to discover. He's always been hard-headed that way." She laughed, a tiny snort, and looked around the restaurant at other diners. "Kind of ironic that he now finds himself surrounded by them. Dr. Getty told me his cholesterol count was through the roof."

"But I thought he—"

"No, Jer. Your father hadn't had a checkup in years, probably hadn't had his cholesterol levels checked in close to thirty years. Dr. Getty told me that with some people, it doesn't matter how well they maintain their diet or how much exercise they get, their livers are prone to producing large amounts of the bad cholesterol . . ."

I knew this, of course, since my doctor had told me pretty much the same thing. I had been on Pravachol for a couple of years now to help keep my cholesterol in check. I just assumed that Dad had been taking something similar. But then, we never discussed such things.

". . . Dr. Getty says that's the case with your father. I tried to talk some sense into him over the years, but your father would just show me his flat stomach and lean muscles and say he had it all under control."

I shook my head, wondering about Dad's short-sightedness. I was very different from him with regard to my health. There had been times when I thought I might be a borderline hypochondriac, my health neurosis forcing me to rush to my doctor anytime I had some weird, inexplicable symptom. Maybe that hadn't been such a bad trait after all.

Suddenly, I heard my cell phone ring. I pulled the phone from my belt pouch and answered it. Barbara chattered excitedly.

"Jerry, it's wonderful! Dad just pulled out of it! He's asking for you and Mom."

"Fantastic!" I nearly shouted, giving my mother the thumbs-up across the table. "We'll pay our check and be right there."

Mighty Methuselah Dahlbeck was back among the living. There was a spring in our steps as Mom and I left the steakhouse and headed back to the hospital.

* * *

Dad was sitting up in the bed. Some color had returned to his face, though it was blotchy. Mom went to him first and kissed him on the cheek, rubbed his arm affectionately. Then I approached him and he smiled, which made my heart soar. He reached out to me and I grabbed his hand. His grip was weak but responsive. He pulled me down closer to him and whispered something unintelligible, his voice a husky murmur.

"What's that, Dad?" I said.

"No more . . . mess . . . you low . . ."

He was trying so hard to tell me something, but I just couldn't understand him. He repeated the same undecipherable phrase several more times, the effort obviously exhausting him. In frustration, I turned around and searched the faces of Mom, Barb, and Louise, who were standing around the bed.

Mom said, "I think he's trying to tell you that there's no more Methuselah, Jer."

I turned back to Dad, who was nodding in the affirmative. I knew he had loved my column about him. With great difficulty, he told me he loved the Methuselah reference, but that he felt he couldn't live up to it. Something very primal touched me deep inside, and I felt tears welling up in my eyes.

"That's okay, Dad," I told him. "You don't need to be Methuselah. You just need to be yourself."

He clutched my hand again and pulled me close. "I love you, Jer."

I told him that I loved him, too, but he never heard it. He had drifted off to sleep.

The doctors told us that though Dad was now out of danger, he would have a long road of physical rehabilitation and speech therapy ahead of him. The Mighty Methuselah was no more, but Peter Dahlbeck—Dad—was still with us, and that's all that really mattered.

THE END

About the Author

Jeff Dennis was born under a full moon on New Year's Day, 1953. Since setting out in pursuit of fame and fortune, he has worked a wide assortment of jobs, including hotel night auditor, department store Santa Claus, college textbook salesman, paper salesman, computer software telemarketer, bookstore clerk, award-winning magazine editor/publisher, rock musician, soccer coach, and technical writer. Some of these "professions" even paid him for his efforts.

He is the author of the dark fantasy collection, *WHEN THE SANDMAN MEETS THE REAPER* (WordCraft Resources Books, 1996). The author is also half of the power acoustic rock duo, The Jeffs, who play clubs around the Atlanta area. Currently Jeff resides in the North Atlanta suburbs with his wife, Cheryl, hyperactive chocolate Lab, Desi, and narcoleptic cat, Smudge.